THE BRANCH

Other books by Mike Resnick

Novels:

THE BRANCH
MIKE RESNICK

WILDSIDE PRESS
Berkeley Heights, New Jersey

First Wildside Press edition: July 2000

The Branch
A publication of
Wildside Press
P.O. Box 45
Gillette, NJ 07933-0045

www.wildsidepress.com

SECOND EDITION

To Carol, as always,

*And to Josep Guirao, for devotion and dedication
above and beyond the call*

Prologue

*I*t was not the best of times; it was not the worst of times. It was the *dullest* of times.

By rights, it shouldn't have been. The first half of the twenty-first century was an age of fantastic, glittering cities that spread like creeping cancers across the face of the planet. It was an age of bold new art forms, darksome pleasures, and bizarre indulgences. Every day saw the discovery of a new perversion, every month revealed the creation of a new spectator sport, every year boasted splendid new forms of entertainment. The fact that the perversions and sports and entertainments ultimately proved not to be so new after all, but merely the recycling of old mundane diversions, could hardly be blamed on society, which continued its quest for the new and the unique with unrestrained vigor, while its members, individually and collectively, came to the unhappy realization that an excess of leisure was not quite the Valhalla that they had anticipated.

Religion had recently made a big comeback. So had philosophy. So had anything else that took up time. Every city possessed baseball, football, hockey, basketball, rugby, soccer, and lacrosse teams, as well as scores of professional and amateur golfers, bowlers, boxers, wrestlers, tennis players, and martial arts experts. Handicrafts were unbelievably popular — and the more complicated and time-consuming, the better. Watercolors and acrylics had given way to a resurgence of interest in oils among amateur painters; origami was sweeping the nation; indoor gardens, especially those requiring constant attention and uncommon conditions, were the order of the day.

Only the rich could afford clothing made of wool, cotton, or other natural fibers; but even the rich designed and sewed ail their own garments, usually choosing the most colorful fashions from past eras.

Scarcely a household was without a pet. Cats were the most popular, since they adapted easily to the mile-high million-windowed hovels that formed the supercities, but a few breeds of dogs — Keeshonds, Shih Tzus,

Lhasa Apsos, and a handful of others still existed in some quantity. These, like the cats, the rats, the mice, the fish, the birds, the crickets, and every other form of animal life, were inbred, linebred, outcrossed, shown, trained, and pampered.

Of course, to the people living through it, there was nothing very special about their day and age. They accepted what came, as people always have, hopeful of better and fearful of worse. None of them were hungry, few of them were oppressed, most of them were at least minimally employed, and all of them were bored.

They were not to remain bored for long.

December 11, 2047, seemed neither better nor worse, neither more nor less interesting, than any other day of recent vintage. Certainly the two men who were to change the face of their world seemed quite ordinary at first glance: one of them was a criminal, and the other a beggar. Nevertheless, although no one was aware of it — and least of all the two principal players — this day marked the onset of a tapestry of events that would soon jolt Earth's unhappy and apathetic billions loose from their lethargy, never to return.

It began, appropriately enough, at a circus. . . .

PART I

1

*L*ike most of the others in the crowd, the young man was attracted by the huge neon signs and electric calliopes. They had come for pleasure, he for business, but all were drawn like suicidal moths to the artificial flame.

A huge, luminescent banner, fluttering slightly in the cold breeze, proclaimed to all and sundry that this was the

NIGHTSPORE AND THRUSH
INTERNATIONAL TRAVELING CIRCUS
AND THRILL SHOW

Direct from Vienna, as circuses of old used to proclaim, though this one was less circus than thrill show, and more recently from Cleveland than Vienna. It was huge, as it had to be, for the people came out of Chicago and its environs by the tens of thousands, wild-eyed and hopeful as they maintained the frantic pace of their lifelong quest for amusement and diversion.

The barkers, the grifters, the hookers, the musclemen, all the night people had assembled there to meet the challenge.

"This way, ladies and gentlemen!" called the barkers. "This way to Madam Adam! Is she a man? Is he a woman? Step right up, come right in, let's keep it moving. The world's only authenticated hermaphrodite, a compendium of all that's most voluptuous and sexciting in man and woman, is onstage right now, waiting to . . .

"Three throws for twenty dollars, three for only twenty dollars! Hurt? Sure it hurts 'em, mister! Ask your girlfriend how she'd like to have you hurl a dart into her naked, pulsating flesh! Listen to them scream, watch 'em writhe! Six throws for . . ."

The young man paused for a moment before the Living Dartboards, then continued walking down the seemingly endless rows of sheds, games, and exhibits.

"Mister Blister, that's what we call him — Mister Blister! No, he doesn't do any childish stunts like eating fire or walking on hot coals. No, sir, not Mister Blister. Now folks, do you see this blowtorch I have in my hand? Well, step a little closer and . . ."

"First time ever onstage: a full-scale production of Leda and the Swan. Now, I know there are doubters out there, I know there are skeptics. So I'll tell you what I'm gonna do. If any of you feel cheated after the performance, if anyone can honestly state that we don't deliver the goods, I'm gonna refund not just *your* money, but each and every . . ."

The young man turned up another aisle, past the Chamber of 1,000 Pains, with its shrieks and groans coming through loud and clear over a pair of outside amplifiers, past the even more exotic pleasurepain palaces.

Tonight would be a good night; he felt it in his bones. The crowd was immense, as well it should be. There were just so many Madam Adams and Sin Shrines and Pervo Palaces in the world, and when the thrill shows made their rare appearances the money flowed like water — and there was no reason why he shouldn't be able to siphon some off for himself.

The young man continued walking past the gaudy, exotic exhibits, fighting his way through the crowd. Finally he came to a small, unoccupied space about a quarter of a mile from a windowless office building, unloaded his backpack, withdrew a pair of very dark glasses and a white cane, and went to work.

There was a bit of work going on inside the office building too — as Mr. Nightspore and Mr. Thrush were finding out. A tall, slender man, immaculately but archaically clad in the fashion of more than a century ago, sat with his feet on Mr. Thrush's desk. His long, lean fingers were covered by white dress gloves, he wore a double-breasted navy-blue pinstriped suit, and his black leather shoes were covered by shiny white spats. He pulled a large cigar from his lapel pocket and placed it in his mouth; it was immediately lit by one of the four burly men standing behind him.

"So you see, gentlemen," he said calmly, puffing thoughtfully on the cigar, "it's not that I have any aversion to your company, or wish you to vacate the premises and set up shop elsewhere. Chicago is a big city, big enough for all of us."

"Then why did you force your way in here?" demanded Mr. Nightspore.

"Please don't interrupt," he said with a smile that began and ended at the corners of his mouth. "As I was saying, there's money enough for everyone here: money for you, money for your employees, and money for me. Frankly, I'm at a loss to see what your problem is. If anyone will suffer because of your presence here, it will be me. After all, there's no more money to be spent today than there was yesterday, but now there are two more hands reaching out for it — *your* hands. I've looked your operation over, and it's my conservative opinion that you'll take in about nine million dollars a week." He paused, staring coldly at them. "That, gentlemen, is nine million dollars I *won't* be taking in. Do you begin to appreciate my concern?"

Mr. Nightspore started to say something, then thought better of it, and nodded.

"Well," continued the man, with another nonsmile, "I'm delighted to see that we understand each other. After all, we're not enemies: we're on the same side of the fence. It's the people out there" — he waved a hand in the general direction of the midway — "who are our opposition. They've got something we both want and there's no sense working at cross-purposes to get it. The three of us are operating on the same basic premise: if God didn't want them fleeced, He wouldn't have made them sheep." He swung his feet to the floor and leaned forward on the desk. "Now, shall we get down to business?"

"How much do you want?" asked Mr. Thrush suspiciously.

"You make it sound like a gift," replied the man. "Let me hasten to assure you that Solomon Moody Moore takes charity from no one. No, gentlemen, you still misunderstand me. My organization will perform certain necessary services, according to a contract that we'll draw up, and we will receive only a fair and reasonable payment."

"What services?" asked Mr. Thrush.

"A very good question," said Moore. "To begin with, my representatives will police your grounds day and night, serving as what might be called combination caretakers and security officers. You've got a lot of valuable equipment, gentlemen," he added pointedly. "Any vandal could do untold damage to it in a matter of minutes." He paused and took another puff of his cigar. "Furthermore, I noticed a number of gambling games as I toured your circus; upward of eighty, I would estimate. Most of them are designed to break between ten and fifteen percent in favor of the house. You've got them rigged for thirty, of course, but you've been taken in by a bunch of clumsy amateurs. They're robbing you blind and giving the suckers too close to an even break. My people, at no extra charge, will set your games for a fifty percent break, and will operate them for you."

"If all this is free, what's the final bill going to run us?" asked Mr. Nightspore suspiciously.

"One-third," said Moore.

"One-third of what?"

"Everything." Moore's cigar went out, and he waited patiently for one of his men to light it again. "View it as a business investment that will pay off in large dividends. I'll double your gross by the end of the week, so it will cost you virtually nothing, and when you leave town, all of my improvements will leave with you."

"And then our partnership is ended?"

Moore smiled. "Oh, no. That, like diamonds, is forever." He held up a hand to stifle their protests. "Believe me, gentlemen, if we find that you're not making more money than before, we can always renegotiate our contract." He took another puff of his cigar, then placed it in an ashtray. "Now let's get down to business. How many drug emporiums are you operating here?"

"None!" said Mr. Nightspore emphatically.

"I would prefer a little more honesty now that we're going to be partners," said Moore calmly. "I counted six, but I might have missed a couple. I repeat: how many are there?"

"Seven," said Mr. Nightspore with a sigh.

"That's better," said Moore. "There is absolutely nothing like openness among friends. I'll take you at your word that there are seven. If we find any more, we'll assume they're not operating under your auspices and will appropriate their stock. Now, how much do you cut your hallucinogens and your harder drugs?"

"Not at all!" snapped Mr. Thrush.

Moore stared curiously at him for a moment. "You know, I think you're just stupid enough to be telling the truth. We can be of service to you there, as well. Next point: how many people die here every week?"

"We're covered for that," said Mr. Nightspore defensively. "No one enters the scare shows or the sado tents without signing an ironclad release. We've been to court four times in the past two years, and won all four cases."

"You didn't answer my question: how many people die at your circus every week?"

"About ten."

"Not enough."

"What?" shrilled both partners in unison.

"Not enough," repeated Moore. "People love blood even more than they love the grotesque. They're not coming here to see your Four-Headed Baby or your Vaseline Corpse. They want death. The more you give them, the more they'll talk about it and come back for seconds. Take your Russian Roulette exhibit: you've got a nine-cylinder gun with one bullet in it and you're offering a lousy thousand dollars to the man who'll play the game. Starting tomorrow, you'll put three bullets into a six-cylinder gun, offer a ten-grand prize, and triple your admission price. Ditto with your Pervo Palaces and all the other crap like that. Agreed?"

The two partners nodded reluctantly.

"As for your girls, get more of them. Prettier, too. And the place reeks of Caucasians. I want to see blacks, browns, reds, yellows, albinos, and polka-dots. If you can't get them, let my people know and we'll hunt them up. If they don't know the meaning of the word 'normal,' so much the better. Also, I want you to start two exhibits for women only; I'll supply what you need for them. Can do?"

"Well, I don't know . . . that, is, I'm not —" began Mr. Nightspore.

"Can do?" repeated Moore coldly.

Mr. Nightspore nodded.

"Excellent," said Moore. "All the members of my organization will wear red armbands with your logo printed on them." He paused. "They are not to be interfered with. Is that absolutely clear?"

The partners assured him that it was.

"My people will be armed for your protection," continued Moore. "I think it would be best if no one else carried any type of weapon, and that includes any security men you may now have on your payroll. It will avoid unpleasant misunderstandings. If any member of my organization abuses your hospitality, or if every last penny is not accounted for, I will expect you to report it to me." He stood up and stretched.

"And now, if you gentlemen will excuse me, I'd like to take another walk around our circus. My associates will provide you with the proper contracts. I had a feeling that we could come to an equitable agreement, so I took the liberty of having them drawn up before I left my office. My men," he added meaningfully, "will keep you company until the contracts have been signed. Since you won't be needing me for the next few minutes, I think I'll take my leave of you. I find these interviews personally distasteful."

He put on his bowler — another anachronism — and walked out of the building.

It was not, he reflected as he mingled with the crowd, a bad night's work. Nightspore and Thrush ran the same kind of show as everyone else: it was geared for fear, lust, and greed, with a fair share of side trips into the bizarre. It was also rigged to the teeth, which made it fair game for him.

He looked up at a Eurasian girl proudly displaying her four nipples as a come-on for the Freak Show. Yes, he reflected, people would shell out all kinds of money just to see something different, to get out of their ruts and worship somewhere other than at the altar of Humdrum. And as long as people like Nightspore and Thrush were willing to bilk them, he'd stay solvent by bilking the bilkers.

Of course, there were legitimate business interests to be considered too, and he'd been buying into quite a lot of them lately: a leatherworks factory in New Hampshire, a computer plant in Pittsburgh, thoroughbred yearlings in Kentucky and California, a professional basketball team in Albuquerque. With more and more time to fill, there were more and more ways to capitalize on the needs of one's fellow man. Although,

Moore acknowledged grimly, even the capitalizers had to battle against boredom. He himself had more money than he could hope to spend in one lifetime, and a reputation that would take him several lifetimes to expunge, and yet he kept at it.

And why not? After all, what else was there to do? The moment he stopped feeding off humanity he would become indistinguishable from them, ripe for somebody else to come feed off him. He had started as a small-time burglar, learned the ropes, began gathering a meticulously selected organization about him, had been careful never to move prematurely, and because he was a little smarter and a little hungrier and a little more ruthless than the next guy, had taken over the next guy's territory, and the next guy after that, and after that. He had a good, solid structure behind him, peopled with the best men and women that money and the opportunity to escape from boredom could buy. Every one of them wanted his job — he had no use for anyone who willingly settled for second-best — and it kept both him and them on their toes, a reasonably healthy state of affairs in this day and age.

He'd been uncommonly successful in his chosen field of endeavor, although that didn't really surprise him. When all was said and done, everyone else was running away from dullness and drudgery, while he was running *toward* his problems, molding men and situations to fit his various needs.

A shrill yell broke his train of thought, and he looked up to find himself in front of the Chamber of 1,000 Pains. He grimaced. Why people would pay perfectly good money to have the hell flailed out of them was beyond his capacity to understand, and he had no greater empathy for the hundreds of spectators who shelled out still more money to watch. He shook his head, shrugged, and continued walking.

He circled the entire Thrill Show, feeling increasingly unclean from his proximity to the marks, and finally decided to return to the office building to pick up the contracts. As he approached it, he noticed a small crowd gathered around a young man with dark glasses. The man had a moth-eaten top hat in one hand and a white cane in the other, and was singing psalms in a less-than-outstanding tenor.

Moore stopped and looked into the hat. "Not much of a haul," he remarked. "You'd do better with bawdy ballads."

"You want one, you got one," said the young man, breaking into one of the three million or so verses of "The Ring-Dang-Doo."

"Enough!" laughed Moore a moment later, flipping a coin into the upturned hat.

"You don't like the songs of the masses?" asked the young man with a smile.

"I don't like anything about the masses," replied Moore. "Want to make some real money?"

The young man nodded.

"Five hundred dollars says you're not blind."

The young man felt around in his hat, fingering the coins. "Sixteen dollars and seventy-three cents says you can't prove it."

Moore lit a match and casually tossed it toward the young man's face. There was no reaction.

"Not bad," said Moore, suddenly releasing a blow to the young man's midsection. The air gushed out of him and he fell to his knees. Some of the change rolled out of the hat, and his fingers traveled frantically over the ground, trying to retrieve the lost coins. Moore walked over to him and faked a kick at his face, which went unheeded.

Finally Moore helped him to his feet, then dug a wad of five-dollar bills out of his pocket, counted ten of them off in front of the young man's face, and placed them in the hat.

"Thank you, sir," wheezed the young man.

Moore paused a moment, then took the money back, withdrew his wallet, peeled off ten fifty-dollar bills, and dropped them into the ragged top hat.

"I was wrong," he said, giving the young man a pat on the shoulder and walking off toward the office building.

Then, as he reached the door, the young man called out after him: "Hey, Plug-Ugly, where the hell did you ever buy those godawful white spats? They make you look like a goddamned faggot!"

Moore wheeled around, but the young man had already vanished into the crowd.

And *that* was the first meeting between Solomon Moody Moore and Jeremiah the B.

Most historians would have swapped their fortunes, their spouses, and their eyeteeth to have been there.

2

*T*uesday was smut day.

Or, more properly, Tuesday was the day of the week when Moore went over the reports of his publishing corporation and its affiliates and issued his directives for the coming week.

He sat now in what was quite possibly the most Spartan office in the entire Chicago complex. Unlike most executive suites it contained no televisions, no radios, no sound systems, no paintings, no couches, no exercise areas, no handicrafts alcoves, no wet bars. It was spare and barren, like the man who worked in it. There was one large desk, made of artificial mahogany, which supported a computer terminal, three telephones, and a quartet of intercoms. Facing it were six chairs, none of them very comfortable. There were doors on three of the walls, two of which were rarely used, and one of the walls contained a small built-in safe. There was only one window in the room, albeit a huge one, and the view was invariably obscured by a row of blinds that had been layered between the inner and outer panes of glass. What pleasures Moore sought were found elsewhere; his office was a place for work, and nothing else.

"The reports, Ben, if you please."

The man sitting across the desk from Moore handed him a sheaf of computer readouts, along with a large breakdown sheet. Ben Pryor, his clothing as loud as Moore's was muted, his wavy blond hair a stark contrast to Moore's straight steel-gray, was Moore's second-in-command, in charge of the day-to-day management of all Moore's enterprises. He was shrewd, highly intelligent, and totally competent, possessed of a master's degree in business administration and another in economics. He was also openly ambitious, which was natural but regrettable; he knew far too much about the operation for Moore ever to let him go, and the day wasn't too far off when Moore would have to eliminate him in a more permanent manner.

Moore began reading the reports, making an occasional comment, issuing a rare order. The pornography industry was doing very well these days, as usual, and the problems of management had more to do with the vast size of the operation than with any legal or sales problems. Indeed, sometimes the scope of it amazed even Moore: he owned three publishing companies that specialized in erotic books, magazines, and newspapers, and two others that churned out pornographic videotapes and computer disks. Between them, they produced some three hundred different titles each month, with sales in excess of eighty million units.

But that was just the beginning. Pornography, though going through one of its cyclic periods of legality, was still far from being socially acceptable and was subject to occasional harassment, which meant that the huge, monolithic distributors who monopolized service in the densely populated metropolitan areas didn't care to handle the stuff, or at least didn't push it with the same verve and zest that they applied to the more suitable publications. So Moore had quietly bought up a number of existing secondary agencies and created still more, each of them specializing in the type of material the large, independent distributors didn't want.

From there it was just a small step to buying and building some four thousand pornographic emporiums that specialized in carrying his merchandise. Since many of them catered to prostitution and the more bizarre sexual desires of the public, Moore had also branched out very thoroughly into such services. Finally, he had purchased a huge printing plant that not only sufficed for all his needs but also printed a goodly portion of his rivals' output as well, and had built a small factory that manufactured most of the sexual gadgets he carried in his stores.

The money didn't just roll in; it *poured*. The average publisher needed to sell about forty percent of his print run to break even; Moore, who owned the publishing company, the printing press, the distribution agencies, the bookstores, and all the associated items, broke even with a sale of five percent. He sold more than five percent, though; more than eighty percent, in point of fact. It wasn't that his products were superior; they weren't. But when you control the distribution lifelines, you control the industry, and when you have the power to fire any distributor who puts a single copy of a rival's publication on display before all of your own are sold, you are a lead-pipe cinch to wind up with the lion's share of the market. Moore not only had the lion's share of the market, but held on to it with the tenacity of a lion defending his kill from all the scavengers of the jungle.

The orders came slowly as Moore studied the reports: fire this man, promote that woman, sell this store, print more copies of that magazine, kill this line of plastic sex aids, place ten more girls in that city. Pryor took it all down on a pocket computer and left to set the wheels in motion. He returned a few minutes later, a beer in his hand, and sat back down opposite Moore.

"That's your fourth today," noted Moore disapprovingly, gesturing toward the beer.

"Haven't your spies got anything better to do than measure my alcoholic consumption?" asked Pryor with no trace of surprise or concern.

"They're doing it."

"Maybe you ought to send them over to the Thrill Show. Your new partners have already been pulling strings to get out of their contract."

"Let 'em," said Moore coldly. "This is my town." He paused. "If they want to mess around with me, they'd better choose a city where I don't own half the politicians and all of the coroners."

"What's the show like?" asked Pryor. "I haven't had a chance to get out there yet."

"Maybe if you'd stop trying to seduce my secretary and my stockbroker and every other woman who's ever had anything to do with me, you could find the time," said Moore with a mirthless smile.

"Can't blame a guy for trying," replied Pryor easily. "Besides, not everyone can lead your ascetic life."

"That's what keeps us in business," said Moore. "The way *I* live, and the way *they* live."

Pryor stared across the desk for a long moment, mystified as always by the concept of a criminal kingpin who grew rich off his victims' lusts and seemed violently opposed to displaying any of those drives himself. Finally he shrugged.

"You still haven't told me what the show is like," he said, taking a swallow of his beer.

"Pretty typical," said Moore. "They're selling dreams, just like all the others."

"That's a good commodity these days."

"It always was," said Moore. He clasped his hands together and stared thoughtfully at his fingertips. "I wonder if there isn't a cheaper way to go about it, though."

"What are you talking about?" asked Pryor.

"Dreams."

"We're already in it, except that we call them drugs."

Moore shook his head irritably. "Drugs *create* dreams. I want to *fulfill* them."

"You mean like putting a harlot in every room?" chuckled Pryor.

"I'm being serious, Ben," said Moore coldly.

"You always are," sighed Pryor. "But I haven't got the foggiest notion of what you're talking about."

"Just what I said: Dream Come True, Inc. I wonder if it's feasible?"

"How the hell should I know? What's the angle?"

"The angle is simply this: we'll fulfill any dream for a price. After all, the Thrill Show isn't going to be here forever, and besides, they're long on promises and short on results."

"Give me a for-instance."

"Okay," said Moore slowly. "Let's say some guy finds his life unbearably dull . . ."

"Which he probably does."

"And he wants to have one all-out fling at some excitement."

"Such as?"

Moore shrugged. "I don't know. Let's say he wants to rob the First National Bank."

"You're not seriously suggesting that we do it for him?" said Pryor incredulously.

"No. But what if we help him do it for himself? We make up the plans, help him case the joint, supply all the muscle and expertise he needs, and guarantee that he gets away scot-free."

"There's got to be a gimmick," said Pryor skeptically. "Why do we take all the risks so he can grab all the dough?"

"Of course there's a gimmick," said Moore patiently. "We're not altruists, Ben. What if we charge him a flat fee of half a million, hold his take down to a hundred thousand, and split our fee sixty-forty with the bank? Everybody's happy, nobody goes to jail, and we all get a little richer." He paused. "Anyway, it's got possibilities. What do you think?"

"I think you picked a loaded example," said Pryor. "There are something like nine elephants left in the world, all worth tens of millions. What if he wants to shoot them all in one afternoon? Or take an example closer to home: I would love to kill my ex-wife and sire fifty bastard children within a year. What can this outfit do for me?"

"We could certainly supply you with fifty women over a three-month span; the rest would be up to you. As for killing your ex-wife . . . well, that could probably be arranged for a substantially higher fee." Moore smiled. "Of course, you'd have to tell us exactly which of your many ex-wives you had in mind."

"And the elephants?"

"He'd have to be a very rich daydreamer," said Moore with a shrug. "Anyway, have our people work out a *schema* of what is actually possible with this notion, and have them get it back to me in a day or two. Why should I split all the dreamers' money with Mr. Nightspore and Mr. Thrush?"

"Are those really their names?" asked Pryor with a disbelieving grin.

"What's in a name? It's their business that interests me."

Pryor left a few minutes later, and Moore took a brief lunch break, after which he began working on some of those enterprises that the government did *not* know about. Most of it was accomplished by telephone, through so many middlemen that nothing could be traced back to him. No records, written or computerized, were kept anywhere, and even Pryor didn't know the full extent of the operation, though Moore knew that he spent a lot of his own time and money trying to find out.

Moore left the office in late afternoon, as was his custom, boarded an underground monorail, and, accompanied by a solitary bodyguard, went to the center of town. The area had once been called the Loop, because of the elevated train tracks that encircled it, and the sobriquet still held, though the tracks had long since been torn down and the vast business buildings, all interconnected on every level and covered by an enormous dome, took up three square miles of incredibly valuable real estate. The suburbs might know rain and snow, but the inner city was always clear and pleasant.

He rode the slidewalks and escalators until, half a mile above the ground, he came to his regular Tuesday-evening eateasy, a swank and illegal little restaurant with a grubby exterior that proclaimed to all nonmembers that it was a branch of a silicone surgery beautification chain. The government had been rationing meat and most other non-soya products for more than a decade, but men and women of means soon found entrepreneurs to cater to their tastes and hungers, and the eateasies had become some of the more affluent pillars of the huge underground economy.

Moore left his bodyguard outside and his umbrella at the door — it never rained within the enclosed downtown section of the city, but he carried it religiously — and was ushered to a small table in the back, where he dined on a felonious meal of genuine veal cutlets and whipped potatoes. He ordered blueberry pie for dessert (six months for selling it, one thousand dollars for eating it, courtesy of the United States Fair Food Administration), capped it off with a cup of real coffee, and paid the standard flat fee of six hundred dollars. Then, sated, he picked up his umbrella and, joined by his bodyguard, he reentered the world of soybean by-products and flavored water.

He toyed with the idea of returning to the Thrill Show, hunting up the phony blind man who had duped him yesterday, and offering him a job in the organization, but concluded that the man was sharp enough to have a different gimmick for every night of the week and would be impossible to spot.

He decided to go home for the night instead. As he approached the monorail station he reached into his pocket for a token, and felt his fingers come into contact with a piece of paper. He pulled it out and saw that it was a business card:

THE BIZARRE BAZAAR
Specialists in the Unusual
461 N. LaSalle – 5ᵀᴴ Level

Scrawled across the back of it, in nearly illegible handwriting, were the words: "Come alone."

It could be a trap, of course; after all, if his life weren't in continual danger, he wouldn't require a bodyguard in the first place. However, most of his bigger deals were consummated in just such a manner — a politician who couldn't be seen going into Moore's office, a rival's underling with some information to sell, a deserted lover ready to turn against a man or woman Moore was out to ruin. After a moment's debate with himself, he dismissed his bodyguard and rode the escalator to the fifth level of Wabash Street. Then he took a slidewalk to Randolph Street, transferred to a northbound slidewalk, got off at LaSalle, and began walking north on a stationary ramp.

When he crossed over the long-dry bed of the Chicago River, which now housed a park and a huge sporting complex, he became aware of a subtle change in the stores and shops. Gone were the huge, brightly lit department stores, the plush, velvet-walled jewelers, the fashion shops and gift emporiums and other high-quality specialty shops. In their place were grubby little antique stores, secondhand bookstores drowning in stacks and stacks of dusty, moldy volumes, bars and brothels and warehouses.

Finally he came to the address he sought. It looked like a little hole in the wall, a storefront out of some Western ghost town. The windows were covered by dark, opaque shades, there were no signs, stating either the name of the establishment or what it dealt in, and a distinct smell of incense emanated from its half-open doorway.

He took one last took around to make sure he hadn't been followed, then walked into the store. He found himself in a dimly lit maze, with the walls blackened up to the ceiling, and followed it carefully as it continued to turn back upon itself. Finally he emerged into a long, narrow room that was illuminated only by an occasional red light bulb.

There were two glass showcases, one running down each side of the room. On display in them were various grotesque torture devices: spiked necklaces, tongue ties, exotic branding irons, razor-sharp chastity belts, instruments for piercing or removing all limbs and organs not essential to the minimal maintenance of life. Hung on the walls (or nailed to them; he wasn't sure which) were shriveled human heads, hands, legs, fingers, genitalia, noses, eyes, and ears. Stacked neatly in a corner were dozens of spears, spikes, and prods.

"May I help you?" said a hoarse voice from behind him.

He turned and found himself confronted by a little man with a satin patch over one eye. The man extended a hand, which was missing two fingers and part of a thumb, and Moore mechanically took and shook it.

"Welcome to the Bizarre Bazaar," said the man. "My name is Krebbs. If there is anything you don't see, just ask. We have many more rooms, each designed around a single theme."

"I'm not a customer," replied Moore, showing the card to Krebbs.

"Ah, well," sighed the man, "there was no harm in asking. One must try to make a living." He smiled. "Surely you, of all people, can appreciate that."

"You sound as if you know me."

"I know *of* you, Mr. Moore," said Krebbs. "You're one of my idols, if truth be known. Ah, to wield such power, to maim and kill and destroy! It must seem like paradise itself!"

"You must have me confused with someone else," said Moore in cold, level tones. "I'm just a businessman."

"Whatever you say, Mr. Moore," said Krebbs with a grin.

"*That's* what I say. Now, why did you ask me to come here?"

"Oh, but I didn't," said Krebbs. "I assure you, Mr. Moore, that I am content to worship you from afar."

"Then who did?"

"I can take you to her if you like," offered Krebbs.

"To who?"

"Why, to the young lady you've come to see."

"What's her name?" asked Moore.

"You needn't be coy with me, Mr. Moore," said Krebbs. "I told you — I'm on *your* side. If you wish to conduct your liaisons in my place of business, I'm only too happy to oblige."

"Where is she?" asked Moore, deciding that further questions would be fruitless.

"She wasn't quite sure when you'd arrive," replied Krebbs, "so I had her wait for you in our Unique Boutique. I'm sure she'll find something suitable to wear there, and there's a huge bed just across the hall." He gave Moore a sly wink with his only eye and took him by the arm, leading him to a curtain of hanging beads. "Fifth room on the right."

Moore shook his arm loose and walked down the corridor until he came to the fifth, and last, right-hand door, then opened it softly and walked in. The room was as poorly lit as the rest of the shop, and seemed to be composed of nothing but clothes racks and mirrors. It was actually quite small, but the mirrors, which covered the walls, ceiling, and floor, gave it the appearance of extending to infinity in all directions.

A blond girl stood at the far end of the room, about twenty feet from him. She wore leather hip boots with long, sharp heels, shoulder-length leather gloves, a black waist cincher, and nothing else. In her left hand she held a small cat-o'-nine-tails, which had bright little metal prongs at the end of each tail. Her face was covered by a catlike mask, replete with silver whiskers.

"I had a little time on my hands," she said in a low, husky voice, "so I decided to try out some of the merchandise." She turned around gracefully. "Do you like it?"

"I don't buy this shit; I sell it," said Moore distastefully. "Am I supposed to know you?"

"Would you like to?"

"Not especially," he replied. "Did you place the card in my pocket?"

"No."

"But you had it placed there?"

"Yes." She moved a bit closer to him, making the tails undulate rhythmically with a flick of her wrist.

"Why?"

"I have something to give you."

"What?"

"This!" she whispered, suddenly bringing the whip down toward his face.

Moore reached out his arm instinctively and absorbed most of the blow's force on the fleshy part of his biceps. He backed away, startled, and the girl came after him.

"Who sent you?" he demanded, dodging another blow. "What the hell is going on here?"

There was no response from the girl, except for a renewed effort to rip his face apart with the whip. He knew better than to keep using his arm as a shield, and he turned and ran down the narrow corridor to the room where he had met Krebbs. Once there, he looked around for the one-eyed proprietor, but the place was deserted. He raced to the stacked weapons and pulled a hooked spear off the top of the heap.

"All right," he said, leveling the weapon between her breasts as she entered the room. "Are you ready to tell me what this is all about?"

The girl screamed an obscenity and swung the whip again. He ducked and prodded her shoulder with the spear. A little trickle of blood appeared, but the girl didn't seem to notice it. Unmindful of the spear, she continued chasing him around the room. Finally he decided that he had no choice but to start defending himself in earnest, and he cut her twice on the arm, once deeply. She fought on like a cornered beast, totally ignoring the wounds. He practically severed her ear with the next swipe of his weapon, again with no effect.

"Of course!" he said suddenly. "You're one of the Living Dartboards!" He ducked as she picked up a glass jar from the counter and hurled it at him. "Who put you up to this — Nightspore or Thrush? Or was it the pair of them?"

Her only response was to kick out with her boot, trying to stab him with its long, murderously sharp heel. He stepped aside, grabbed her leg, and twisted it. She fell heavily to the floor, and he leaped on top of her, turning her onto her stomach and holding her motionless. It took six sharp blows to the base of her skull before he finally managed to render her unconscious.

He dragged her over to one of the red light bulbs and examined her back and neck very carefully. Yes, there were the tiny, almost invisible scars from the nerve-severing operation that had rendered her insensitive to pain.

He decided against waiting to question her when she awoke. After all, if she didn't want to talk, nothing he could do was going to change her mind — and for all he knew, Krebbs was still lurking around somewhere, waiting to put a bullet in his back. He toyed with the notion of covering the girl with a blanket, slinging her over his shoulder, and taking her with him, but he knew he wouldn't be able to control her if she regained consciousness, so he decided to leave her to the tender mercies of one of his security squads. Still worried about Krebbs, he pulled out a cellular phone and called Pryor.

"Ben? Moore here. It appears that one of our new partners has gotten delusions of grandeur. Maybe both of them. . . . Yeah. Right. . . . You won't believe me. . . . A naked blonde with a whip, if you must know." He grimaced at Pryor's reply. "I *told* you you wouldn't believe me. Anyway, I want you to collect the muscle and find out which one tried to whack me. And while you're at it, send a squad to a little joint on LaSalle Street called the Bizarre Bazaar, at 461 North on the fifth level, and do a job on it. You'll find the girl there. I think she's got an accomplice — a guy with a maimed hand. Bring him in if you find him hanging around the place. . . . No, I'll be fine. Catch you in the morning."

He hung up, walked to the nearest monorail platform, and within ten minutes was approaching the entrance to his apartment, part of an exclusive complex at the south end of the inner-city dome. He nodded to his security men and went in, locking the door behind him. Then, being a thorough man, he began a methodical search to make doubly certain nothing had been stolen or tampered with. When he was finally satisfied that everything was as it should be, he sat down in an antique leather chair, put his feet up on a stuffed armadillo that he used for a hassock, and mentally reviewed the events of the evening.

His conclusion was that they just didn't make any sense. Any fool would know that sooner or later he'd be able to spot the girl as being from the Thrill Show — and Nightspore and Thrush, while certainly malleable, hadn't struck him as fools.

Suddenly restless, he arose and began stalking around the apartment. Like his office, his personal dwelling was modestly furnished and did not interface with the outside world except for two telephones, both unlisted. Remaining aloof from the masses that he victimized had become almost a fetish with him, and he allowed himself none of their vices for fear that their accompanying weaknesses might rub off on him. Once, as a surprise, some of his bodyguards had imported a pair of women and ensconced them in his bedroom before he got home; he had rushed to the phone and fired them on the spot, then ordered Pryor to come over and take the women away. Sex, especially the kind the women had promised him in low, sultry voices, was hardly apt to be boring, but he was in the business of selling sex — among other things — and bartenders don't drink when on duty. For one week every three months he packed up and left everything in Pryor's charge. He never said where he went or what he did on these quarterly trips, nor did anyone ask him, but the betting around the office was that the bartender went on a binge four times a year.

The apartment contained no drugs, no alcohol, nothing that could possibly be construed as a means of escaping from reality. When he worked at selling fantasies he practiced only austerity: he partook of no sex, no stimulants, no hobbies or crafts. He had two indulgences: one was gourmet food, and the other was his library. From floor to ceiling all the walls were lined with books, some new, some incredibly old. They were neither neat nor ordered, but he knew where every title was, what knowledge or emotion each author had to impart to him. There were poets and playwrights, philosophers and biographers, modern fiction intermixed with ancient and future fact, and even an old, timeworn copy of the Bible.

It was to his library that he now turned for relief and relaxation. He picked up a couple of works by Wilde and Austen, chronicles of more civilized eras that had no need for a business such as his, returned to his oversized leather chair, sat down with a grunt, and prepared to read himself to sleep.

He was drifting in the halfworld between clarity and slumber when the buzzing of the phone brought him to instant wakefulness.

"Moore here."

"This is Ben. How's the ravisher of Living Dartboards?"

"Knock it off and get to the point."

"The point is that we've got a couple of problems," said Pryor.

"You've been to the Thrill Show?"

"Yes."

"And the Bizarre Bazaar?"

"No such place."

"The hell there isn't!" snapped Moore. "It's at" — he pulled the card out of his pocket "461 North LaSalle, on the fifth level."

"The hell there *is,*" replied Pryor, not without a trace of enjoyment at Moore's distress. "We went through the whole four-hundred block, both sides, and it's just not there."

"I was there two hours ago!"

"You're sure it wasn't *South* LaSalle, or 461 North on some other street — Clark or Wells, maybe?"

"Damn it, Ben — I know where I was and I know what happened to me!"

"I'm sure you do," said Pryor. "But the fact remains that the store isn't there. Besides, the whole thing sounds like some adolescent fantasy. If I didn't know you better, I'd say you'd been drinking."

"I'll take you there myself, first thing in the morning," said Moore disgustedly. "What about Nightspore and Thrush?"

"I know this is going to sound like we're operating in two different worlds, but they didn't know anything about it."

"Horseshit!"

"That's the strongest word I ever heard you use," said Pryor, amused.

"They had to know something," persisted Moore, ignoring him.

"We were pretty thorough."

"*How* thorough?"

"You are now the sole surviving partner of the Nightspore and Thrush International Traveling Circus and Thrill Show."

"Great," spat Moore. "Just what I always wanted." He sighed. "Damn it, Ben, I told you to *question* them, not kill them!"

"You also told me that one of them was behind all this, so we used enough force to get the answers we needed. It was just their hard luck that they happened to be innocent. I've got our legal eagles down at City Hall smoothing things over. I think we can handle it."

"Operating on the assumption — probably erroneous — that our muscle didn't kill them before they could tell the truth, who the hell sent this girl after me?"

"The only thing to do is find the girl and beat it out of her," replied Pryor. "I'd love to try."

"Lots of luck," said Moore, repressing an urge to laugh. "You've got a remarkably single-minded approach to problem-solving, Ben." He paused. "As for identifying her, hell, I probably wouldn't recognize her with her pants on. Check the Thrill Show and find out which of the Living Dartboards was missing for a couple of hours starting at about six o'clock this evening. Track her down and bring her back to the office. Then check out the Bizarre Bazaar again, and if it's really not there, assemble some muscle in my office tomorrow morning at nine sharp and we'll go hunting for it. And Ben?"

"Yeah?"

"Unless you want to find out what happens when I become seriously displeased with someone, don't mess up again."

He placed the receiver back on the hook, picked up Jane Austen, and tried to read himself to sleep again.

It wasn't so easy this time.

3

"You look even more frazzled than usual for this time of day," remarked Moore as Pryor entered his office the next morning. "Shall I assume that we haven't accomplished a hell of a lot?"

"A fair assumption," admitted Pryor. "I did manage to assuage the high moral principles of the city fathers, though. They now agree that both Nightspore and Thrush died of heart failure."

"Well, that's something, anyway," said Moore. "What about the girl?"

"We checked out the Living Dartboard show, and it seems that one of them — a Lisa Walpole — has been missing since four o'clock yesterday."

"Blonde?"

Pryor nodded. "And from what I can tell, she's just the type who'd rather whip you to death than stand back and shoot you. I've got a couple of men trying to pick up her trail, and we've stationed agents at all the airports and bus stations. If she's anywhere in the Chicago complex, we ought to turn her up in a day or two." He paused. "We learned one other thing about her, too: she was sleeping with Thrush."

"Are you sure?" asked Moore, frowning. "I thought when they severed the pain receptors, it deadened the capacity for pleasure as well." He paused, then shrugged. "Oh, well, I suppose there's no law that says a girl who sleeps with her boss has to enjoy it. But I still can't figure out the connection. If Thrush didn't put her up to it, then what the hell was she doing there?"

Pryor shrugged. "I imagine we'll have to catch her to find out."

"While you're at it, I've got someone else who needs a bit of catching: an old man named Krebbs, sixtyish, about five foot seven or eight. He's wearing a patch over one eye — I can't remember which — and his right hand is missing a couple of fingers and part of the thumb. Real slimy type."

"I'll skip the slimy part, and get the rest of the description to our men right away," said Pryor, entering the information on his ever-present pocket computer.

"How about the Bizarre Bazaar?"

"I checked it out again myself, and it's simply not there. The phone book doesn't have it listed either. Are you absolutely sure of that address?"

Moore produced the card and slid it across the desk to Pryor. "We'll make that our next order of business. Leave someone here to keep an eye on things, gather up half a dozen security men, and let's get this show on the road."

Half an hour later Moore, Pryor, and six security men turned onto the North 400 block on the fifth level of LaSalle Street. They walked past two back-number magazine shops and an exceptionally dirty soya restaurant, and then Moore pointed to a building some fifty yards away.

"There it is!" he exclaimed. "What the hell were you talking about, Ben?"

"All I see is an old religious-goods shop," said Pryor , quickening his pace to keep up with Moore. "I checked it out this morning, and it's legit."

The windows of the store were no longer covered, and as Moore looked in he saw nothing but a tiny shop, no more than fifteen feet deep, its walls and counters covered by Bibles, crucifixes, and other denominational keepsakes. An elderly woman stood behind one of the counters, looking through a pile of papers which Moore took to be invoices or index cards.

"May I be of some help to you gentlemen?" inquired the woman as Moore and Pryor entered the store, followed by their security men.

"Where is Krebbs?" demanded Moore.

"Krebbs?" repeated the woman thoughtfully. "He must be one of our newer authors. I don't believe we have any of his works, though you are of course welcome to browse through our stock of books yourself."

Moore unrolled a large wad of bills and laid them on the counter. "Last night there was a man named Krebbs working here. I want to know where he is."

"Here? Last night? You must be mistaken. No one works here except me and my daughter-in-law. We have no one named Krebbs here."

"Let's try another one." He stared coldly at her. "Does the name Solomon Moody Moore mean anything to you?"

"No."

"Lie to me once more and it will," he promised. "How do I get to the back?"

"The back of what?"

"The back of the store," he replied. "It goes on for hundreds of feet."

The woman stared at him as if he could be expected to fall to the ground and begin foaming at the mouth at any moment.

"The store ends at the wall right behind me," she said at last, speaking

as if to a child. "That's all there is, except for a bathroom over there."
She indicated a door on a side wall.

"I told you that's all there was," grinned Pryor.

"How long have you been in business at this location?" continued
Moore .

"Thirty-seven years."

"Where were you last night?"

"Right here, of course."

"How late?"

"Until nine o'clock, as always," she replied. "Are you sure you're
feeling well?"

"No, I am not feeling well!" snapped Moore. "I am feeling angry as
all hell, and getting angrier by the second!" He gestured to the bills lying
on the counter. "I'm going to ask you one last time: where is Krebbs?"

"I keep telling you — I don't know anyone called Krebbs."

Moore picked up his money and put it back into his pocket, then
turned to the head of his security team.

"See that wall?"

"Yes, Mr. Moore."

"Break it down," he said, stepping back out of the way.

"Have you gone crazy?" said Pryor. "It's a goddamned Bible shop,
nothing more!"

"If you talk like a fool, I'm going to have to start treating you like
one, Ben," said Moore, deciding that it really was getting near time to
dispose of Pryor. "I was here. I know what I saw."

"If you don't get out of here and stop harassing me right this minute,
I'm going to call the police!" shouted the woman.

"On the contrary," said Moore. "You're going to stay right where you
are until I say otherwise." He turned to his security team. "One of you
men come over and keep an eye on her."

"Will a laser be okay, sir?" asked the man who was examining the
wall.

"I don't care how you do it," replied Moore. "Just get it done."

The man pulled out a laser device and began tracing a line from left
to right, about twenty inches below the ceiling. He came to a weak spot
a couple of feet before reaching the southernmost corner.

"That's it!" he said, throwing a shoulder against the wall. It crumbled
like the thin plasterboard it was, leaving a doorsized hole through which
Moore, Pryor, and five of the security men passed.

They found themselves in the main room of the Bizarre Bazaar, with
its weapons and torture devices and grisly souvenirs. Moore walked
through the room and went down a dimly lit corridor to the Unique
Boutique.

"What do you think of my adolescent fantasy, Ben?" he asked with grim satisfaction.

Pryor shook his head. "I was wrong. But if it had happened to me and I'd found this Bible shop here the next morning, I would have thought I dreamed it all."

"That's why I'm the boss of this outfit."

"I don't follow you."

"I never fantasize," replied Moore.

One of the security men approached them. "There's no one in any of the rooms, sir," he announced. "We did find a number of long black boards, though, which must be the maze you described."

"Look around and see what else you can dig up," said Moore, dismissing him. "Ben, if you're all through sounding like a complete idiot, suppose you tell me what you think is going on here."

"Someone tried to kill you and missed," replied Pryor, "and then decided that it wouldn't be real healthy to stick around and wait for us to show up." He shrugged. "Makes sense. I don't imagine Al Capone ever gave anyone a second chance at *him,* either."

Moore shook his head. "Too simple. There's a lot more to this than meets the eye. Let's have a little chat with our religious fanatic up front and see if we can get some answers."

When they got back to the false front of the Bizarre Bazaar they found their security man lying dead in a pool of his own blood, a bullet lodged in his temple. The woman was nowhere to be seen.

Moore yelled for other security men, who arrived seconds later.

"Who knows anything about gunshot wounds?" he demanded. "Did the old lady do this?"

One of the men examined the corpse. "Not a chance," he announced after a brief inspection. "This came from an awfully powerful handgun. If she'd fired at close range, it would have taken most of his head off. I'd guess that somebody opened the door and fired from there. There must have been a silencer, too, or we'd have heard one hell of a bang."

"So we can assume Krebbs or the Dartboard was keeping the place under surveillance, just in case I came back," said Moore. He turned to Pryor. "Ben, you got a good look at the old woman; see what you can do about tracking her down. Two of you men take this place apart and see if you can turn up anything that might explain what's been going on. When you're through, rig the whole place up with an electronic watchdog system. You other three, come with me and see to it that I get back to the office in one piece."

He walked warily to the monorail system, half expecting to be shot down at any moment and cursing the day that individual transportation had been outlawed within the city limits, but nothing unusual happened and he was back in his office fifteen minutes later.

The moment he arrived he ordered round-the-clock security forces to be posted throughout the building and had sleeping quarters set up just down the hall from his office. Then, because he was nothing if not thorough, he ordered still more security men to patrol all the possible approaches to the building.

Pryor and his other agents reported in regularly, but nobody seemed able to turn up any information. Finally, when he found himself unable to concentrate on the mundane aspects of his business, he kept himself occupied by working out the basic details of Dream Come True with a few members of his staff, and ordered them to put it into operation.

Anyone would be able to walk in and order up a dream – but if the dream was illegal, as he expected most of them to be, a rigid check would be run on the potential customer to make sure he wasn't working for any of the government or law enforcement agencies. If he was cleared, preliminary plans would be worked out, after which a price would be agreed upon. Moore decided to set up the first office at the Thrill Show on the assumption that a lot of people would go there with money to spend, and he wanted a broad cross-section of dream requests to see which particulars of the operation still had to be smoothed out.

He spent the next two days involving himself in the administration of his little empire, and the next two nights tossing uncomfortably on rollaway bed in the adjoining office. Then, when he had just about made up his mind to go home, one of his security men entered the office.

"Yes?" said Moore.

"We've got her, sir."

"The old woman?"

"Lisa Walpole."

"Better and better," commented Moore. "Where was she?"

"At the airport. She had a one-way ticket for Buenos Aires."

"You did a good job," said Moore. "There'll be a bonus for everyone involved. Bring her in here, and then send for Abe Bernstein."

"Your doctor?"

Moore nodded.

"Any instructions for him, sir?"

"He'll know what to bring."

Lisa Walpole, dressed conservatively this time, was ushered into the office, her hands securely tied behind her back. Her left ear was swathed in bandages. Moore gestured toward a chair, and she walked over to it and sat down, glaring venomously at him.

"Please leave us now," said Moore to the security man. "Miss Walpole and I would like to be alone for a while."

As the door slammed shut, Moore leaned forward and studied the Living Dartboard. "I was right," he said with a smile. "I would never have recognized you with your clothes on."

She stared defiantly at him, her lips pressed together.

"I have a few questions I'd like answered, Lisa," he continued. "For starters, suppose you tell me who hired you to kill me three nights ago."

"Go fuck yourself!"

"Was it the late unlamented Mr. Thrush?"

"You'd like to know that, wouldn't you?" she said contemptuously.

"Indeed I would," agreed Moore. "And what's more, I *will* know very shortly."

"Are you going to torture it out of me?" she asked with a sarcastic laugh.

He shook his head. "No. I don't think a little thing like torture would bother you, even if you hadn't had your pain receptors severed. Of course," he added conversationally, "I could always slash an artery or two and threaten to let you bleed to death if you didn't tell me what I want to know, but it would stain the carpet — and besides, I suspect that you're just a little too infatuated with death for a stunt like that to serve any useful purpose. And your unfortunate condition precludes the use of our Neverlie Machine; after all, there's not much sense in shooting an electrical charge through your body every time you lie if you can't even feel it."

"Then how do you expect to drag it out of me?"

"I'm not going to drag it out of you at all," said Moore. "You're going to tell me of your own volition."

"Hah!"

Moore pressed a button on his intercom. "Is Bernstein here yet?"

"Yes," replied a feminine voice. "He's waiting in your outer office."

"Send him in."

The door opened a moment later and a small, portly, silver-haired man entered the room, carrying a dark leather bag in his right hand.

"Thanks for coming so fast, Abe," said Moore.

"I was downstairs in the sauna, sweating off another one of my wife's parties," replied Bernstein with a smile. "I hear you had a pretty exciting weekend, Solomon."

"I'll tell you about it later," said Moore. "In the meantime, we seem to have a little problem that requires your talents," he added, indicating Lisa Walpole.

"I saw Ben on my way in, and he told me about it — though I assumed as much when you couldn't use the Neverlie Machine." As he spoke, Bernstein opened his bag and withdrew a syringe and a small bottle. He filled the syringe, walked over to the girl, and injected its contents into a vein in her forearm.

"Give her about two minutes," he told Moore. "Her eyes will glaze over a bit, but she'll be able to speak cogently. Ask direct questions, and try to finish up within ten minutes."

"Thanks, Abe," said Moore. "You'd better leave now."

Bernstein nodded and walked out of the office, as Moore counted off two hundred seconds on his watch, just to be on the safe side.

"All right, Lisa," he said, rising and walking over to the girl. "We're going to have a little talk now. Did Thrush put you up to killing me?"

"No," she said emotionlessly.

"Nightspore?"

"No."

"Then it was Krebbs!" he exclaimed. "But why?"

"It wasn't Krebbs."

"Who was it, then?"

"Jeremiah."

"Jeremiah?" repeated Moore. "Who the hell is Jeremiah?"

"He's a young guy who hangs out around the Thrill Show," said Lisa, her voice a droning monotone.

"What's his last name?"

"I don't know. He calls himself Jeremiah the B."

"I never heard of him in my life," said Moore, frowning. "What has he got against me?"

"Nothing."

"Then why did he have you try to kill me?"

"Thrush told me that you had forced your way into the business, and that you had plenty of money."

"And you relayed that to Jeremiah?" asked Moore.

"Yes."

"When and where?"

"In bed, the same night Thrush told me."

"He's a fast operator, I'll give him that," said Moore. "Now suppose you tell me exactly what I was being set up for."

"Jeremiah figured you'd carry a big roll of cash with you."

"Then you were just going to rob me?" said Moore dubiously.

"No. A plain robbery wouldn't have been safe. We felt we had to kill you first."

"*We?* Does that mean you and Krebbs?"

"No. Jeremiah and me. He was in one of the other rooms, hiding."

"Brave fellow," Moore commented dryly. "How about Krebbs? Where does he fit in?"

"Jeremiah knew him, and promised him a piece of the action if we could use the Bazaar."

"And the little old lady in the religious shop?"

There was no answer.

"Did you know that Krebbs camouflaged his store as a religious-goods shop the next morning?"

"No."

"Do you know of an elderly woman who was involved with either

Krebbs or Jeremiah?"

"No."

"One last question: where can I find this Jeremiah?"

"I don't know. Probably at the Thrill Show."

"Thank you, Lisa," said Moore, pressing a button on his intercom system that signaled for two security men. "You did very well. The fact that I'm going to let you live, at least for the time being, should not imply that I am a forgiving man. You'll remain here, in this building, until I decide what to do with you."

He cut her bonds and ordered the security team to incarcerate her on another floor, then summoned Pryor to his office.

"Abe mentioned that you were in. Any news?"

"None," replied Pryor. "I think we must have checked out every Krebbs in the city, and I had one of our porn artists, of all people, render a sketch of the old lady that I passed out to all of our agents. There's nothing left to do now but sit and wait." He lit a cigarette. "By the way, did you learn anything from the Dartboard?"

"Plenty," said Moore. "For one thing, Nightspore and Thrush had nothing to do with it."

"I told you they weren't lying," said Pryor smugly.

"And *I* told *you* that you killed them for nothing," replied Moore irritably.

"What's done is done," said Pryor, shrugging off their deaths with a single sentence. "Did you find out who's behind it?"

"It's hard to believe, but some Thrill Show grifter found out I carry a big bankroll, and the whole thing was just a setup to roll me."

"It must be catching," remarked Pryor cheerfully.

"What are you talking about?" said Moore.

"Just that this grifter isn't the only guy who's decided to spread the wealth around. Dream Come True had its first customer this morning." He withdrew a sheet of paper from his notebook and handed it to Moore. "Take a look."

Moore read it, then read it again to make sure his eyes weren't playing tricks.

DREAM COME TRUE, INC.
PRELIMINARY APPLICATION FORM

HEIGHT: 6 feet, 2 inches
WEIGHT: 187 pounds
HAIR: Brown
EYES: Blue
DISTINGUISHING MARKS: None
AGE: 22
NATIONALITY: American

```
RELIGION: None
CURRENT ADDRESS: Refused to divulge
MARITAL STATUS: Single
FINANCIAL STATUS: Unclear at present
FIRST CONTACT: December 15, 2047
DREAM DESIRED: To murder Solomon Moody Moore and take over sole ownership
       of Dream Come True, Inc.
SIGNATURE: Jeremiah the B
```

"Persistent son of a bitch, isn't he?" said Moore, replacing the form on his desk.

"I don't think I follow you," said Pryor.

"Jeremiah the B just happens to be the guy who tried to set me up at the Bizarre Bazaar."

"And now he's trying to use Dream Come True to do the same thing?" said Pryor, greatly amused by this revelation.

Moore nodded. "He's got guts, I'll give him that."

"Are we going to do anything about him?"

"I think we'd better — before he gets around to doing something about me. As soon as the Thrill Show shuts down for the night, send some muscle over to pay our friend Jeremiah a friendly little visit."

"And?"

"And kill him," said Moore.

4

*T*he young man sat up in bed, fondly patted the bare, rounded buttocks of his still-sleeping partner, and began putting on his clothes. He knew they'd be coming after him before long, and the Thrill Show was the first place they'd look, which meant that it was time to make himself scarce.

He stuck his head out the door of the trailer, made sure that no one was lurking in the shadows, and slipped out into the night, avoiding the bright lights and gaudy neon signs.

Jeremiah had confidence in his ability to escape detection for as long as need be. Moore might own or control most of the vice dens in the Chicago complex, but he didn't know them. Jeremiah did, and that was all the advantage he needed.

Moore would turn the city upside down trying to find him, but it wouldn't do him any good. Jeremiah could stay buried until Moore gave up the search, and then make his pitch: a one-third partnership. He'd learned enough about Moore to know that he never destroyed what he could assimilate, and if Jeremiah could hold off the entire force of Moore's organization, he would have shown all the boldness and resourcefulness that Moore could demand of a would-be associate.

The setup at the Bizarre Bazaar had been just that — a setup. He hadn't expected Lisa Walpole to be able to kill Moore. If she had pulled it off, so much the better; but the likelihood was that she'd fail, and that Moore would find some way to extract his name from her. He knew nothing of her current whereabouts, but felt reasonably certain that Moore had her by now. However, he viewed the Dream Come True application as his masterpiece. If there was a better way of announcing his presence, he couldn't think of it.

The trick now was to stay alive, to keep Moore constantly aware of the fact that he was still in Chicago, and to wait him out. He'd been playing for pennies long enough; this was his chance to make the big time in one giant step, and he had no intention of blowing it.

He had already decided where to hole up: Darktown, that sleazy underground section of the city, just west of the old Loop, with its tawdry subterranean dens of drugs and sin. Whether you wanted to buy a woman, a man, a child, a murderer, a narcotic, a fingerprint graft, or whatever, if it was illegal or contraband you could get it wholesale in Darktown.

It wasn't an easy place to reach, though anyone who had business there knew the way. It existed, ghostlike and serene, a good quarter-mile below the huge, forty-foot-diameter sewers that ran beneath the city. The service elevators and escalators stopped at the mammoth pipelines, and after that one had to know exactly where to go to find his way into Darktown.

The construction of Darktown had consisted of one disastrous blunder after another. It had originally been commissioned by the city as a stormwater reservoir, then changed to a garbage dump. During the initial drilling and digging the contractors had, not once but three different times, come upon the Lake Michigan water table, practically drowning themselves and their huge work crews. Then, when they finally managed to avoid the water, they created an artificial cavern about half a mile square, only to have it collapse within the first month of its existence. These setbacks were followed by ventilation and temperature-control problems, and finally, as costs continued to skyrocket, the project was abandoned, leaving a massive but empty area one mile long and just over half a mile wide, with heights varying from fifty to ninety feet. It stood deserted for almost a decade, and then the criminal element moved in and took it over.

The first to go underground were the whores, the pimps, and the drug merchants. They were soon followed by the fences, who built long, low warehouses in which furs, jewels, paintings, appliances, and the million and one collectible items that so fascinated the bored multitudes could age before going back on the market.

Then came the dealers in big-ticket contraband products. Robots had made a brief appearance in human society before people discovered that their presence created even more leisure time; they had been outlawed for years, but they could still be purchased in Darktown. Automobiles, either those that ran on fossil fuels or those requiring electric or solar power, were prohibited under most of the nation's domes, but the man who had the room to keep one in secret could buy it in Darktown. Weapon shops abounded, as did those stores specializing in the hardware of the burglar's trade.

The streets were usually empty, for Darktown was not a place for window-shoppers. If a man had business there, he knew where to go; if he didn't have business to conduct, he didn't come to Darktown.

There were no streetlights as such, but a number of argon lamps had been set into the rocky walls of the cavern, giving Darktown a perpetual dull-blue glow.

Jeremiah, all his worldly possessions in his backpack, and his entire bankroll — such as it was — folded in one of his pockets, slunk into Darktown as silently as one of the rats that prowled its alleys. He went straight to a dingy flophouse and, using an assumed name, rented a small room.

This done, he walked down the dank, foul-smelling street to the Bar Sinister, a drug saloon which, despite its relative inaccessibility, had acquired a reputation that extended far beyond the Chicago complex. Here a man could order up a glass of Venusian joyjuice — which did not come from Venus and was not a juice — and go instantly into a hallucinogenic trance that lasted anywhere from ten minutes to two hours. Some of the more notorious concoctions — the Big Bang, the Pulsar, and the ever-popular Dust Whore — were potent enough to burn out every neural circuit of a habitual user's brain in a matter of days; beginners had been known to die from two drinks. Jeremiah was no beginner.

He sat down at a small table and waited for one of the seminude waitresses to come over and take his order. Nobody seemed to notice him for the better part of five minutes. Then a well-dressed man approached him.

"Hello, Karl," said Jeremiah.

"What the hell are *you* doing here?" snapped Karl Russo, who was both the owner and bartender of the Bar Sinister.

"Waiting to order a drink," said Jeremiah.

"What are you using for brains?" demanded Russo. "Don't you know Moore's put out a hit on you?"

"His men will be looking for me at the Thrill Show," replied Jeremiah confidently. "It'll be days before they get down here."

"It will be, huh?" said Russo. "Then how do I know there's a price on your head?"

"What do you mean?"

"Who the hell do you think owns half the joints in Darktown? Moore, that's who! And you, like an idiot, let him get a description of you, right down to the color of your eyes! He's offered fifty thousand dollars to anyone who can finger you, and there's an artist's drawing of you plastered up in every joint down here."

"He works fast, doesn't he?" remarked Jeremiah, obviously unperturbed.

"He sure as hell does," answered Russo. "You'd better leave the city for a while, if you know what's good for you."

"Oh, I don't know. I kind of like it here."

"Then at least get out of Darktown."

"I especially like Darktown," said Jeremiah.

"Have you got rocks in your head?" said Russo. "How many people have you seen since you got here? Five? Ten? Half of them have probably already told Moore's goons where you are!"

"I suppose they have," said Jeremiah. "Now, how about that drink?"

Russo slammed a fist down on the table. "Goddamnit! You're acting like you *want* him to find you!"

"No. But I sure as hell want him to try."

"You're out of your mind! Whatever you think your angle is, forget it. You stay in Darktown two more hours and you're a dead man. Hell, you're probably one already."

"I'll have a Dust Whore, I think," said Jeremiah with a grin.

"You think you've got something Moore wants?" demanded Russo. "Some skill, some information? Forget it! All he wants is your scalp. I don't know why he's after you, but if he's mad enough to put out a hit and a reward, he's too damned mad to deal with."

"Not for a smart young feller like me," said Jeremiah, still smiling. He felt elated. If the whole of Moore's attention was focused on him, that would just make his bargaining position that much stronger later on.

"If you had half as much brains as guts, you'd be scared shitless," said Russo disgustedly. "Now get the hell out of here. They ain't going to shoot up my place just to get you."

"What are you talking about?"

"Get out. I'll give you a five-minute start, and then I'm letting Moore know you were here."

"I thought we were supposed to be friends," said Jeremiah.

"Only when it's good for business. And right now, being your friend is about the worst thing in the world for my business, to say nothing of my health." Russo pointed to a clock on the wall. "Four and a half minutes left."

Jeremiah shrugged, then stood up and walked to the door, giving one of the waitresses a salacious wink as he passed her.

"I'll be back next month," he said to Russo. "I figure you owe me a couple of freebies for this." He turned to the waitress. "I'll see *you* then, too."

He went to three more boardinghouses, rented a room at each of them, and was heading toward a fourth when he saw a number of men clambering down the stone stairs that were carved into the side of the wall behind the Bar Sinister. He ducked behind a small warehouse and scrutinized them carefully. They were dressed neither like wealthy slummers nor like the usual inhabitants of Darktown, and coming in quantity like this, they could only be Moore's men.

He was surprised that they had arrived so quickly, but not dismayed. It had been said, back before deer became extinct, that one such animal could easily hide from two armed hunters on a mere acre of forested ground; he was a hell of a lot smarter than a deer, and Darktown was a hell of a lot larger than an acre.

He removed his shoes and shoved them into his backpack, then donned a pair of rubber-soled sneakers and ran silently at right angles to the gunmen. He continued at top speed past a lengthy stretch of brothels and drug parlors, then ducked in between a pair of buildings to see if he was being followed.

So far, so good. He clambered up the side of one of the buildings and soon reached the roof, some twelve feet above the ground. Then, removing his backpack, he laid it down and stretched out, using it as a pillow. It would take them hours to check out the dozens of flophouses, and he'd be as safe here as anywhere. Food would be no problem, either; after he'd gone to Dream Come True, he had placed a number of small retort pouches of concentrated soya products in his backpack, enough to last him for more than two weeks, three if he was careful.

Some time later he awoke with a start. There was no way of measuring the passage of time in the subterranean chamber, but he was sure he couldn't have been dozing for more than a couple of hours, for he felt neither stiff nor refreshed. One of Moore's men was walking slowly down the street just in front of the building, and the hollow clicking of his feet on the damp pavement had awakened Jeremiah.

He arose and walked silently over to the edge of the roof. It would be an easy matter to jump down on top of the man; the force of the fall alone would probably be enough to kill him. But he rejected the idea; he wasn't out to fight a war, but rather to impress Moore with his ability to survive. Besides, if he killed the man, Moore would just send more.

He observed Moore's man for a few more minutes, then decided to go back to sleep. He turned and began walking back toward the middle of the roof. Suddenly his foot crashed through a weak section of rotting boards.

The man in the street turned and fired four quick shots in his general direction. Jeremiah raced to his backpack, picked it up on the run, and hurled himself off the back of the building. He landed on his feet and raced into the alleyway, zigzagging in and out of the long, eerie shadows.

He ran until he reached the end of the alley, then turned to his right past the nondescript building that constituted the unofficial headquarters of the city's unofficial murderers' guild. Nobody shot at him, which meant that they were either unaware of his identity or — far more likely — had no intention of helping a man who kept gunmen on salary. He ducked into a small abandoned firearms factory, raced to the back of it, and eased himself out through a broken window. He stopped for a moment, listening for footsteps, but couldn't detect any. Slowly, cautiously, he peeked out around the corner of the factory, trying to see what he could of the street. It seemed deserted.

Then, after stepping back out of sight, he turned and headed off in the opposite direction. He stopped when he came to the corner, and barely avoided bumping into another of Moore's men, who was advancing down the street, gun in hand.

He waited until the man was more than two hundred yards past him, then crossed the intersection. He had almost made it back into the dim shadows when he heard the sharp report of a gun, and little pieces of stone sprayed his face, ripped off from the edge of a building by the bullet.

He started running again, darting in and out of warehouses, changing directions every half-block or so, slowing to a walk whenever he dared. In less than an hour he had made an almost complete circle of Darktown, and now he could see the Bar Sinister glittering just ahead of him.

He got to within three hundred yards of it, panting heavily, then saw two of the gunmen standing in front of the entrance. Turning once more, he ducked into an alley that led him behind a row of drug parlors. When he came to an open back door he stepped through it, leaning against a wall and gasping for air. He could hear strange, gurgling moans ahead of him, and decided not to risk cutting through to the front.

Chances were that the sounds were coming from someone who was too far gone in a featherheaded trance to be much of a threat, but he couldn't be sure that the person was alone, and it wasn't worth the risk.

He eased himself out through the back door, then saw a man coming down the alley toward him. He began running in the opposite direction, heard a number of shots, and felt a burning sensation just above his left elbow. He cursed, increased his speed, and ducked into the first building he came to that had a door in the back.

Without hesitating, he ran to the front of the building, out the front door, and across the street. Two more shots rang out from a new direction, and he darted into another structure.

It was large and well-appointed, with a circular staircase ascending to some upper level that was lost in shadows. He raced up the stairs, taking them three at a time, and burst through a door at the top. It closed automatically behind him, and he found himself in a sumptuously furnished drawing room. The rug was plush and deep, the wallpaper was flocked velvet, a number of tufted loveseats lined the walls, and soft recorded music was being piped in through a hidden speaker system.

"Welcome," said a deep, resonant voice.

He jumped and looked behind him. The room was empty.

"You have just entered the Plaza Gomorrah, the ultimate experience in bordellos."

He ran to the door through which he had entered, but it was locked.

"We commend you on your selection of the Plaza Gomorrah, where sensual experiences undreamed-of await even the most jaded hedonist. Except for your fellow seekers after fulfillment and gratification, not a living soul is in attendance. Even the voice you are now hearing is a recording. You need fear no embarrassment here, no humiliation, no threat of public disapproval. Be wild, be wicked, be inventive, be uninhibited, be yourself! We ask only that you allow us to demonstrate our unique ability to serve you and cater to your every desire." There was a momentary pause. "Rooms four, fifteen, eighteen, and twenty-four are currently available. All can be found down the corridor to your left. Payment will be made on your way out. We accept every form of currency and credit card currently in use in Europe and the Western Hemisphere, as well as any properly endorsed corporate bonds rated double-A or better. Alternative forms of payment can be made by special arrangement."

A door on the left side of the room swung open, and Jeremiah shot through it. He tried the first room he came to, found that it was locked, and raced to the end of the long, dimly lit hallway, where he found a door with the number 24 affixed to it in blinking diodes.

He opened it, stepped through a dressing area, heard the door close and lock behind him, and walked swiftly toward a window on the far wall.

"Hi, good-looking," said a soft, sultry voice.

Jeremiah stopped in his tracks and saw a voluptuous redhead, totally naked, standing by the foot of a king-size brass bed.

"Not today, sister," he said. "I'm in one hell of a hurry."

"I'm glad you could make it tonight," said the redhead in level tones, reaching out and taking his arm.

"Look!" he snapped. "I told you — I've got no time for this now!"

He tried to pull his arm loose, and was astonished to discover that he couldn't.

"I've been waiting all week for someone like you," said the redhead, pulling him over to the bed.

He heard a door crash down in the distance.

"Damn it, they're here already!" he snarled. "Let me go, you stupid bitch!"

"If there is anything special you'd like me to do, you have only to ask," said the redhead, lying back on the bed. "I am programmed to perform any act in *The Kama Sutra, The Perfumed Garden,* or the works of Krafft-Ebing."

"*Programmed?*" shrieked Jeremiah, as two more doors caved in. "Oh God, let go of me, you damned machine!"

He began smashing his fists into the robot's face. She smiled and nibbled gently on his ear.

"Let me go!" he begged. "They're coming to kill me!"

She drew him down on top of her, wrapping her arms and legs around his body, moving her hips and torso rhythmically.

He drove a knee into her inner thigh, bit her neck, and poked his thumb into her left eye.

"Oh, you're going to be good, baby," she whispered mechanically. "Better than all the others."

He heard the door to his room cave in, heard the footsteps as five of Moore's men walked over to the bed.

"LET ME GO!" he screamed.

"Oh, baby, you're the greatest," droned the robot, as five guns went off in unison.

5

*T*he roar of the shot was deafening.

"Where's the bullet?" asked Moore, lowering the gun to his side.

Pryor walked across the room. "Flattened out against the safe," he answered.

Moore turned to the eight security men who were standing uncomfortably in front of his desk.

"Gentlemen," he said, trying to control his temper, "using one of your own weapons I managed to hit a small wall safe at a distance of about twenty feet — and I am not a professional gunman. Now, has anyone got a reasonable explanation for what happened?"

There was no reply, and he stared directly at his chief of security.

"Montoya, you were the one who chased him into the Gomorrah. How did he get out?"

Montoya, a small, wiry man with dark, sunken eyes, just shook his head and shrugged.

"All right," said Moore, pacing up and down in front of the eight men. "Let me see if I've got this straight. Jeremiah raced up the stairs and went into one of the rooms, while Montoya waited for reinforcements. By the time four more men arrived, a robot was holding him totally helpless. The five of you walked in, surrounded the bed, leisurely took aim, and fired a total of forty-three bullets. Am I correct so far?"

"Yes, sir," said Montoya.

"You fired from no more than ten feet away?"

Montoya nodded.

"And five of the best-trained gunmen in the city, shooting at point-blank range, failed to kill or even maim a man who was right in front of them," continued Moore in a cold fury. "Not only that, but you blew the robot's head off, thus allowing Jeremiah to jump free, leap out the window, and completely evade you. To which I repeat: has anyone got a reasonable explanation?"

"I would be happy to undergo a session with the Neverlie Machine, Mr. Moore, if you feel that anything we've told you is false or incomplete," said Montoya.

"It's already been arranged," said Moore. "Each of you, when you leave here, will report to the Neverlie room. I might add that the voltage will be very close to lethal. Something funny is going on here, and I mean to get to the bottom of it." He turned to Pryor. "Ben, I want that room at the whorehouse examined. See how many slugs you can find in the walls, the robot, everywhere."

"I've already ordered it," replied Pryor. "We ought to be getting in the results shortly."

"I also want to know how the hell he got out of Darktown after the shooting."

"Right," said Pryor, nodding.

Moore turned back to the eight men. "All right — get out of here," he said disgustedly.

As they filed out, Pryor's pocket computer came to life.

"Got it already," he announced.

"Got what?" asked Moore.

"A report from the Gomorrah. They found thirty-two bullets in the head, arms, and legs of the robot, and four others in the mattress."

"And the other seven?"

"No trace. But we know Jeremiah was wearing a backpack. It was probably filled with retort pouches and maybe even a weapon or two. It's not inconceivable that four or five of the bullets got lodged in the pack."

"Why just four or five?" asked Moore. "Why not all seven?"

"Because there were traces of blood on the floor and the windowsill. He had to be hit at least once, maybe a few times."

"But not enough to slow him down," said Moore. "Damn it, Ben, the whole thing is unbelievable!"

"I agree," said Pryor. "But since he made a clean getaway, maybe we'd better start believing it unless you want to believe that a penniless beggar could somehow buy off five men who have been loyal to us for years." He paused to light a cigarette. "As nearly as I can reconstruct it, our other three men must have headed over to the Gomorrah as soon as they heard the gunfire, and Jeremiah evidently managed to slip by them and get out of Darktown while they were all still trying to figure out what had happened." He shrugged. "It's crazy, but that's the only way everything fits."

"It doesn't make any sense!" repeated Moore. "How could five crack shots fire forty-three bullets from less than ten feet away and not even slow him down? Hell, you'd think the noise alone would be enough to scare him to death."

"From what our men say, he was damned near out of his mind with fear even before they started shooting," said Pryor.

"I just can't find any rational explanation for it!" growled Moore. "I mean, it's not as if he has a surplus of brains. Look at what's happened. First, he sent a hundred-and-ten-pound woman to try to kill me with a weapon that required her to get within reach of me. That was just plain dumb. Second, he tried to camouflage the Bizarre Bazaar while I still had a business card with the address on it. Dumber still. Third, he used a maimed man and a Dartboard as his confederates — not the hardest people in the world to identify and track down. Fourth, he filled out the Dream Come True application form, which told us exactly what he looked like. Fifth, he walked into Russo's joint and let himself be seen. Sixth, while trying to hide from our muscle he climbed on top of the most dilapidated warehouse in Darktown and had the roof cave in under him. Seventh, he walked into a room with a robot whore and let it hold him helpless while our men came in and shot at him. Hell, a bona fide imbecile would have behaved more intelligently! And yet, he's still at large, and our entire organization looks like a bunch of incompetents."

"You do make it sound like something more than luck," remarked Pryor wryly.

"Do you call it luck that three-quarters of the bullets hit the robot?" retorted Moore. "These guys are specialists, Ben. They *couldn't* have missed!"

But the Neverlie Machine soon verified that the men had indeed told the truth, and Moore had no alternative but to order the manhunt to continue.

"Also, turn Lisa Walpole loose," he ordered Pryor, "and put a tail on her."

"If she knew where to find Jeremiah, she'd have told you while she was under the truth serum," said Pryor.

"I know," replied Moore. "But *he* might have some reason to see *her*, and if and when he does, I want to know about it." He paused. "Also, there must have been some fingerprints in the whorehouse. Check them out, and see if we can't find out just who the hell this guy is. Does he have a last name? Where does he live? And why is he after me? He can't be as dumb as he seems, or he wouldn't be able to dress himself in the morning without help. I want to find out everything we can about him."

Pryor nodded, then left the office to carry out his orders.

Moore punched a button on his intercom. "Send in Montoya."

The security man entered a moment later, and stood uncomfortably before Moore's desk.

"Sit down," said Moore, gesturing toward a wooden chair. "Difficult as I find it to believe, it appears that you were telling the truth, so we're back where we started. I still want to know why Jeremiah isn't dead."

"I honestly don't know, sir."

"Did you notice anything unusual, either about Jeremiah or about the room in general?"

"Not a thing," replied Montoya, shaking his head. "Hell, sir, he *couldn't* have known where he was going! I was hot on his tail, and he ducked into the first place he came to."

"Are you sure he didn't plan it to look that way?" suggested Moore.

"Absolutely."

"All right. Off the record, what would you say went wrong?"

Montoya shrugged eloquently. "I wish I knew."

"Could it have been the robot? Could it have been treated to attract bullets in some manner?"

"Not a chance. I *know* some of those bullets never touched the robot."

Moore grimaced. "Eleven of them." He paused. "How badly wounded was he?"

"Not so bad that he couldn't jump out of a window and hit the ground running." Montoya shook his head. "I still can't believe it, sir."

Moore dismissed him, toyed with questioning the other seven men, and decided against it. After all, they couldn't tell him anything more than they'd told the Neverlie Machine. Finally he summoned Pryor back into his office.

"Ben, we can't just sit here and wait for Jeremiah to make the next move. I want you to hunt up an actor who looks like me, dress him in my clothes, and send him around to all my usual places: restaurants, gymnasiums, bookstores, anywhere that I might be expected to go."

Pryor looked dubious. "I don't think he'll bite, but we can try it if you like."

"I like. And find out why the hell we're having so much trouble coming up with Krebbs. God knows he shouldn't be hard to spot."

"It would help if we had a picture."

"Hell, he's missing an eye and some fingers! Isn't that enough to go on?"

Pryor shrugged. "I'll pass the word that we're still interested in him."

"Also," added Moore, "from what little we know about Jeremiah, I'd say he can't seem to pass up anything that twitches. Check around and see if we can come up with a couple of girls who know him."

"Can I offer an inducement?"

"Five thousand dollars for any information." Moore paused. "No, make that ten. He's like an itch I can't scratch. The sooner we get something concrete on him, the better."

Pryor nodded and left.

Next on Moore's agenda was the girl from Dream Come True who had taken Jeremiah's application, but she couldn't add anything to the small body of knowledge they possessed about him. Nobody at the Thrill Show remembered him, either. He had no police record. Karl Russo knew him as a customer, but could provide no useful information. Even Moore's contact inside the murderers' guild couldn't help.

The first break came in midafternoon, when his private telephone began flashing. He picked up the receiver.

"Mr. Moore?" said a feminine voice.

"Who are you?" demanded Moore. "How did you get this number?"

"An employee of yours named Visconti gave it to me," she replied. "He told me you might have something for me."

"Such as?"

"Such as fifty thousand dollars."

"You know Jeremiah?"

"Yes."

"Why didn't you give the information to Visconti?"

"Because he didn't have the money," she replied.

"Come on over and I'll have it waiting for you."

"No, thank you. If Solomon Moody Moore is willing to shell out that much money just for information, then Jeremiah must be a pretty dangerous man. I don't want to be seen anywhere near your office."

"You name the time and place," said Moore. "I'll be there."

"Alone?"

"Absolutely not," said Moore. "I'm not going to be suckered twice in one week."

"I'll have to think about it."

"Sixty thousand," said Moore instantly.

There was a momentary silence. "All right," she said at last.

"Fine. Where do we meet?"

"The Museum of Death."

"Never heard of it. Is it far?"

"It's in Evanston. You can find the address in the phone book."

"When?"

"Ten o'clock tonight."

"What if the museum's closed then?" he asked.

"It will be."

"Then how —?"

"Just be there at ten, Mr. Moore," said the voice. "I'll take care of the rest. And Mr. Moore?"

"Yes?"

"Don't be late. I don't like to be kept waiting."

She hung up the phone.

Moore pressed another intercom button. "Get Visconti on the phone."

A few moments later his agent called in.

"Who is this woman who contacted you about Jeremiah?" demanded Moore.

"I don't know. She wore sunglasses, and the brightest red wig you ever saw. She wore real heavy makeup, but I have a feeling that she was pretty pale underneath it."

"Did you try to follow her?"

"No," answered Visconti. "I figured that if she really knew anything, I didn't want to scare her off."

"How did she know to contact you in the first place?"

"We sent the word out through the usual channels. It wouldn't have been too hard. After all, we're looking for Jeremiah, not hiding from him."

"True," said Moore. "Okay. I want you and Montoya in my office at eight this evening."

"Anything special?"

"I'm meeting the girl tonight, and I want you to confirm her identity, if you can."

He broke off the connection, and kept busy with his legitimate interests for the remainder of the day. He was just getting ready to leave with Montoya and Visconti when Pryor buzzed him on the intercom.

"What's up?" asked Moore.

"We just found Maria Delamond."

"Who the hell is she?"

"The old lady from the religious shop," replied Pryor.

"Good! Where is she?"

"Lying in an alley behind the third level of Monroe Street, with her throat slit from ear to ear."

6

Moore and his two security men walked up to the large, darkened building.

"Jesus, it's cold!" muttered Visconti, turning up his collar as the December wind blew in off Lake Michigan.

"It's been a long time since I was outside the dome during the winter," agreed Montoya, blowing on his hands. "I'd forgotten what it was like."

"Both of you are getting soft from too much city living," said Moore.

"Doesn't the cold bother you, sir?" asked Visconti.

"Not enough to complain about it."

"Look at those spires and turrets!" exclaimed Montoya. "The damned place looks like a gothic castle."

"More likely a reconditioned mansion, or perhaps a school building from the old Northwestern University," replied Moore. "I count at least six different doors. Visconti, pull your gun out and start trying them, one by one. Montoya, stick with me and keep your eyes open."

As Visconti, a huge, muscular man with close-cropped blond hair, strode up to the main entrance, Montoya turned to Moore.

"I haven't had a chance to ask you since the problem in Darktown," said the security chief in low tones. "What do you want us to do about Mr. Pryor, sir — keep up our surveillance, or concentrate everything we've got on Jeremiah?"

Moore considered the question for a moment. "Leave two men on Ben," he said at last. "Put everyone else to work on Jeremiah."

"Are you sure that's wise, sir?"

"Ben doesn't present an immediate problem," replied Moore. "Jeremiah's after me right now."

Visconti rejoined them a moment later.

"No luck," he announced. "The building's got six doors; I tried them all." He paused thoughtfully. "She knows you've got the money with you. Do you suppose this could be a setup?"

"You're the one who put her on to me," responded Moore. "Do you think we're being suckered?"

"I doubt it," answered Visconti after some consideration. "What's to stop us from walking away right now?" He shook his head decisively. "No, if she wanted to set you up, I think she'd do it inside the museum, not here."

"It makes sense," agreed Moore. "However, all the logic in the world won't make the slightest bit of difference if we're wrong." He glanced at his wristwatch. "It's five minutes to ten. I think we'll check the doors again at ten sharp."

Five minutes later Visconti walked up to the building and returned shortly thereafter to report that one of the side doors was now unlocked.

The three men walked up to it and paused. Moore looked inside, but could see only a darkened corridor.

"All right," he announced after a moment. "Montoya first. Visconti, you bring up the rear. And remember — your job is to protect me, not avenge me."

They entered the building and had taken a few tentative steps forward when a feminine voice spoke out:

"Close the door behind you and walk straight ahead."

Moore nodded to Visconti, who did as the voice directed. The corridor turned sharply to the right after about forty feet, opening into a small room that was totally devoid of furniture. Standing in the middle of it was a woman with the whitest skin Moore had ever seen. She had short black hair, very dark eyes, high prominent cheekbones, and a figure Jeremiah couldn't have ignored. Moore guessed that she was in her late twenties, but wouldn't have been surprised to discover that she was pushing forty.

"Have your men put their guns away," said the woman. "Weapons make me nervous."

"Clandestine meetings make *me* nervous," replied Moore. "The guns stay out." He turned to Visconti. "Is this the woman?"

"The hair and makeup are different, sir," said Visconti, "but it sure sounds like the same voice."

"Did you bring the money?" asked the woman.

Moore withdrew it and held it up for her to see.

"Good. Let's go to my office. We can sit down there and speak in comfort."

"Lead the way," said Moore, as he and his men followed her through a door at the back of the room. It led into a large hall that was filled with glass cases, each illustrating a scene of doom and destruction.

"This is our most popular exhibition room," said the girl, slowing her pace to allow Moore to study the displays more closely.

Case after case displayed life-sized figures in varying states of suffering and death. Here was Mussolini hanging by his heels, there was John Kennedy getting the top of his head blown off, over there was Lincoln a microsecond after John Wilkes Booth had fired his pistol.

"Very realistic," said Moore, pausing to examine Julius Caesar's death throes.

"We're especially proud of this one," said the woman, pointing to Marie Antoinette's head, which dripped a trail of blood and ganglia as it hung, suspended in time and space, midway between the guillotine blade and the small basket that awaited it.

"Not bad," commented Moore. "Have you got Braden anywhere?"

"In the next section," she replied, leading him through another doorway and stopping before a representation of James Wilcox Braden III, the forty-eighth President of the United States, and the only one ever to commit suicide in office.

"He doesn't look quite the way I remember him," remarked Moore. "Still," he added, staring at the blood that seemed to be flowing con-tinuously from his wrist into a bowl of warm water, "it's impressive."

They walked on past the other exhibits. De Sade was again trying to find the ultimate breaking point of the human soul and body, Martin Luther King was staring in disbelief as the blood spread over his shirt, Nikolai Badeliovitch still had an uncomprehending expression on his face as a failing life-support system ended the first manned expedition to Venus.

Another room. Here there were plagues, famine, leprosy. The Andersonville prison. Auschwitz. Vlad the Impaler busy earning his sobriquet.

Still another room, and they came to the Christians falling beneath the fangs and talons of the lions, the huge dogs ripping children to shreds during the Calcutta riots of 2038, heroes and martyrs and star-crossed lovers — and, in a tall display case that took up fully a quarter of the room, Jesus writhed once again on his cross, his eyes asking in mute agony why God had forsaken him.

"What do you think of it?" she asked, when they had passed through the last of the displays.

"I find it fascinating," he answered. "Whoever created it certainly had a morbid preoccupation with death." He looked around. "How long has this place been here?"

"The building itself is almost two hundred years old," she said. "As for the Museum of Death, it's been in business just under five years."

"Who frequents it?" asked Moore. "I wouldn't have thought you could draw enough people to warrant the expenditure."

"We manage to make ends meet," she replied. "We draw a goodly number of tourists and sightseers. And of course we've also got a pretty steady clientele: historians, artists, costumers, and a fair share of freaks." She led the three men through a small doorway and up a flight of stairs to a row of offices. The first four doors, which seemed to lead to the same oversized chamber, were labeled STOCKROOM.

"What do you keep in there?" asked Moore.

"Future exhibits. Would you like to see some of them?"

"Very much."

She unlocked one of the doors, and a rush of cold air hit them. Moore stepped inside and found himself staring at perhaps fifty corpses, all neatly labeled and lying on slabs.

"We keep them refrigerated until we need them," explained the woman.

"Then those *weren't* wax or plastic figures I saw."

"I should say not."

"Where do you get your bodies?" he asked.

"Originally the morgue supplied all our needs, but most of the specimens were too badly damaged to use. Recently we've been obtaining them elsewhere."

"For instance?"

"Trade secret," she said with a smile, ushering the three men out of the. chamber. "My office is the last one on the left."

"I take it that you're something more than just a tour guide," remarked Moore dryly.

"Oh, I'm a little of everything," she replied, walking up to her office and inserting a computerized card in the lock. Moore got a brief glimpse of the gold lettering on the door before he followed her inside:

MOIRA RALLINGS
TAXIDERMIST

The woman turned to Moore. "Have your men inspect the office and then wait outside for us."

Moore nodded to Montoya and Visconti, who gave the room a thorough going-over and then reported that it seemed secure. Moore motioned them into the hall and closed the door behind them.

"Sit down, Mr. Moore," said Moira Rallings, seating herself on a wooden rocking chair in a darkened corner of the small, cozy office. Moore walked past a large bookcase that was filled to overflowing with anatomy and taxidermy texts and an occasional illustrated history book, then sat down on the edge of her cluttered desk.

"Shall we get down to business?" he asked.

"That's what we're here for."

"Fine." He leaned forward. "Who is Jeremiah the B? What's his real name?"

"I don't know."

"Where does he live?"

"He used to have an apartment in Skokie, but it's empty now."

"Why does he want to kill me?"

She looked surprised. "I didn't know he wanted to."

"Perhaps we're going about this the wrong way," suggested Moore. "Suppose you tell me what you do know about him."

"I know that I'd like to see him dead fully as much as you would," said Moira with obvious sincerity. "And I know that you can't trace him through the normal channels. He has no criminal record, and he once told me that he'd never been fingerprinted or voiceprinted."

"How about retina identification?"

"If you get close enough to him to take it, I don't imagine you'll need it," she replied with a smile. "Besides, they've only been doing it for eight or ten years. My guess is that he's not on record."

"You said you wanted to see him dead. Why?"

"He stole my life savings."

"How?"

She sighed deeply. "I'd better start at the beginning. One day, about three months ago, I saw him picking pockets right here in the museum and threatened to report him. He offered to split the money with me if I kept quiet about it."

"Did you?"

"I kept quiet," said Moira, "but I didn't take any of the money. He moved in with me a couple of days later."

"Into your apartment, not his?" asked Moore.

"That's right."

"Then for all you know, the Skokie address might not exist at all."

"It exists," she replied bitterly. "I went there five weeks later, right after he cleared out with my savings and my jewelry."

"I assume you didn't find him?"

She shook her head.

"How was the apartment registered?"

"In the name of Joseph L. Smith."

"Joe Smith!" said Moore incredulously. "How can an amateur like that still be on the loose? *Joe Smith,* for Christ's sake!" He shook his head in disbelief. "Well, let's get on with it. What did you learn about him while you were living with him?"

"He was born in Tel Aviv."

"I thought he was an American citizen," interrupted Moore.

"He is. His mother was an American archaeologist. They stayed in Israel until he was ten or eleven, then went to Egypt."

"Is she still alive?"

"No. Both of his parents died in an accident when he was fourteen, and he was sent back to the States to live with an aunt. I don't know her name. He left her house after a couple of months and has been on his own ever since."

"Where?"

"Let me think for a minute," she said, lowering her head. Finally she looked up at him. "Manhattan, the Denver complex, Seattle, and then here. He used to work in a library, but I don't know which city it was in. I got the impression that his duties were pretty menial."

"How long has he been in Chicago?"

"A little over a year," replied Moira.

"What did he do before he latched onto you?" persisted Moore.

"Begged, hustled, robbed. A little of everything — except work."

"Where is he likely to hang out?"

"I don't know."

"What are his interests?"

"He hasn't any," said Moira. "He knows a lot about archaeology, but that's probably just from his upbringing. He once told me that he speaks Hebrew and Arabic as fluently as English, but he may have been lying." She smiled ruefully. "He lies a lot."

"Has he got any aliases?"

"I only know of one — Manny the B. But I got the feeling that he had a lot of others."

"Does he gamble?"

She shook her head. "He didn't during the time I knew him. I gather he once lost his bankroll on a fight that he thought was fixed, and he hasn't made a bet since."

"How big a bankroll?" Moore asked sharply.

"I don't know, but from the way he talked about it, it must have been pretty substantial."

"What fight?"

"I don't know anything about boxing. He mentioned the names of the fighters as if everyone should know them, though. It would have been, oh, nine or ten months ago."

"That would probably have been the Tchana-Makki heavyweight title fight," said Moore. "We'll be able to check with our bookmaking agencies, and see if we can get a lead from them. As for his parents, we'll just have to do it the hard way and check out every American archaeologist who was in Israel twenty years ago and died in Egypt during the past decade."

"Can an organization like yours *do* something like that?" she asked curiously.

"You'd be surprised what we can do when we set our minds to it," he replied with a grim smile. "Or, rather, when *I* set *my* mind to it." He paused. "Do you know if he's ever been married?"

"He never mentioned it," she said with a shrug.

"Any kids, legitimate or otherwise?"

"None that I know of."

Moore stared at her for a long minute.

"You seem like a reasonably bright, reasonably attractive, reasonably selective woman," he said at last. "Why the hell did you ever shack up with a dumb hustler like Jeremiah?"

"I really don't know," she said uncomfortably. "It just happened."

"He must be an attractive man."

"Not especially," said Moira, her expression puzzled. "That's the funny part of it. He's not even very good in bed. Looking back on it, I'm even more surprised at myself than you are."

Moore stood up, stretched, and walked to a window that overlooked the darkened suburb. "From what you know of him, why do you think he might want to kill me?"

"I don't think he wants to," she replied thoughtfully. "If he did, you'd be dead by now."

"Who are you kidding?" said Moore with a contemptuous laugh. "He couldn't shoot a fish in a barrel without blowing off half his foot."

"He's a very unusual man," said Moira. "I don't know why or how, but he always seems to get his way. Call it luck if you want, but if he truly tried to kill you I think he'd succeed."

"I don't believe in luck," said Moore, trying not to think of the episode in the Plaza Gomorrah.

"That's up to you," she said. "But whether it's luck or something else, things have a way of working out for him."

"Then why is he still a small-timer?" asked Moore.

"I don't know."

"What are his ambitions? What is he after?"

"I don't think even Jeremiah could answer that. He just seems to live from one minute to the next. I've never seen him worried or upset. If he needed money, he just went out and got it."

"Why did he need money?" asked Moore quickly. "Was he feeding some kind of habit?"

"I know he used to go to Karl Russo's place down in Darktown, but I wouldn't say that he was addicted to anything."

"Then you think if I checked out all the local pushers I'd come up empty?"

She paused to consider the question.

"Probably," she said at last.

"If you're right about his not wanting to kill me, just what *does* he want?"

"Knowing the way his mind works, I'd say he's trying to impress you enough so that you'll give him a top job in your organization."

"Do you really believe that?" asked Moore skeptically.

"It's an educated guess, nothing more," said Moira.

"How the hell did they ever let him out of kindergarten?" said Moore, shaking his head in amazement. He walked back to the desk. "If I told you he was wounded, where do you think he'd go to get patched up?"

"I don't know that he'd bother," replied Moira. "If he was healthy enough to elude whoever shot him, he's probably healthy enough not to risk visiting a doctor."

"Has he got any friends that you know about?"

She shook her head.

"Does the name Krebbs mean anything to you — an old man missing an eye and a couple of fingers?"

"No."

"How about Maria Delamond?"

"No."

"Lisa Walpole?"

"I've never heard of any of them."

"From what you know of Jeremiah, would you say that he's capable of slitting an old woman's throat?"

She considered the question for a minute. "I don't know if he'd do it himself, but he certainly wouldn't have any moral compunctions about getting someone to do it for him."

"You know," said Moore, "somehow I don't feel I'm getting my money's worth from you."

"You know more about Jeremiah now than you did twenty minutes ago," replied Moira. "And if you want him as badly as I think you do, you've gotten your money's worth and then some. After all, Solomon Moody Moore isn't exactly hurting for money."

"True," agreed Moore. "However, I figure you've only given me a thousand dollars' worth. Now you're going to earn the other fifty-nine."

She eyed him suspiciously. "How?"

"You're coming to work for me."

"The hell I am!"

"Let me make my offer before you refuse it," said Moore. "I'll pay you the sixty thousand now, and two thousand a day until I catch him."

"What do I have to do for it?"

"Just hang around and look pretty."

"As a decoy?" She laughed sarcastically. "Do you really think Jeremiah will swoop down and try to rescue me from your dastardly clutches?"

"Not at all," replied Moore. "I very much doubt that Jeremiah gives a tinker's damn whether you live or die. But on the other hand, I think he'll care quite a lot about what you may have to say to me."

"But I've told you everything I know about him."

"Perhaps," said Moore, "though we have a painless psychoprobing device at my office that will make sure of it. However, what you know and what Jeremiah thinks you *may* know are two different things."

"It won't work," said Moira adamantly.

"If it doesn't, you've got a guaranteed income for the rest of your life."

"All I would have to do is be seen in public with you?" she asked suspiciously.

"That's right."

"I won't have to sleep with you?"

"Absolutely not," Moore assured her. "I never mix pleasure and business. You'll be provided with your own private quarters in my office building."

"That's a lot of money," she said thoughtfully. "And I want to see Jeremiah dead as much as you do. But I'd have to leave the museum and give up my work until he was caught, wouldn't I?"

"Yes, you would."

"Couldn't I spend a few hours a day here?"

He shook his head. "For two thousand dollars a day, you'll stay where I want you to stay."

"There's a special exhibit I've been working on for the past two years," said Moira. "You'd have to let me take it along so I can continue working on it."

"Which one was it?" asked Moore. "The Crucifixion?"

"It's not on public display. Would you like to see it?"

Moore shrugged a semi-assent, and she led him out of the office. Montoya and Visconti fell into step behind them as they walked down the corridor to a large metal door.

"Just you," she said, and Moore nodded to his men, who returned to their places outside Moira's office.

She unlocked the door, then pushed it open and stepped into the darkened room. Moore followed her, and she immediately closed the door behind them.

"Are you ready?" she whispered.

"I'm ready," he replied in bored tones.

She switched on the colored overhead lights, and there, mounted on various platforms and podiums, were forty lifelike corpses. Grouped in twos, threes, and fours, nude or clad in kink, all were frozen into positions of almost unbearable ecstasy. Fellatio, cunnilingus, homosexuality, lesbianism, sodomy, bondage, flagellation, all were meticulously displayed, as were some aspects of the sex act that made even the raunchier performances at the Thrill Show look mundane by comparison.

"Do you like it?" asked Moira at last, her face suddenly alive with excitement.

"It's . . . ah . . . impressive," said Moore, mildly surprised that he could still feel shocked about anything sexual, and idly wondering what kind of mind could conceive and create such a display.

"It's my own project," she said proudly. "No one else has been allowed to work on it, and only a handful of people have even seen it." She lovingly stroked a nude male of Homeric proportions. "It's all mine, and I won't leave without it."

"You could only work on it when I didn't need you," said Moore.

She lowered her head in thought for a long moment. "I don't think I'm interested," she said at last. "My work is more important to me than your money."

"Then let me offer one final inducement," said Moore, who had been observing her carefully. "After I'm through with Jeremiah, you can have what's left of him for your project."

"Do you really mean that?"

Moore nodded.

A look of exaltation spread slowly across her chalk-white face, and her dark eyes widened with an unfathomable expression that almost scared him.

"Mr. Moore, you've got yourself a deal," said Moira Rallings.

7

*N*eptune's Palace was crowded, as usual. Big-time gamblers and top-dollar prostitutes rubbed shoulders (and other things) with Chicago's leading social gadflies, most of whom were looking for one last thrill on the way to senility or a first thrill on the road to adulthood. Painted transvestites, leather-clad exhibitionists of both sexes, the newly wealthy who now disdained their prior association with the proletariat, all spread money through the ranks of the Palace staff to secure prominent tables at which they could preen and be seen.

Ben Pryor and Abe Bernstein sat in a small, unobtrusive booth at the back of the huge room, sipping a pair of Water Witches and watching the unpaid clowns outdraw the professional ones. There were half a dozen empty glasses on the table in front of Pryor, and his ashtray was filled to overflowing with half-smoked cigarettes.

"So what do you think?" Pryor was saying.

"About this place?" replied Bernstein with a smile. "Give me a chance to make up my mind, Ben. I've only been here for five minutes. But off the record, I suspect my wife would kill me if she knew I was enjoying myself at Neptune's Palace while she was baby-sitting for two of our grandchildren." He paused for a moment. "And while we're on the subject of this place, exactly why *am* I here?"

"It's easier to talk in comfortable surroundings."

"You call *this* comfortable?" repeated Bernstein. "Unusual and exciting, maybe, but . . ."

"Well, *I'm* comfortable, anyway," said Pryor defensively. He dumped his ashtray into an empty glass and lit another cigarette.

"As long as you're paying the bill," said Bernstein with a shrug. He forced himself to stop staring at the patrons and turned to Pryor. "I don't imagine you invited me here to talk about this Jeremiah person that Moira used to live with, so what's on your mind?"

Pryor chuckled. "I'm sick to death of Jeremiah. He's just a goddamned beggar with delusions of grandeur." He suddenly became intent. "Tell me about Moira."

"About Moira? What's to tell?"

"You had her under the psycho-probe," persisted Pryor. "What makes her tick? I've met a lot of strange people in my life, Abe, but she's as weird as they come!"

"We probed her for information, nothing more," replied Bernstein. "She did tell me about her — what would you call it? — her *collection*, if that's what you're interested in." He took another sip of her drink. "Did Solomon really empty a four-room office suite so she could move it in?"

"It makes her feel at home," said Pryor, signaling a nude prepubescent boy in a turban to bring him another drink. "I wonder why Moore agreed to it, though. It's not like him to go around doing people favors."

"Who knows?" shrugged Bernstein. "I'm sure he had his reasons."

"I just wish I knew what they were," muttered Pryor.

"What difference does it make?"

"You've got to know your enemy before you can take him on."

Bernstein frowned. "Enemy?" he repeated. "What kind of talk is that?"

Pryor downed his drink and stared directly into Bernstein's eyes. "I'm going to take the organization away from him some day." Bernstein opened his mouth to protest, and Pryor held out his hand. "Don't act so surprised, Abe. Moore knows it and you know it, so let's just lay our cards on the table."

"I don't want to hear this," said Bernstein.

"Of course you don't," said Pryor with a smile. "You've Moore's man, Abe."

"Funny," replied Bernstein, startled. "That's the way I always felt about *you.*"

Pryor shook his head. "Uh-uh. The organization is your only client, and you're as high up the ladder as you planned to go. You're fat, overpaid, and underworked — meaning no offense. You belong to a temple and a country club, you've put your kids through college, you own a big house out in Lake Forest. You've got what you want out of life, Abe. But I'm in a different position: *Moore's* got what I want."

"Even if that's so," said Bernstein, "what makes you think he'll give it to you?"

"He won't. That's why I'm going to have to take it away from him."

"That's dangerous talk," said Bernstein uncomfortably.

"Nonsense. It's business talk. I've put nine years of my life into this organization, Abe. I've worked more eighty-hour weeks than you can count and had three marriages fold out from under me." He paused. "I didn't do it so I could take orders from Moore for the rest of my life."

"If I'm Solomon's man, why are you telling me all this?"

Pryor smiled. "Like I said, I'm not telling you anything he doesn't know. And don't look so damned suspicious: I don't plan to preside over a pile of rubble, so I'll do the best job I can until I get rid of him."

The nude boy returned with his drink. "And in the meantime, I've put a couple of things together on the side."

"Such as?"

"Who the hell do you think owns Neptune Palace?"

"Does Solomon know?" asked Bernstein.

"Of course."

"Then it would seem that you're doing all right on your own," noted Bernstein, waving a hand at the crowded room.

"Moore goes for the common man's dollar; as another guy named Abe once pointed out, there are so many of them. I wanted to show him we could go after the rich man's money, too. It spends just as well."

"And you've obviously become successful," noted Bernstein, taking another sip of his drink.

"Only because Moore isn't interested," said Pryor. "Otherwise, he'd buy Naomi off in a minute."

"Who's Naomi?"

"Naomi Riordan. Her professional name is Poseidon's Daughter."

"I've heard about her," said Bernstein, displaying some interest. "She's something of a sensation, according to the people I've talked to."

"You can decide for yourself," said Pryor. "Her act's due to start very soon now."

In less than a minute the house lights dimmed, and a huge aquarium tank, housing hundreds of exotic fish and a pair of large jeweled sea castles, rose up out of the center of the floor.

"Watch," said Pryor.

Music from an unseen harp soon permeated the room. Then a spotlight hit the aquarium, the door to one of the castles opened, and Poseidon's Daughter made her entrance, wearing only a pale-blue mermaid's tail, which she soon removed. She began swimming around the tank, her movements taking on the fluid grace of some long-lost Lorelei of the sea, her muscles rippling exotically beneath her unblemished skin. Her long, flaming red hair trailed out behind her, undulating sensuously through the water as her body arched and banked and circled in intricate interlaced patterns. Soon the fish, attracted by her hair, fell into a synchronous choreopattern, and suddenly the girl, the hair, the fish, and even the air bubbles had formed an hypnotically whirling, swirling unity that transcended Grace and achieved Art.

And then, before the stunned audience could rise in thunderous applause, Poseidon's Daughter had disappeared beneath the second sand castle and all that remained of the performance was a small school of fish. Oblivious to the screaming, cheering spectators, they clustered just above the sand in a far corner of the aquarium and pursued their fruitless quest for algae.

"What did you think of her?" asked Pryor, when the applause had subsided and the tank had sunk back into the floor.

"Absolutely fantastic!" enthused Bernstein. "I've never seen anything like it!" He turned to Pryor. "Could I possibly meet her? I'd like to tell her how much I admired her performance."

"Perhaps some other time," replied Pryor ruefully. "We had a little disagreement last night."

"Oh?"

He nodded. "Yeah. We've been living together ever since I hired her, and I lost track of the time and didn't get home until sunrise."

"What could keep you away from something like that?"

"As a matter of fact, I was with Moira Railings," said Pryor with no trace of embarrassment.

"I never thought of you as a man of poor taste before," said Bernstein. "But if you prefer that bloodless lunatic to —"

"It was strictly business," interrupted Pryor.

"If it was strictly business," replied Bernstein firmly, "Solomon would have been there first."

"There are certain problems I'm better equipped to handle than he is," said Pryor, not without a touch of pride. "I wanted to find out what she had on Jeremiah."

"To help Solomon or harm him?"

"To help him. Give me credit for a little intelligence, Abe. Being Number Two with Moore is better than being out on the street with Jeremiah. Anyway, nothing happened."

"Nothing?" said Bernstein dubiously.

"Nothing that I was personally involved in," amended Pryor slowly. "She's a pretty strange woman."

"*How* strange?"

Pryor stared at him for a moment, as if debating whether or not to answer the question. Finally he shrugged. "Abe, she's a goddamned necrophile!"

"I find that a little difficult to believe."

"So did I, until last night."

"I find it even harder to envision," continued Bernstein. "Making love to a dead woman may have its drawbacks, but at least it's possible, however disgusting the thought. But for a woman to have sex with a male corpse . . ."

"She's a taxidermist, remember?"

"Just the same . . ."

"Damn it, Abe!" snapped Pryor. "I was there! I watched her!"

"And you say *she's* weird!" laughed Bernstein contemptuously.

"It's the way she gets her kicks. She wouldn't talk to me *unless* I watched."

"Well?"

"It was fascinating. And I've got to admit it was exciting as all hell. If we could get some films or tapes of her, we'd sell five million copies."

"That's not what I meant," said Bernstein. "What does she have on Jeremiah? I put her through the psycho-probe and couldn't find a damned thing that Solomon hadn't already gotten from her."

"Nothing."

"I take it back," said Bernstein after a moment's consideration. "She did tell me one item of importance."

"Oh?" said Pryor quickly. "What was it?"

"She told me why Solomon runs this organization and you don't."

"Yeah?" said Pryor suspiciously. "Why?"

"Because she made a similar offer to him yesterday, and he turned her down flat. He went home to work in an empty apartment, while you left Naomi Riordan to spend the night with her."

"What does that prove?"

"Ben, whether you did it for kicks or you did it for Solomon, it comes to the same thing. All he wants is power; if you're interested in anything besides power, whether it's pleasure or perversion or money, you're going to stay in second place because you haven't got the single-minded intensity that he has."

"I *told* you why I was there," said Pryor defensively. "It's hardly my fault if I enjoyed it."

Bernstein shook his head. "That's a lousy answer, Ben. If Solomon knew going there wouldn't help, then so did you — and if you say otherwise, you're just lying to yourself." He stared severely at Pryor. "Solomon lies to a lot of people, but he's never yet lied to himself. *That's* why you're never going to be able to take this organization away from him."

"We'll see about that!" said Pryor hotly.

"So we shall," agreed Bernstein.

"But in the meantime," continued Pryor, his attention suddenly captured by a top-heavy blonde who had just walked into the club unescorted, "we're all teammates. It's Jeremiah who's the enemy. We'll talk more about it tomorrow."

He signed for the tab, nodded pleasantly to Bernstein, and set off on an arduous and ultimately successful pursuit of the blonde.

And, as Pryor's thoughts turned once again to sexual conquest, Moore sat alone in his apartment, considering various ways to bring Jeremiah out into the open. A few minutes later one of his agents called to tell him where Pryor would be spending the night. He smiled, shook his head in wonderment, and returned to his planning.

8

*M*oore spent the next four weeks being visible.

With Moira Rallings in constant attendance at his side, he spent the bulk of the first week touring the legion of underworld dives and drug dens that flourished beneath Chicago's shining exterior, simultaneously shutting down the security — or at least that portion of it that was obvious — around his office building and his apartment.

There was no sign of Jeremiah.

The following week he began a systematic tour of the local retreats, those incredibly valuable pieces of real estate that extended from the westernmost portions of the Chicago megalopolis halfway to the Mississippi River. He went to the health farms, where the truly sick died in luxury and the hypochondriacs were soon convinced that they were truly sick. He went to the diet farms, where the results of years of boredom and inactivity could be starved and sweated off at a rate of five thousand dollars a pound (or ten thousand dollars a week, which usually came to the same thing). He went to the dryout farms, where the aromas of fruit juice and coffee assailed his nostrils from hundreds of yards away, and where repentant alcoholics and unrepentant but dying alcoholics were never more than a short walk from the church and all-purpose temperance lecture of their choice. He went to the R&R farms for tired businessmen, which were dedicated to letting their patrons win at rigged sporting games all day and score with rigged sporting women all night, and he went to the R&R farms for tired businesswomen, which were, if anything, even more wildly enthusiastic about providing for their patronesses. He went to the religious camps, the nature camps, and all the multitude of country estates that had been set aside, not to eradicate mankind's boredom, but merely to channel it in new directions.

Jeremiah remained in hiding.

Next came a series of visits to the sites of the city's most expensive diversions. He went to the Obsidian Square, the huge, almost legendary casino where everything from the chairs and tables to the very walls was made of shiny black volcanic glass, and which stood, with only a mild attempt at camouflage, at the very center of the old Loop. He went to the Sky Links, the most exclusive nine-hole golf course in the world, located a half-mile above the ground (and covered by an immense net, lest stray shots kill unfortunate passersby on the lower levels). He went to the Little K, the miniature nondenominational Kremlin that could be rented, at great expense, for weddings, funerals, baptisms, festivals of the arts, or just about any other function desired, including an occasional orgy.

Jeremiah was nowhere to be seen.

He went to Veldtland, that extremely costly and exclusive ranch in the northwestern portion of the state, which possessed fifty of the last three hundred lions left on Earth, all roaming at large over a thirty-mile tract. For the modest stipend of two million dollars, a man could shoot one of them; or, for one-tenth of that amount, he could strip himself naked and go armed with only a spear. He even promoted a welterweight championship fight, and used himself as bait by taking over the ring announcer's duties.

But as the month drew to a close there was still no sign of Jeremiah.

"Maybe those gunshot wounds really did kill him after all," mused Moore, sprawling on an overstuffed leather chair in his temporary living quarters down the hall from his office.

"Not a chance," said Moira firmly. "If he was dead, the body would have turned up."

"Lots of people die every day in this town," said Moore dubiously.

"You have your sources for hunting down the living," replied Moira, "and I have mine for finding the dead. If Jeremiah dies, I'll know of it the same day."

"Well, alive or dead, I wish to hell he'd become a little more visible," said Moore. "I'm running out of ideas." He shrugged. "Getting hungry?"

"Yes."

Under the watchful eyes of his well-hidden security men, Moore and Moira took a monorail to Randolph Street, then transferred to an escalator that took them to the upper levels.

"Where are we going this time?" asked Moira, who during the past month had grown increasingly used to splendid food splendidly served.

"A little place that specializes in French cuisine," replied Moore. "Have you ever had Oysters Bienville?"

"I've never even heard of them," said Moira. "What do they taste like?"

"You'll see," said Moore with a smile. "We're only a block away, and —"

Suddenly he froze.

"What is it?" asked Moira. "Is something wrong?"

"That man!" said Moore, pointing toward an elderly man walking toward them on the opposite side of the street. "It's *him!*"

"It's *who?*"

"Krebbs — the old guy from the Bizarre Bazaar. Come on!"

Moore broke into a run, and instantly three large, well-dressed men emerged from the throng of shoppers to join him. They reached the old man in a matter of seconds. Moore's quarry made no attempt to evade him, but merely stared blankly ahead with dull, lusterless eyes.

"All right!" snapped Moore, unmindful of the crowd that was gathering around them. "Where is he?"

The old man gazed off into space.

"Where is Jeremiah?" demanded Moore.

The old man smiled vacantly. His face displayed no sign of intelligence or recognition.

"Just a minute," said Moira, finally catching up to Moore. "Isn't Krebbs supposed to be missing an eye?"

Moore stared at the old man's two eyes in surprise.

"Maybe the eyepatch was a disguise," he said.

"How about his hand?"

Moore reached out and grabbed the old man's right hand. It possessed a thumb and four fingers.

"You've made a mistake," said Moira.

He shook his head savagely. "This is Krebbs, all right. I can't explain his hand or his eye, but this is the man."

"You must be wrong," persisted Moira. "The eyepatch may have been a disguise, but people don't grow fingers upon request."

"I'm telling you this man is Krebbs! Call Ben and tell him to have Abe Bernstein in my office in twenty minutes."

"Okay — but I think you're crazy."

"Then humor me!" he snarled, leading the old man to the nearest monorail as his security men made sure he wasn't interfered with.

He reached his office in fifteen minutes and gestured to the old man to sit down. The old man remained on his feet, staring expressionlessly at a wall.

Bernstein arrived a few minutes later.

"I'm glad you're here, Abe," said Moore. "We've got a little problem on our hands."

Bernstein took an ophthalmoscope from his bag and shone the light into the old man's eyes. Finally he looked up at Moore.

"Correction: you've got a *big* problem here. What happened to this man, Solomon?"

"I was hoping you'd be able to help me find out."

"Who is he?"

"Krebbs," said Moore.

"The old man who tried to set you up?" asked Bernstein. "I was told he was —"

"Missing an eye and some fingers. I know."

"Have you any reason to believe that you might have been mistaken about that?" asked Bernstein.

"None whatsoever."

"Then this man can't be Krebbs."

"He's Krebbs," said Moore firmly.

"What makes you think so, Solomon?"

"I don't think so. I *know* so. Hell, I'm not likely to forget what he looked like."

"A lot of old men look alike," suggested Bernstein.

"This isn't a lot of old men," snapped Moore. "This is one particular old man — an old man named Krebbs, who happens to be my only link to Jeremiah!"

"Why don't you pick up the phone, call the nearest hospital, and ask them when was the last time they had a case of digital regeneration in a human being?" said Bernstein in exasperation.

"A little less patronizing and a little more medicine," said Moore. "I say he's Krebbs, you say he isn't. Fine. We'll let it pass for the moment. Can you tell me what's wrong with him?"

"On the spur of the moment?"

"If not sooner."

Bernstein examined the old man again, checking pulse, heartbeat, respiration, and reflexes. Finally he stepped back and sighed deeply.

"You've come to the wrong kind of doctor, Solomon. For a man of his age, he's in excellent health. I'd say you need a good psychiatrist, and I emphasize the word 'good.'"

"Why?"

"Dr. Freud, may he rest in peace, would say that this is a classic case of hysteria. Since the word has come to mean screaming and ranting, I would amend it to say that he is suffering from extreme shock."

"How extreme?"

"Bluntly, it seems to have blown every neural circuit in his brain. This, of course, is only my own semiskilled opinion. Possibly a man versed in the field would totally disagree and bring him out of it in five minutes' time."

"How long will it take *you?*" asked Moore.

"I don't think you understand," said Bernstein. "Curing, or even diagnosing, mental cases isn't my field."

"You didn't answer my question," said Moore. "Look — this man is no use to me like this. You've got to find a way to make him rational. A couple of minutes is all I need."

"First, I am not a psychiatrist. And second, this man is not Krebbs." Bernstein paused. "I don't know how you can be so sure about something that is so obviously wrong."

"Either you believe in your instincts and your judgment, or you don't. I do."

"But —"

"You're still not helping me," said Moore impatiently. "I know a psychiatrist would be better, but I don't happen to have any on my payroll, and I don't have any time to waste. Now, what's the best way to bring him out of this trance?"

"You're asking me to do something very unethical, Solomon."

"Wrong," said Moore. "I'm *telling* you to."

Bernstein looked back at the old man, grimaced, and shook his head. "I'm just not well versed enough in the field. Let me call in someone who is."

"All right," Moore assented. "Get him here with everything he'll need in thirty minutes."

Bernstein walked to the phone, made a quick call, and hung up the receiver.

"All right," he announced. "I've called in Neil Procyon. He's on the staff of the Elgin Mental Hospital, and from what I hear he's pretty good with shock therapy."

"Do you know him personally?" asked Moore.

"Socially," answered Bernstein. "He and my son go skiing together up in Michigan."

"Well," said Moore ominously, "let's hope he knows his stuff."

Procyon showed up some twenty-five minutes later, carrying a small plastic case under his arm. He was a young man, intense and unsmiling, with the body of an athlete and the drawn face of a man who didn't know when to stop working. He greeted Bernstein formally, allowed himself to be introduced to Moore, and walked briskly to the old man. He conducted a brief but thorough examination, and then turned to Moore.

"What caused this man's condition?" he asked.

"I don't know — but there's a blank check waiting for you if you can snap him out of it."

"I'll send a team from the hospital out here to pick him up later this afternoon," said Procyon.

"Now," said Moore coldly.

"I beg your pardon?"

"Don't send any teams, Doctor. Cure him now."

"What makes you think you can give orders to me?" demanded Procyon hotly.

Moore made no reply, but pressed a button on his intercom console. Two armed security guards immediately entered the office and stationed themselves by the doorway, their weapons drawn.

"Dr. Bernstein, what the devil is going on here?" demanded Procyon.

Bernstein shrugged. "I'd suggest that you attempt to bring the old man out of his daze here and now, Neil. Mr. Moore is not known for playing practical jokes."

"And, knowing that, you called me in?"

"*I* would surely have killed the patient," said Bernstein. "*You* might not."

"I intend to make a full report of this as soon as I get back to Elgin."

"As you like," said Moore. "But in the meantime . . ." He gestured toward the old man.

"All right," said Procyon. "I just want it clearly understood that I am doing this under threat of death, and for no other reason."

Moore fumed to one of the security men. "Get Moira and Ben in here. I want them to hear anything Krebbs might say."

"If he says anything at all," commented Bernstein, "It'll probably be that his name isn't Krebbs, and that he's been a wino or a junkie for the past five years."

"We'll see," said Moore.

"I'll need some help," announced Procyon.

"Anything you wish," said Moore, as Moira and Pryor entered the office.

"I want this man tied securely — and I mean *securely* — to his chair."

The security men, at a signal from Moore, holstered their weapons and carried out Procyon's instructions. The young doctor then unlocked the small case he had brought along and withdrew four transistorized devices, each about the size of a penny. He affixed one on each of the old man's temples, one over the heart, and the fourth on the roof of the man's mouth. He then withdrew a tiny control panel from the case.

"Stand away from him," he ordered. Then he turned to Moira. "You may want to avert your eyes."

"Fat chance," muttered Pryor.

Procyon pressed a button on the panel, and the old man's body began jerking spasmodically. A few seconds later the doctor removed his finger from the button, and the old man sagged limply in his bonds.

Bernstein walked over to the old man, lifted an eyelid, took his pulse, and measured his respiration.

"Well, he's still alive," he announced at last. "But that's about all I can say for him."

"Do it again," said Moore.

"But Mr. Moore . . ." protested Procyon.

"Again."

Procyon pressed the button, and the old man's body almost flew out of the chair.

"No reaction," said Bernstein, after examining him again.

"Once more," said Moore.

"Solomon, it'll kill him!" said Bernstein.

"You heard me," said Moore to Procyon.

The young doctor started to object, then took another look at the security men, sighed, and pressed the button again.

This time, after twitching furiously, the old man opened his eyes and glanced about the room, the total absence of expression giving way to a look of bewilderment.

"Krebbs, can you hear me?" said Moore, kneeling down beside the chair.

"Krebbs? Krebbs?" repeated the old man, mouthing the word uncomprehendingly.

"Where is Jeremiah?"

"Jeremiah?" said the old man, his face puzzled.

"Yes, Jeremiah!" snapped Moore. "Where is he?"

"Krebbs? Jeremiah?"

"You're Krebbs, and you tried to set me up for Jeremiah," said Moore. "I'll let you off the hook, but you've got to tell me where Jeremiah is!"

"Hook? Hook?" The old man repeated the word as if it were a name he couldn't quite recall.

"Give him a little time to recover," urged Bernstein. "He's awfully weak right now."

"Five minutes, no more," said Moore. "Unstrap him."

Bernstein untied the old man, then helped him to sit up more comfortably. A shock of white hair, wet with perspiration, fell onto the old man's forehead, and he reached up with his right hand to brush the hair back. As the hand came within his field of vision he stared at it with growing confusion, wiggling each finger in succession.

"Oh my God," he muttered.

"What is it, old man?" asked Bernstein.

"Oh my God!" he repeated, staring at his fingers.

"Where is he, Krebbs?" persisted Moore.

The old man gingerly raised his left hand and touched first one eye and then the other.

"Oh my God!" he shouted. *JEREMIAH!*"

With a shriek of pure terror, he toppled off the chair and fell heavily to the floor. As quick as Moore and Bernstein were, Moira was even quicker, and was instantly kneeling over him.

"Is he alive?" asked Moore.

"No," answered Moira, her face flushed with excitement.

"Damn!" said Moore. "Just when he was getting cogent enough to tell us something!"

"I wouldn't say he was cogent," interjected Bernstein. "I'd say he was scared out of his wits, and I mean that quite literally. I think he died of fear."

"What scared him?" asked Moira, lovingly stroking the dead man's face and hair.

"I'm almost afraid to think about it," said Bernstein. He bent over and examined the old man's right hand closely. "There are no scars of any kind."

"What does that imply?" asked Moore.

"Let's allow Dr. Procyon to take his leave first," suggested Bernstein. "Then we can all speak a little more freely."

Moore signaled the security men to escort Procyon out of the office.

"I'll need the body for my report," said the young doctor, visibly shaken.

"No!" said Moira suddenly. "*I* want it."

"What on earth for?" asked Procyon, curious in spite of himself.

"She's kind of a collector," said Pryor with a grin.

"Very funny," muttered Procyon. "Now will you please have someone help me transport it back to the hospital?"

"That wasn't a joke," said Moore. "The lady is keeping the body."

Procyon took two steps toward the corpse, found his way blocked by the security men, then turned on his heel and left.

"He's going to get you in a hell of a lot of trouble, Solomon," said Bernstein.

"It's nothing we can't handle," said Moore, dismissing the subject. "What were you saying about his hand?"

"There are no signs of any skin grafting," said Bernstein. He lifted each eyelid in turn. "Neither eyeball is artificial, either. Let me ask you once more: could you possibly have been mistaken about his eye or his hand?"

"Absolutely not," replied Moore. "Ben, have this man's fingerprints checked out and see what we can dig up on him — and when you're through, have Moira show you where she wants you to stash the body."

Pryor nodded and summoned two more men to help with the fingerprinting, while Moore seated himself behind the desk.

"Well, Abe," he said, "are you finally willing to admit he was Krebbs?"

"I lean in that direction," replied Bernstein. "Tell me a little more about this Jeremiah. Moira made him sound like just another grifter, and not very bright at that."

"A little more is all that I *can* tell you. He's a normal-looking young man in his early twenties, or so I'm told. He's a con artist and a ladies' man. He's been known to frequent Karl Russo's place down in Dark-town, but he's probably not an addict. He did his damnedest to set me up for a mugging, he's dumb as all get-out, and he's the luckiest son of a bitch I've ever come across."

"How so?"

"Five of my men cornered him in a room and fired at him at point-blank range. He not only came out of it alive, but managed to escape as well."

"Why does he want to kill you?"

"I don't know. In fact, Moira is of the opinion that he's just trying to scare me."

"And why do you say he's stupid?"

Moore launched into his explanation, and by the time he was done Pryor was back in the room with a computer readout clutched in his hand.

"That was fast," remarked Moore.

"Ex-cons are a little easier to identify than most," replied Pryor.

"What do you have on him?"

"Plenty," said Pryor, looking at the readout. "His name is Willis Comstock Krebbs, Caucasian male, age sixty-three, born in Tucson, Arizona. He served time for rape, arson, extortion, blackmail, bigamy, and second-degree murder."

"Nice fellow," commented Moore dryly.

"I'm not finished," said Pryor. "His identifying marks are as follows: he lost his left eye during a prison brawl in 2027, and lost the thumb and portions of two fingers of his right hand in a monorail accident in 2031."

"That's all?" asked Moore.

"So far."

"Okay, Abe, you're the expert — just what the hell are we dealing with here?"

"I'm not at all sure I want to know," said Bernstein.

"Could Krebbs have been a mutant?"

"Not a chance," replied Bernstein.

"You're sure?"

Bernstein nodded. "First of all, most mutations — well over ninety-nine percent of them — are so small and meaningless as to go completely unnoticed. And the remainder, almost without exception, don't make the mutant any more viable. They might consist of an extra finger, or one less vertebra in the spine, or a hair color that wasn't in the gene pool. Only writers dream up mutants who can control minds or breathe underwater; Nature hasn't gotten that far yet. Furthermore, if Krebbs had the power of regeneration, why did he go twenty years without an eye and sixteen without a couple of fingers before he decided to grow them back?"

"How about Jeremiah?" asked Moira, finally looking up from the body. "Could *he* be the mutant?"

Bernstein shook his head. "Once and for all, forget about mutants. The two of you keep assuming that a mutant would have the power to regrow lost organs and limbs, and I assure you that it just isn't so. And certainly no mutant, even if he possessed that power, could will regeneration upon someone else."

"Could Jeremiah be an alien?" suggested Moira.

"You've been watching too many bad television shows," said Bernstein. "I very much doubt that an alien would bear such a resemblance to us, and I find it just a little difficult to believe that an alien would spend all his time swindling our men and fornicating with our women." He paused and smiled. "I can also give you half a hundred sound scientific reasons to support my position, if you would care to hear them."

"Could a mutant — or a man, if you prefer — be able to control random chance, to make his own luck?" asked Moore.

"No more than you can," said Bernstein. "Whatever the reason for Jeremiah's escape from your men, it wasn't because he consciously or unconsciously willed them to miss him."

"Have you got a better explanation?"

"Not yet," admitted Bernstein. "At the moment, I'm much more concerned with how Krebbs regrew his missing parts than with Jeremiah."

"Don't be so sure that the two aren't related," said Moore. "After all, he screamed Jeremiah's name after he saw that he was whole again."

"That doesn't mean there's a connection," said Bernstein doggedly.

"It doesn't mean there's *not*, either," responded Moore.

"Jeremiah once told me that the ancient Egyptians had all kinds of magical healing arts," offered Moira. "Maybe he found out what they did and did it to Krebbs."

"Horseshit!" snapped Bernstein. "There's never been a case of regeneration in the history of humanity. What does a carnival grifter know about Egypt, anyway?"

"He lived there," said Moira.

"He's been to Egypt?" asked Bernstein, suddenly interested.

She nodded.

"And Israel too?"

"He grew up in the Middle East," said Moore. "How did you know that?"

"I didn't," said Bernstein thoughtfully. "Let's call it a lucky guess."

"Have you got any more guesses?" asked Moore.

"None that I care to put on the record."

"You look very disturbed, Abe."

"I am."

"If you know something, I think you'd better share it with us."

"I don't *know* anything. For just a second I had a crazy notion. Let's forget it."

"It's probably not any crazier than a man regrowing an eye and some fingers," said Moore. "Let's hear it."

Bernstein shook his head firmly.

"All right," said Moore with a shrug. "In that case, we'll operate under the assumption that Jeremiah is either a mutant of as yet unknown powers, or an incredibly skilled surgeon, which seems like the least likely explanation of all. I'll have Ben dig us up a scientist or two who knows something about mutation."

"It won't help," said Bernstein.

"Besides, Jeremiah hasn't been seen since Darktown," added Moira. "Why don't we just assume he's left the city? Then you can get back to work, and I can go home to the museum."

"Because if I let one guy get away with trying to kill me," explained Moore, "how long do you think it will be before others start lining up to take a crack at it?"

"Well, I don't like it," said Moira.

"You don't have to like it; you just have to do it," retorted Moore.

Suddenly Bernstein walked to the door.

"Where the hell do you think you're going?" demanded Moore.

"I've got a lot of thinking to do," replied Bernstein uncomfortably.

"You look like you're scared shitless."

"If truth be known, I am."

"You didn't answer my question. Where can I find you if I need you?"

"I'll be at my temple," said Bernstein.

Moore uttered a sarcastic laugh. "What kind of crap are you handing out here? I know you: every time you get scared you threaten to quit and move to Florida."

"I don't think quitting will help this time."

"And going to temple will?" asked Moore with a smile.

"Yes," answered Bernstein seriously. "I think it will."

9

"We've got him surrounded, sir!"

"Where?"

"Lakeport."

"I'm on my way."

Moore slammed the phone down, summoned Moira, Pryor, and half a dozen security men, and headed for Lakeport, the huge airport complex that floated atop Lake Michigan, some ten miles off Chicago's shoreline.

When they arrived they found that Jeremiah was trapped inside an empty hangar. As far as Moore could tell, there was no possible means of escape. Thirty armed men encircled the building, their weapons trained on every door and window. Still more men were backing up the first group, and the remainder of his security force was carefully checking the passengers on all incoming and outgoing boats and planes.

Furthermore, the city — or those members of its government who were personally obligated to Moore — had blocked off all other means of ingress and egress: the ramps, the tunnels, the monorails.

"How did you spot him?" Moore asked the man in charge.

"He tried to buy a ticket to Cairo."

"Egypt or Illinois?"

"Egypt. A couple of our agents identified him."

"You're sure it's Jeremiah?"

"Him or his twin brother," came the reply. "He fits the description we've got to a T, and he raced off like a bat out of hell when we called him by name."

"And he's still in the hangar?"

"Right."

"Moira, you come with me," said Moore. "I want to be absolutely certain we've got the right man."

"I don't think you should go in," she said. "He could be more dangerous than you think."

"I want to make sure that what happened last time doesn't happen again," said Moore. "Or if it does, I want to see it with my own eyes."

He took a handgun from one of the guards and, gesturing to his own security team to accompany him, entered the hangar.

It was quite large, almost four hundred feet long by two hundred wide and eighty high, and displayed no sign of life. Moore directed one of the men to turn on the lights, but found that the additional illumination didn't make much difference. He looked up at a number of ramps that ran along the inside wall of the hangar at a height of about fifty feet, trying to locate a likely place of concealment. There was none.

"All right," he announced at last. "It's obvious that he can't get out past our men, so we can take our time about this. We'll proceed as a unit and go over every inch of the damned building."

They began following the wall to the left, moving slowly and carefully, looking under, behind, and inside every object large enough to hide a man. They had gone about two hundred feet when they heard a shuffling sound from the far wall of the hangar.

"Over there!" shouted Moore, racing in the direction of the noise.

He and his men got to within fifty feet of a large baggage carrier when a young man stepped out from behind it, his hands above his head.

"Is that him?" Moore asked Moira.

"Yes," she replied.

"You're sure?"

"Absolutely."

Moore stared at the young man for a long moment. Finally he shrugged.

"Kill him," he ordered.

"No!" screamed Jeremiah. "I'm unarmed! You can't do this! I'm —"

Seven guns exploded in unison, Moore's included, and Jeremiah was flung some thirty feet away by the impact of the bullets. As soon as he stopped rolling over he got groggily to his feet and began running.

"What the hell is going on here?" muttered Moore. He fired again at Jeremiah, who was limping painfully but rapidly toward a door at the far end of the hangar as a hail of bullets struck the walls around him.

Moore took up the chase, shooting as he went. Jeremiah fell twice more, but each time managed to regain his feet and continue running toward the door. He reached it mere seconds ahead of Moore and raced out into the sunlight.

Moore stepped through the doorway just in time to see an airplane skid off a runway and head directly toward the hangar. He took in the situation at a glance, then ducked back inside the hangar and threw himself to the floor. There was a loud explosion an instant later, followed by two smaller ones and a burst of heat and smoke.

The hangar caught fire instantly, and beams and girders began falling to the floor. Moore got to his feet and began running to the undamaged end of the building. Moira and two of the security men followed him, but the others had disappeared under the rapidly accumulating rubble.

When he reached the door through which he had entered, he stepped outside, checked himself for injuries, found nothing but some superficial bruises and abrasions, and circled around the hangar to view the carnage. The air stank of burning flesh, and fifty of his men lay dead or severely mangled near the wreckage of the plane. A rescue crew was already on the scene, and half a dozen more were speeding toward the scene.

"Where is he?" demanded Moore, trying to spot Jeremiah's corpse in among the other bodies.

"He couldn't have survived that," replied one of the security men firmly. "He was right in the middle of it. You'll be lucky if you can find the fillings from his teeth."

"I hope you're right," said Moore, "but I want the entire area checked anyway. And I want somebody to find out what happened to the plane — what made it skid and crash." He turned to Moira, who was bleeding from her mouth. "Are you all right?"

"I will be, after I see a dentist," she said. "I have a couple of teeth loose." She looked down at her torn, grime-covered suit. "I think I could probably use a change of clothes, too. How about you, Mr. Moore? You look dreadful."

"I'm okay. Just shaken up a little," he said. "Let's get back to the office. There's nothing much we can do here."

They arrived, patched up most of their wounds, and changed into fresh clothes just in time to receive Pryor's first report from Lakeport: the plane's landing gear had failed to function. A brief preliminary investigation hadn't turned up any signs of sabotage.

Ten minutes later there was a second call from Pryor. A horribly mangled young man who matched Jeremiah's description had managed to board an airliner at gunpoint, and was, according to the pilot's radio message, preparing to parachute down somewhere over the Pocono Mountains.

"I wish I knew what the hell is happening!" snapped Moore after hanging up the receiver.

"I don't understand," said Moira.

"Your boyfriend has more lives than a goddamned cat."

"You don't mean to say that Jeremiah is alive?"

"Alive and free," said Moore. "The son of a bitch not only lived through that holocaust, but he managed to hijack a plane."

"But that's impossible!" exclaimed Moira.

"Evidently not," replied Moore. "I seem to remember Sherlock Holmes telling Dr. Watson that when you eliminate the impossible, whatever remains must be the truth. If we apply that to Jeremiah, the one thing that remains is that there's no way in hell that he can be a normal man with normal abilities — if he's a man at all."

"I don't care if he's a man, a mutant, or an alien," persisted Moira. "No one could have survived that!"

"Someone did," said Moore. *"Him."*

"There must be some mistake," she insisted. "Probably they identified the wrong man as Jeremiah."

"I don't believe that, and neither do you," said Moore soberly.

"But there's no other rational explanation!"

"You've noticed," he said wryly.

"He's *got* to be dead!"

Moore stared at her as if to argue, then shrugged. "I've been letting too damned many subordinates check up on Jeremiah. I think it's time that I did a little homework myself."

"Beginning where?" asked Moira.

"At the beginning," said Moore. "We've had people working around the clock trying to find out something about this guy. I want to go over every last shred of information they've put together. And I want *you* to submit to the psycho-probe again, once you get your teeth fixed. Maybe it can drag something out of you that it missed the first time around."

Moira left the office, and Moore waited until all the material, sparse as it was, had been assembled on his desk. Then he locked the door and began going over it slowly and methodically.

There still wasn't much.

To those few tidbits of information he already possessed were added the following:

- ◆ Jeremiah's parents were agnostic Jews, and he himself was an atheist.
- ◆ Jeremiah had had a vasectomy two years ago while living in Seattle.
- ◆ Jeremiah had not only had the normal childhood diseases, but had actually contracted typhoid and an unknown sleeping sickness. In both cases he was near death, but miraculously recovered.
- ◆ Jeremiah's mother had published two small monographs concerning some obscure theories about the ancient Mesopotamians. Neither had received any coverage whatsoever from the academic community.
- ◆ Jeremiah's full name was Immanuel Jeremiah Branch, and he was the son of Marvin H. Branch and Linda Branch.

And that, in a nutshell, was that. The sum total of his knowledge of Jeremiah wouldn't fill two sheets of typing paper. In fact, the only thing Moore had learned — or, rather, deduced — was the genesis of the names Jeremiah the B and Manny the B.

He heard nothing further from Pryor, and Moira was still undergoing the psycho-probe, so he decided to return to his apartment for the first time in days, hoping that in the comfort of his library he might be able to sort out the day's events and perhaps make a little sense out of them.

When he arrived home, he took a hot shower and tended to his wounds once again. Then he prepared a quick dinner consisting primarily of non-soya vegetable products, and spent two hours sitting on his old leather chair, pondering over the few notes he had scribbled and wondering what they had in common with a man who could survive gunfire and plane crashes with equal facility. It wasn't as if he had done it with style, either; Moore was certain that Jeremiah was fully as surprised at his ability to cheat death as everyone else was.

Moore stared at the notes for a few more minutes, and finally three words caught his attention: Immanuel Jeremiah Branch.

Somewhere, deep in the forgotten recesses of his mind, that name rang a bell, or perhaps a series of them. It seemed familiar, though he was sure he had never come across it before.

Curious, he walked over to a long-unopened copy of *Burke's Peerage*, and was not surprised to find that there was no such name listed there. He then pulled down a couple of books devoted to coats of arms, with the same results. He even tried the Chicago and Manhattan phone directories, still with no luck.

And then, on a hunch, he picked up a copy of the Bible. As far as the name Immanuel went, he knew of only one place where he could recall seeing it, and he turned to the Book of Isaiah, thumbing through it until he came to Chapter 8:

"Behold, a virgin shall conceive, and bear a son, and shall call his name Immanuel."

"Well," he muttered, "so much for Immanuel."

The hoped-for Immanuel, Isaiah went on to say, would eat butter and honey and learn to refuse evil and choose the good — which certainly didn't sound like the Immanuel that Moore was after.

He was about to put the book back when he riffled through the pages once with his thumb to shake the dust loose.

That was when he saw it, flashing briefly before his eyes. He bent back the leather cover and let the pages race by again, but couldn't pick it out, so he began turning them one at a time until it reached out and hit him right between the eyes, capital letters and all:

"Here now, O Joshua the high priest, thou, and thy fellows that sit before thee: for they are men wondered at: for behold, I will bring forth my servant The BRANCH.*"*

It was the Book of Zechariah, and he read on, searching for some other reference to The Branch.

He found it.

". . . Thus speaketh the Lord of Hosts, saying, behold the man whose name is The BRANCH; *and he shall grow up out of his place, and he shall build the temple of the Lord; and he shall bear the glory, and shall sit and rule upon his throne. . . ."*

Two minutes later he was on the phone to Bernstein.

"Abe, I'm sorry to bother you, but I've got to ask you a couple of questions."

"Did Moira give us something new?" asked Bernstein.

"I don't care what the hell she gave us. How conversant are you with the Bible?"

"I knew you'd ask sooner or later," sighed Bernstein, "but I never thought it would be this quick."

"You didn't answer my question."

"I grew up with the Old Testament. I'm not as well acquainted with the other one."

"That's okay. The Old Testament is what I'm interested in. What can you tell me about The Branch? All capital letters. It's in Zechariah."

"Hold on while I get my copy," said Bernstein.

Moore waited impatiently while Bernstein, with a great deal of noise and a muffled curse as he bumped into a chair, walked across his room, picked up a Bible, and limped back to the phone.

"I'm back," he announced painfully.

"Have you got the place?" asked Moore.

"Zechariah. Right."

"Fine. Who is The Branch, and why is he called that?"

"It's a guarded reference to the Messiah," said Bernstein, after reading the chapter half aloud, half to himself. "The Branch refers to his being a fresh branch from the withered Davidic family tree."

"Why the Davidic tree?"

"Because one of the few things the Messianic prophets agreed upon was that the Messiah — which is simply Aramaic for Anointed One — would come from the line of David."

"Ready for another question?"

"Go ahead," said Bernstein.

"How many present-day Jews can trace their ancestry back to David?"

"None."

"Then it's a dead line?" asked Moore.

"I have no idea. But I know that no one can trace his lineage back that far. You're talking three thousand years or more."

There was a long, uncomfortable pause.

"Are you thinking what I'm thinking?" asked Moore at last.

"It's crazy, Solomon."

"I know. So is everything else that's been happening lately."

"It's so farfetched that I'm embarrassed to even admit that the thought had crossed my mind," said Bernstein.

"Me too."

"He's more likely to be a man from Mars."

"I agree," said Moore. "But I want you to do me a favor anyway."

"If it's within my power."

"Meet me at my office tomorrow morning at eight o'clock sharp."

"That's all?"

"Not quite."

"What else?" asked Bernstein.

"Bring your rabbi."

10

"Solomon, allow me to introduce you to Rabbi Milton Greene," said Bernstein.

Moore arose and stared at the young man who stood before him in a striped, floor-length robe.

"Call me Milt," said Greene, extending his hand.

"That's quite an outfit you've got there," commented Moore, taking his hand.

"My coat of many colors?" replied Greene with a smile. He turned around once. "I wove it on my own loom."

"It must wake them up during your sermons," said Moore.

"Oh, I dress a little more formally for work," said Greene. "Actually, I'm going over to the Sky Links when I leave here."

"Surely you can't swing a golf club in *that*," offered Bernstein.

"I keep a sweater and a set of knickers in my locker," replied Greene, sitting down on one of the wooden chairs that were lined up in front of Moore's desk. "Well, Mr. Moore, what can I do for you? Abe told me to bone up on the Messiah before I came, but as yet I have no idea what for, since I'm probably the last person you'd want to see about converting to Christianity."

"I've got some questions to ask you," said Moore. He paused, staring at Greene again. "I don't mean to hurt your feelings, but you seem awfully young to be a rabbi."

Greene shrugged and smiled. "Well, if it comes to that, you seem awfully young to be a criminal kingpin."

"I'm just a businessman."

"That's not what the media thinks."

"Then why did you agree to see me?"

"Why not?" Greene smiled again. "Somehow, I have a hard time envisioning your organization muscling in on the God racket."

Moore turned to Bernstein. "I like him," he said approvingly.

"That's why I left my old temple and joined his," agreed Bernstein.

"Tell me, Rabbi —" began Moore.

"Milt," interrupted Greene.

"Tell me, Milt, what kind of advice does a guy like you give to an old-timer like Abe?"

"That's what you got me down here to ask?"

Moore shook his head. "Just curious."

"I tell him the usual crap about living a good life and worshiping the Lord," replied Greene. "Then, whenever I think his guard's down, I tell him to throw his son out of the house before he turns into a full-time deadbeat."

"Now, just a minute!" said Bernstein hotly.

"Abe, the kid is twenty-four years old and he's never done an honest day's work. All he does is go skiing on your money. You've really got to put a stop to it," said Greene, and Moore found himself agreeing silently.

A secretary entered the office just then and handed Moore a sealed report telling him where Pryor had spent the night and estimating when he could be expected at the office. Moore opened it, read it over, and put it in a desk drawer. As the secretary left the room, he told her to make sure he wasn't interrupted until his meeting with the rabbi was over.

"Well," he said, turning back to Greene, "shall we get down to business?"

"Fine," replied Greene. He pulled out a huge cigar. "Mind if I smoke?"

"Be my guest," said Moore. "Abe told you that I needed some information, right?"

"That's correct."

"Good," said Moore. "Let's start with an easy one: are you still waiting for the Messiah?"

Greene laughed. "You mean, right this minute?"

"It's pretty unlikely that he's going to walk in through the door while we're speaking," said Moore, resisting the urge to knock on wood. "I mean generally."

"Do you want a personal answer or an official one?" asked Greene.

"Take your choice."

"Personally, no. Officially, yes."

"Okay, let's keep it official for a while," said Moore.

"Assuming that in your official capacity as a rabbi you believe in the Messiah and the Messianic prophecies, why don't you believe that Jesus was the Messiah?"

"There have been about ten thousand books that address that very subject," replied Greene. "Maybe I should just loan you a couple of the better ones."

"Could you condense them into a couple paragraphs for me?"

"I'll do better than that: I'll give it to you in a single sentence. Jesus didn't fulfill the Messianic prophecies."

"Almost four billion people think that he did," said Moore. "Why?"

"Some people are stupider than others," replied Greene easily. "Look, the first thing you've got to understand is that the Messianic prophecies aren't anywhere near as simple as the King James Version of the Bible would lead you to believe. Even before the discovery of the Dead Sea Scrolls, we know of three separate and distinct Messiahs that were expected by the ancient Jews."

"Three?" said Moore, surprised.

"At least. Probably there were more. The word 'Messiah' — which comes out as 'Kristos' in Greek, if you want to know how Jesus got his name — merely means 'anointed,' and anointed is what a king was supposed to be. The Messiah of the Jews was to be a king who would restore the race to its former glory, and of course Jesus failed to do this. In fact, the Jews were driven from Jerusalem in 70 A.D., only forty years after his death, and didn't reestablish themselves there for almost two thousand years."

"What else was expected of him?" asked Moore.

"Not a goddamned thing," interjected Bernstein.

"Abe's quite right," said Greene. "The only thing the Messiah had to do was establish an all-powerful kingdom in Jerusalem."

"Just a minute," said Moore. "I've been going over the Bible all night, and I've found a lot of other things he was supposed to do."

"No you didn't," said Greene, puffing on his cigar. "I told you that things aren't as simple as the New Testament makes them sound. What you're referring to are a number of signs by which the Messiah could be identified, but these were all preliminary. His only purpose was to establish a kingdom in Jerusalem." He shook his head sadly. "I never could understand how so many people could worship a man who delivered the preliminaries and blew the big event — meaning no disrespect if you happen to be one of them."

"Then why is he worshiped as the son of God?"

Greene shrugged. "Beats me. The Messiah's only got supernatural powers in the New Testament; in the prophecies he was just a man. A very special man, to be sure, since he had to possess even greater wisdom than Abraham and David, but a man, nonetheless."

"Let's get back to the signs for a minute. I was under the impression that Jesus had fulfilled them — riding into town on a white ass, being resurrected, and so forth."

"More smokescreen," said Greene firmly. "There were hundreds of signs predicted in the books of the prophets and other ancient Hebraic literature. The white ass was mentioned exactly once — and even that was probably added a century or two after the Crucifixion to agree with prior events."

"What are you talking about?"

MIKE RESNICK   85

"There hasn't been an awful lot written in stone since the Ten Commandments," explained Greene in amused tones. "The Bible was rewritten every generation or two, and usually changed to agree with the dominant beliefs of the period. As for the signs, his resurrection was never once prophesied. Don't forget — his kingdom was to be here on Earth. Heaven was, so to speak, God's domain."

"Then what signs would the Jews have accepted as proof of his Messiahship?" asked Moore in frustration.

"The most telling sign would have been the establishment of his kingdom. I know it's becoming repetitive, but setting up shop in Jerusalem is what being the Messiah is all about."

"Let me rephrase the question," said Moore. "If the Messiah were to show up during your lifetime, by what signs — short of the establishment of his kingdom — would you know him?"

Greene continued puffing on his cigar as he considered the question for a moment. Finally he looked up. "I think there are probably four signs that would be agreed upon by most Jewish scholars," he answered at last. "First, he'd have to come from the line of David; second, his name would have to be Immanuel; third, he would have to come out of Egypt before establishing his kingdom: and fourth, he'd have to resurrect the dead."

"Didn't Jesus fulfill those signs?"

Greene laughed aloud. "He's lucky if he's batting .250. Jesus is Greek for Joshua, not Immanuel. Nowhere is there any historic proof that he raised the dead. Nowhere is there any proof that he set foot in Egypt. And —"

"Just a minute," interrupted Moore. "The Gospels clearly state that he went to Egypt as a boy to avoid one of Herod's bloodlettings."

Greene turned to Bernstein. "Do you want to tell him, Abe?"

"Solomon," said Bernstein, "read your history books. There were *no* bloodlettings under King Herod!"

"Right," chimed in Greene. "And if this mythical slaughter didn't take place, I can't see any reason to believe that Jesus had to escape from it."

"What about his descent from David?" continued Moore. "Matthew documents it, generation by generation."

"Pure bullshit," said Greene. "Mathew made so many genealogical blunders that even the writers who codified it in his Gospel couldn't tidy it up."

"For instance?"

"For instance, he claims that Joram begat Ozias. But recorded history shows that there were four generations between Joram and Ozias, and that Ozias was actually the son of Amaziah. You know," he added, "when you write a Holy Book, the very first thing you should do is make sure that it can't be contradicted by the record. Matthew blew it." He paused to relight his cigar, which had gone out. "His biggest blunder was trying to place Joseph, and hence Jesus, into the Davidic line. I know of no Biblical scholar, Jewish or otherwise, who can substantiate that little tidbit."

"So you're saying that Mathew lied."

"Not necessarily. The damned thing was probably rewritten twenty or thirty times before the end of the Dark Ages. I'm saying that *somebody* lied. Which," he added, "is perfectly understandable. They had to twist certain facts and fabricate other ones if the Gospels were to establish Jesus as the Messiah."

"And what is the Jewish view of Jesus?" asked Moore.

"Mine, or the official one?"

"Let's keep it official."

"The prevailing view is that he was a good and intelligent man, one of many children of Joseph the carpenter and his wife, whose real name was Miriam, not Mary. It is assumed that he grew up somewhere in Galilee and —"

"Why do you put him in such a broad area as Galilee?" asked Moore. "Why not Nazareth?"

"Because there probably wasn't a Nazareth," replied Greene. "More likely the Nazarenes were a Jewish sect not unlike the Essenes. There were a lot of such sects around at the time, and his later career would certainly imply that he had taken his training with one of them. He was strongly influenced by John the Baptist, and took John's cause for his own. He must have had some basic knowledge of herbal medicine, since he cured a number of illnesses — though of course we don't believe that he cured leprosy or made blind men see."

"You also don't believe that he brought Lazarus back from the dead?"

"Of course not. Do you?"

Moore shook his head. "No."

"Good for you," said Greene. "Moving right along, we believe that Jesus chose his disciples from the lower classes because he himself came from that particular social stratum, that he led them to Jerusalem just prior to Passover, that he was outraged to see money-changing going on in the Temple, and that his subsequent actions caused such a disturbance that both Pilate and the Pharisees felt he must either be discredited or run out of town." He paused. "And of course you know the rest. He was found guilty of treason and executed."

"And the resurrection?"

"A fairy tale. But even if it were true, it wouldn't signify his Messiahship in any way."

"And the Jews have been waiting for more than two thousand years since his death?"

"Some of them have."

"What does *that* mean?" asked Moore.

Greene grinned and leaned back. "I was hoping we'd get around to this subject, since I boned up on it before coming here. Did you think Jesus was the only man who claimed to be the Messiah and picked up a bunch of believers along the way?"

"I had assumed so," admitted Moore.

"Well, assume again, Mr. Moore," said Greene. "There were hundreds before him, and a hell of a lot after him as well. Back in the thirteenth century, a descendant of a noble Spanish-Jewish family named Abraham Abulafia convinced tens of thousands of people that he was the Messiah. In the early 1500s a dark, gnomelike dwarf named David Reuveni had so many followers convinced that he was the true Messiah that he was even granted an audience with Pope Clement VII."

"Really?" said Moore, surprised.

"Wait," said Greene. "It gets better. The most widely accepted would-be Messiah — including Jesus — was Sabbatai Levi, a seventeenth-century Turk. He heard voices exhorting him to redeem Israel, and to fulfill the Messianic prophecies he went to Egypt, where he astounded half a million disciples by promptly marrying an internationally known prostitute."

Moore chuckled. "And that was the end of him?"

"Not quite," replied Greene. "He returned to Turkey amid rumors that he had a huge Jewish army hidden away in Arabia just awaiting his commands, and announced that he planned to depose the sultan."

"So what happened?"

"The sultan offered him a choice: he could publicly convert to Islam, or he could be chopped to pieces — testicles and head first. He converted, and another Messianic hope bit the dust."

"Were there any more recent ones?" asked Moore.

"There was Jacob Frank, a Russian, who declared that anyone could find redemption through purity, but that the true path was through *impurity.* He proceeded to enliven his pseudoreligious séances with sexual orgies, and was later excommunicated by the Turkish and Russian rabbis. He died in — when was it? — 1791, I think. The last of the major pretenders to the Messiahship was Bal Shem Tov, who was born in the Ukraine at about the same time as Jacob Frank. He supposedly had a halo and performed miraculous cures, and by the time of his death in 1780 about half the Jews in Europe believed he was truly the Messiah." He paused and stretched his arms above his head, then relaxed. "So you see, Mr. Moore, while having a Messiah one believes in is a unique experience to Christians, having one who doesn't fulfill the prophecies is nothing new to Jews."

"So I gather."

"And now, Mr. Moore, I feel that I am entitled to ask you a question."

"Go right ahead."

"Who is *your* candidate for Messiahship?"

"I don't believe in Messiahs," said Moore.

"That's a relief," said Greene with a smile.

"Why?" asked Moore. "Wouldn't you like to see the Messiah before you die?"

"Not really," answered Greene. "The Lord, my God, is a jealous God, and not at all above flooding the earth or totally destroying Sodom and Gomorrah. If he's got a Messiah in mind for us, I rather suspect that it will be a Messiah who rejects the power of love in favor of the might of the sword, and will burn the old kingdom down before erecting a new one on its ashes." He paused thoughtfully. "No, if the Messiah ever appears, I for one hope that I'm peacefully dead and settled in my grave before that happy moment occurs."

"One last question," said Moore. "Tell me about The Branch."

"Ah, yes — Abe mentioned that I should read Zechariah. It appears that Zechariah swiped Isaiah's metaphor about a fresh branch coming forth from the withered Davidic line, although later it appears that he's naming Zerubbable as the Messiah."

"Did Zerubabbel fulfill any of Zechariah's or Isaiah's prophecies?" asked Moore.

"Not a one." He paused. "Is that it?"

"Yes."

"Good! Then I can still get in nine holes before lunch. There's a great little Hungarian eateasy two levels down from the Sky Links. Someday if you get a chance, you might —"

"I already have," said Moore. He got to his feet and escorted Greene to the door. "Does your temple have any objections to receiving a donation from me?"

"Probably," said Greene. "If you feel that you must, why not give it to Abe and let him contribute it?"

"I'll do that," promised Moore.

Greene stopped in the doorway and turned to Moore once more. "Is your candidate batting better than .500?"

"I don't know," said Moore. "But I sure as hell doubt it."

Greene left the office, and Moore walked back to his desk.

"Well?" said Bernstein.

"I was hoping he would shoot a few hundred holes in the idea," said Moore, frowning. "Abe, what would you say if I told you that Jeremiah's full name is Immanuel Jeremiah Branch?"

"I wouldn't be surprised."

"Still, it's just too farfetched to believe," said Moore. "I like the mutant theory better."

"I was sure you would," said Bernstein.

"Just what the hell is *that* supposed to mean?"

"Solomon, when people come across something that is contradictory to their training and their experience, they tend to either ignore it or misinterpret it."

"Well, if *you* believe this Messiah crap, why aren't you leading a bandwagon for Jeremiah instead of helping me plot to kill him?" demanded Moore.

"There'll be time for that later," said Bernstein seriously. "Besides, it ought to be apparent to you by this time that no one is going to kill him."

"We'll see about that," said Moore. "In the meantime, he's only batting .500 — his name's Immanuel and he's been to Egypt."

"By the way, I do have one little tidbit of information for you," said Bernstein.

"About Jeremiah?"

"Yes."

"Why didn't you tell me as soon as you got here?" demanded Moore.

"I wanted to wait until Milt Greene left."

"Okay. Let's have it."

"I checked the results of Moira's psycho-probe before Milt showed up this morning," began Bernstein.

"And?"

"Jeremiah once told her that when he was seventeen years old he was swimming with a friend, and the friend drowned after suffering a stomach cramp."

"So what?"

"Jeremiah revived him."

"And you call that resurrecting the dead?" scoffed Moore. "Hell, any Boy Scout can perform artificial respiration!"

"There's nothing in the prophecies that says he has to dig up a moldering corpse and magically return it to life," replied Bernstein. "His companion was dead. He revived him. Q.E.D. — and he's batting at least .750."

"It's a crock of shit, and you know it."

"I *don't* know it and neither do you, or you wouldn't have had me bring Milt over," said Bernstein stubbornly.

"Oh, come on, Abe! Jeremiah's a beggar and a thief, he's as dumb as people get to be, and he's not exactly on the road to establishing a kingdom in Jerusalem or anywhere else. I'd say he's as unlikely a candidate for Messiah as you're ever going to find."

"At the risk of sounding religious," replied Bernstein, "he won't be the Messiah because he's a likely candidate, but because he *is* the Messiah, plain and simple."

"Horseshit. He's no more a Messiah than you or me. If there was a Messiah at all, it was Jesus."

"You don't believe that any more than I do."

"No, I don't," said Moore. "But almost half the people in the world think Jesus was the Messiah. Maybe they know something we don't know."

"To quote my employer: horseshit."

"Then look at it another way. The Jews have been established in Israel for a century, and they've been trouncing the Arabs every decade or so. Maybe the Messiah showed up when no one was looking. Maybe he was David Ben-Gurion."

"An interesting notion," admitted Bernstein. "But unfortunately, it doesn't explain Jeremiah away."

"I don't want to explain him away," said Moore. "I just want to kill him. Hell, your rabbi did a beautiful job of explaining Jesus away, and billions of people still believe in him."

"It doesn't make them right."

"It doesn't make them wrong, either."

"Why should an avowed atheist suddenly defend Jesus' divinity?" asked Bernstein. "Could it be that if you can force yourself to believe in the Christians' Messiah you won't have to face the grim reality of the true one?"

"Perhaps," admitted Moore uncomfortably. He sighed. "I suppose the next order of business is finding out whether or not Jesus was really the Messiah."

Bernstein laughed sarcastically. "Hundreds of thousands of scholars have devoted their lives to finding that out. What makes you think you'll succeed where they failed?"

"They didn't know who to ask," said Moore. "I do."

11

*I*t had achieved a measure of fame out of all proportion to its appearance. It was structurally unimpressive, just a little building divided into a foyer, a file room, and twenty cubicles. It was a branch of the Reality Library, known by reputation to tens of millions of people, and misunderstood by almost all of them.

Moore left his bodyguards at the door, entered the building, and walked up to the sole attendant, a portly, middle-aged man who sat behind a cluttered counter.

"Yes?"

"My name is Moore. Solomon Moody Moore, I made an appointment."

The man typed the name into his computer terminal. "Ah. yes, Mr. Moore. I've reserved cubicle number seven for you."

"Do I pay you now or later?"

"Our fee is twenty thousand dollars an hour, and we require at least two hours' payment in advance."

"Fine," said Moore, scribbling down the identification number of his personal account.

"Thank you," said the attendant. "You can begin in a few moments, just as soon as our computer transfers the funds. Your bank has been notified that this transaction will take place, hasn't it?"

"Yes."

"Have you ever used the Library before?"

"No," said Moore.

"Do you know how it works?"

"Only what I've heard."

"Then perhaps you might appreciate a little backgrounding," said the attendant, producing a pamphlet from behind the counter. "Here. You might want to read through this. If you have any questions after you've finished with it, I'll be happy to answer them."

Moore thanked him, then walked over to a chair, sat down, and began reading.

The Reality Library, said the pamphlet, despite the incredible complexity of its techniques, was basically a form of entertainment, the logical culmination of all that had gone before. Phonograph records and audio tapes appealed to only a single sense, theater and the cinema to only two — but even if one found a medium that appealed to all five senses, as the short-lived feelies had attempted to do back in the 2020s, one would still be only a spectator, a voyeur whose experience would remain totally vicarious.

But the Reality Library had changed all that. When a user (the pamphlet disliked the word *"customer"*) sat down in his cubicle, he would find two nodules that he would attach to his temples, as per the carefully rendered illustration. He then flicked a switch on the right arm of the chair, and contact with the main bank of the Library in Houston was immediately established.

The Library had more than a quarter million works of literature recorded. The user had merely to select any character, no matter how great or small, from any book in the tape catalog, and he would for all practical purposes become that character for the duration of the tape. He would feel exactly what the character was feeling, know what he knew, see what he saw. The user would be unable to act independently or change the prerecorded pattern of what occurred in the chosen work of literature; rather, he would seem to find himself in a secret section of the character's mind, sharing every thought and experience, and following him through to the conclusion of his saga.

The pamphlet went on to explain how actors had originally been tied in to vast banks of machines that sorted and stored their reactions, which were then temporarily transferred to the brains of the Library's patrons. The results were less than satisfactory, since what the patron was then receiving was an actor's interpretation of an author's work, and of course wars and death scenes were almost impossible to manage. Over the years, though, the Library's technology had grown increasingly more sophisticated, to the point where a user could now live a book without having it filtered through actors, directors, adapters, or any other middlemen. A single tape usually took a team of four technicians between two and three years to complete; and with half a million technicians under contract and more being trained each day, the Library's catalog was growing geometrically.

Moore read a little further, found nothing except an inordinate amount of self-congratulatory hyperbole, and finally returned to the counter.

"Any questions?" asked the attendant, taking the pamphlet back and putting it out of sight behind the counter.

"Does it hurt — attaching these things to my head?"

"Goodness, no!" laughed the attendant. "Who would come back a second time if there were any pain involved'?"

"You'd be surprised," said Moore, thinking of some of the more notorious exhibits at the Thrill Show.

"I assure you that you won't feel the slightest discomfort, Mr. Moore."

"I'll take your word for it," said Moore with a shrug.

The attendant's computer terminal beeped twice.

"Ah! Your money has been transferred."

"Your prices must scare away a lot of customers," commented Moore.

"Not as many as you might suppose," replied the attendant. "We offer you experiences that nobody else can duplicate. Have you ever wondered what the female orgasm feels like? You can become Fanny Hill, live her life, feel her sensations. Do you dream of empire? You can be Caesar, Elizabeth, Bonaparte — not just observe them, mind you, but *become* them. Do you fantasize about your physical abilities? Then be Tarzan, locked in mortal combat with Numa the Lion."

"How long does it take to run through a tape?"

"It varies, but by and large you can live a tape in about forty minutes. Of course, if you wish to be Natasha in *War and Peace*, it will take a little longer. And, conversely, if you wish to be a character who appears in only a single chapter of *War and Peace*, it might run only two or three minutes."

"What if I want to be a character at only one point of a story?" asked Moore. "How can I do that?"

"You must signify which portion of the story you want, in advance," answered the attendant. "You will be totally powerless to act independently once it begins. In fact, you won't even be aware that you are living a tape rather than a life. Therefore, all limitations must be decided beforehand."

"Where can I find a list of your tapes?"

The attendant gestured toward a door. "Go through there, and you'll find yourself in our Catalog Room. Write down the titles and code numbers of the tapes you want, as well as those portions of the tapes that you wish to live. Then bring the list to me and I'll feed it into the master computer while you arrange yourself in your cubicle."

Moore went into the Catalog Room and returned with his list half an hour later.

"Ah," smiled the attendant, looking at the titles. "I see you are a religious man."

"Not especially," replied Moore.

"Then you wish to become one?"

"Not especially."

"You'll feel differently after you have died for our sins and risen again."

"I doubt it."

"Then why should you wish to be Jesus?" asked the attendant, curious.

"I don't," said Moore, scribbling down the character whose life he wanted to live. "Let's begin with the Gospel of John."

He went to his cubicle, attached the nodules to his temples as directed, felt a pleasant drowsiness come over him, and . . .

*H**e was Judas Iscariot, and he was furious.* Jesus had entrusted him with the bag that contained the disciples' money, solely so that he would be held accountable if anything was missing, and he resented it. He was a thief, and now there was nobody to steal from except himself.

Why had he ever fallen in with this gentle, white-robed man in the first place? Surely this was no Messiah, but merely a teacher, a rabbi with strange, revolutionary ideas. He should leave, should be out trying to make or steal a living . . . and yet, there was always that chance, that minute possibility.

How long, how many times, had his people implored the God of Israel to unleash His Messiah and reclaim the former glory of the race? Claimant after claimant to the Messiahship had come forth, tried to rally the masses, and been stoned to death or crucified for his trouble. And although he would bide his time before deciding if this man Jesus was the One his people had been awaiting, he felt certain that in the end he would prove no more of a Messiah than any of the others.

Still, while he watched and waited, he had to do his master's bidding, and it enraged him to play the part of a holy man of peace. He sat now in the house of Lazarus, watching while Mary, the sister of Lazarus, took out a pound or more of very costly ointment, placed it on Jesus' feet, and rubbed it in with her hair. Finally Judas could stand it no longer.

"Why was not this ointment sold for three hundred pence, and given to the poor?" he demanded.

He cared no more for the poor than for the Romans, of course; but the profit from the sale would have helped fill out the money pouch — and if Jesus turned out to be nothing but a man, there would have been that much more of a stake for Judas in whatever new life he chose for himself.

"Let her alone," answered Jesus firmly. "Against the day of my burying hath she kept this, for the poor always ye have with you, but me ye have not always."

The other disciples all stared at him in mute disapproval, and for perhaps the hundredth time he cringed in humiliation before his master. He nurtured his hatred, let it grow and blossom within him. Soon they would go to Jerusalem for the Passover. Then he would act. The money he would receive for betraying his master would make three hundred pence seem like so many grains of sand on the desert.

Soon the moment would come. Soon . . .

*A*nd suddenly he was thrust into the hot, barbaric world of Kazantzakis' *The Last Temptation of Christ*. He was huge, rawboned, virile, with the strength of a bull, and a great red beard that was the envy of every man. . . .

*H*e was Judas, and he was impatient. Once, months ago, he had loathed the sight of Jesus, had even gone to a desert monastery to kill him. But the strange, pale-skinned young man with the haunted eyes, the ascetic who seemed always to be running not toward the Messiahship but away from it, had convinced Judas without even convincing himself that he was indeed the One.

And now Judas grew increasingly impatient. Why did Jesus not wield the sword? Why did he not bring the Romans and the Pharisees to their knees? Why did he dance and drink, and rub shoulders with the scum of the earth? This was no way for the Messiah to act! The Messiah must carry the terrible sword of the Lord's wrath and vengeance. They were wasting time, Jesus and his scrawny, flea-ridden, cowardly band of followers, and it was up to Judas to show him the way, to convince him that the time had come to strike the blow that would set his people free once and for all.

But that night Jesus took Judas aside and spoke to him of a vision he had had while lying all alone atop Golgotha. The prophet Isaiah rose up in his mind, holding aloft a black goatskin covered with letters. Suddenly Isaiah and the goatskin vanished, leaving only the letters, which writhed like living beasts in the air.

Sweating and trembling, Jesus had read them aloud: "'He has borne our faults; he was wounded for our transgressions; our iniquities bruised him. He was afflicted, yet he opened not his mouth. Despised and rejected by all, he went forward without resisting, like a lamb that is led to the slaughter.'"

Jesus stopped speaking. He had turned a deathly pale.

"I don't understand," said Judas. "Who is the lamb being led to slaughter? Who is going to die?"

"Judas, brother," said Jesus, trying to control his terror, "*I* am the one who is going to die."

"You? Then aren't you the Messiah?"

"I am."

"I don't understand," growled the redbeard, torn between rage and grief.

"You must help me do what must be done," pleaded Jesus. "You must go into Jerusalem."

"Why do you choose *me?*" demanded Judas.

"Because you are the strongest," replied Jesus. "The others don't bear up."

And because he was the strongest, and the most devoted, he slunk out into the night toward Jerusalem to do his master's bidding. . . .

*A*nd suddenly, instead of the hot, arid streets of Jerusalem, he was catapulted down, down, down, to the depths of the *Inferno* of Dante. . . .

*H*e was Judas Iscariot, and he was in such agony as no man had ever known before.

Above him, beyond him, souls were suffering all the torments of the eternally damned. They endured rivers of fire, hideous mutilations, transformations into serpents, living burials, every monstrous indignity and torture that Hell could provide.

He would gladly have traded places with any of them.

At the very epicenter of Hell squatted Lucifer, the archfiend of all Creation. He had three faces and three mouths. In the mouth on the left was Brutus; in the mouth on the right was Cassius; and in the largest of the three mouths, the one in the center, was Judas.

He had been in that mouth, chewed and mangled by Lucifer and made unthinkably unclean by his very nearness, for all eternity. He would remain there for all eternity. The agony was unendurable, and yet he endured it. He tried to direct his mind away from the pain, but whenever he did so he saw the face of his master looking down at him from the cross, and even the agony of Lucifer's black, jagged teeth was preferable to that.

He screamed.

He had screamed an infinite number of times in the past. He would scream an infinite number of times in the future. He was Judas Iscariot, and he had betrayed his God. . . .

*F*ree from the nethermost regions of Hell, he found himself back in the suffering, oft-raped body of Palestine, the land of Asch's *The Nazarene*. . . .

*H*e was Judah Ish-Kiriot, and he was troubled. The Temple was to be destroyed, and Jerusalem was to be leveled with the earth and trodden underfoot by the gentiles.

"Who has said these dreadful things, man of Kiriot?" demanded Nicodemon.

"My rabbi!" wailed Judah. "He who I believed would bring salvation to Israel!"

Nicodemon shook his head sadly. "Your rabbi has said that he who will not be born again shall not see the kingdom of God. I did not understand this, so I asked him: 'How can a man be born when he is grown old? Can he enter into his mother's body again?' And your rabbi replied, 'He that is born of the flesh, is flesh; but he that is born of the spirit, is spirit.' This is true, but are we born of the flesh alone? Is not the Torah our mother, and are not Abraham, Isaac, and Jacob our fathers? So I said to myself, this rabbi's doctrine is good and great for those who are born without the spirit, or for such as would deny the spirit. And on that day I withdrew from your rabbi."

Judah stared at him uncomprehendingly.

"Is it not possible," continued Nicodemon softly, "that your rabbi has come for the gentiles?"

The more he thought about it, the more likely it seemed to his anguished brain. And yet, to redeem those millions of souls who had been born without the spirit, he would play his part in the tapestry of pain and death that was yet to come. . . .

*A*nd from the house of Nicodemon he journeyed to a Jerusalem suspended in time and space, in Dunn's epic poem, *Satan Chained*. He seemed insubstantial, shadowy, ethereal. . . .

*H*e was Judas, and yet he was not. He was a toy, a pawn in an eternal chess game that had begun when Satan and his demoniac generals had led the revolt. Scenes shifted, time progressed, and yet the battle-game went on, unchanging.

But God had decided to bring a new piece onto the board:

His Son. And so Satan had countered with Judas Iscariot. The Son would try to save the human race; Judas would try to nail Him to the cross.

Judas won, yet in winning he lost, and the setting moved elsewhere. . . .

*A*nd finally, back from Somewhere, he was once again in Jerusalem, living the Gospel of Matthew. . . .

*H*e was Judas Iscariot, and he was tortured. He had sold his master for thirty pieces of silver, and he still didn't know why.

Was Jesus really the Messiah? He didn't know that, either. All he knew was that he could no longer tolerate the possession of the money for which he had made his betrayal. Whether Jesus was man or Messiah didn't matter anymore; whether Jesus lived or died did, and so he determined to sacrifice his own life to save that of his master.

He raced to the Temple and sought out the elders and priests.

"I have sinned!" he cried, hurling the money to the floor in front of them. "I have betrayed the innocent blood!"

"What is that to us?" asked the high priest sardonically.

He knew then that Jesus was indeed doomed, and he left the blood money on the floor and raced out into the night.

He tried once again to examine his motives. Was he trying to force Jesus into some sort of Messianic action? Was he trying to punish him for not being the kind of Messiah he wanted him to be? Or was he merely trying to save the people of Israel from another dashed hope when their new Messiah turned out to be only a man after all? He didn't know. All he knew was that Jesus of Nazareth would die because of thirty pieces of silver.

He found a length of rope on the ground and picked it up, making a slipknot noose at one end of it. Then he went off to find a tree with a sturdy, low-hanging limb. . . .

*M*oore was back in his cubicle. The tapes were over, though it took him a few minutes to acclimatize himself to his surroundings. Finally he emitted a sigh, replaced the nodules, and walked out to the foyer.

"How long was I at it?" he asked.

"Just about ninety minutes," replied the attendant. "A refund of ten thousand dollars will be transferred to your personal account." He paused. "If you don't mind my saying so, you look a little shaken, Mr. Moore."

"I am."

"It's not every day that one gets to betray the Messiah so many times," said the attendant wryly.

"*Was* he the Messiah?" asked Moore.

"I have no idea. I should have thought Judas would know."

"Judas didn't know any more about it than you do."

"Odd," mused the attendant. "I wonder why."

"Maybe he didn't have all the facts before him."

"What fact was missing?"

"A man named Jeremiah," replied Moore.

12

The Golden Lobster, like most other eateasies, was well camouflaged. It was on the fourth level of State Street, and was fronted by a rather plain dry-cleaning shop which seemed to do a considerable amount of business in its own right.

Once inside, though, the decor delivered on the restaurant's promise. The walls were totally covered by gold and yellow Japanese screens and tapestries dating back many centuries, and the chairs and tables were all hand-wrought and gilded. Even the tiles and carpeting glistened like gold, and the dishes and serving carts were gold-plated. Crustaceans of every imaginable size and variety resided in carefully tended triangular golden tanks in the four corners of the room, and the waiters and waitresses were covered with metallic gold body paint and very little else, though each did possess a crown made of glitter-covered seashells.

Moore and Pryor were ushered to a table in the back of the restaurant, where Moore ordered for both of them.

"It's fabulous!" exclaimed Pryor, looking around the room. "I've been meaning to get here for a year now, ever since it opened, but I just never got around to it."

"The food's even better than the surroundings," replied Moore. He waited until a waitress brought Pryor a drink — he himself abstained, as always — and then turned to his assistant.

"You heard where I went this afternoon?"

Pryor nodded. "The Reality Library. Learn anything?"

Moore shook his head. "A waste of time and money. We seem to be running into one dead end after another."

"So we're back to where we started?"

"It's starting to look that way," said Moore grimly. He turned to Pryor. "Ben, what's *your* thinking on Jeremiah?"

"I think he's a hard man to kill."

"Thanks a lot."

"You want a stronger statement?" said Pryor. "Okay. I think that, for some reason we haven't put our fingers on yet, he's literally *impossible* to kill. Personally, I lean toward the mutant theory. It may be weird, but it's a hell of a lot easier to swallow than Abe's Messiah crap."

"I'm open to suggestions," said Moore. "Got any?"

"I'm no scientist," said Pryor. "But then, neither is Abe. I think I'd find a few people, maybe down at the University of Chicago, who know something about mutation and see what they have to say."

"We might as well," agreed Moore. "Take care of it when you get to the office tomorrow morning."

"You look dubious."

"I'm not a betting man, Ben," said Moore. "But if I was, I'd lay plenty at twelve-to-one that they support what Abe says about mutation. Mutants aren't supposed to be able to do what Jeremiah does, and I imagine scientists are pretty much like everyone else — they don't like to come face to face with anything that goes contrary to their beliefs."

"Just like Christians," chuckled Pryor. "Wouldn't it be funny if he was the Messiah?"

"Hilarious," said Moore dryly.

The waitress reappeared with their dinner — lobster tails for Moore and a variety of shellfish in a wine sauce for Pryor — and they spent the next half hour enjoying the delicious and highly illegal meal. After a flaming dessert was brought to the table, Moore turned to Pryor again.

"Even if he can't be killed, I want to keep up the pressure. Put out a contract on him."

"It's already been done."

"A bigger one," said Moore, stirring some sugar into his coffee. "A million dollars. So far we've kept this thing in our organization. Let's pass the word to the freelancers too. Maybe it'll buy us a little more time."

Pryor pulled out a pair of cigars and offered one to Moore.

"No, thanks," replied Moore. "I only use them for props when I'm trying to convince people that I'm a real tough customer."

"I've seen you let them go out just so the muscle can re-light them," said Pryor, returning one of the cigars to his lapel pocket. "It's amazing how much a show of deference from a bunch of three-hundred-pound bruisers can impress people."

"Speaking very calmly helps, too," said Moore. "Most people expect to be yelled at."

"Nothing like keeping them off-balance," agreed Pryor, lighting his cigar. "By the way, you said that you wanted to buy us a little time. What for?"

"Because we've all been overlooking one very important fact."

"Oh? What's that?"

"Jeremiah thinks he can be killed. Once he figures out that he can't, he's going to stop running away from us and start running *toward* us."

Pryor frowned. "I hadn't thought of that." He paused for a moment, then shrugged again. "Still, what the hell can he do?"

"I don't know — and I sure as hell don't intend to sit around and find out."

"So far the only talent he's demonstrated is strictly a defensive one. I think if he had any offensive capabilities he would have demonstrated them by now."

"Maybe he doesn't know what they are," replied Moore. "Remember, we're not dealing with any mental giant here. Whatever else he's got going for him, brainpower isn't a part of his arsenal."

"You hope," said Pryor.

"I *know*," said Moore.

The waitress brought the check, and Moore left seven hundred dollars on the table. He picked up his bodyguards at the door, said goodnight to Pryor, and went back to his apartment, where he spent most of the night reading what he could find on mutation. By the time he arrived at the office in the morning, he knew more about mutants than he had ever cared to know — but he still couldn't decide what Jeremiah was.

He spent most of the morning attending to routine business. Then, just before noon, he summoned Moira, Pryor, and Bernstein into his office.

"What's up, Solomon?" asked Bernstein.

"Abe, could luck be a mutant talent?" asked Moore.

"You mean precognition?"

Moore shook his head. "No. If he had precognition, he wouldn't keep blundering into traps. I'm talking about luck — or, to put it in your terms, an involuntary reaction that enables him to overcome the statistical averages."

"Such as evading forty-three bullets at point-blank range?" asked Bernstein with a smile. "Do you know how silly that sounds?"

"All right," said Moore. "Could he conceivably have developed a skin that is practically impervious to bullets?"

"No," interjected Miora, shaking her head decisively. "I've seen him cut himself shaving."

"Besides," added Bernstein, "that wouldn't explain what happened at the Gomorrah. Those bullets didn't bounce off him, Solomon — they *missed* him."

"Ben," said Moore, "have you got anything from the biologists yet?"

"Too soon," answered Pryor. "They probably won't get back to me for a day or two."

"You're seeking outside council?" asked Bernstein. "What will you do after they agree with me, Solomon?"

"Ask me when it happens," replied Moore.

"I'll be happy to," said Bernstein. "May I make a suggestion in the meantime?"

"Be my guest."

"Since you have to wait a couple of days to evaluate the mutant theory, perhaps you should consider the alternative in the meantime?"

"Damn it, Abe — he doesn't *act* like a Messiah! Even when he's done something that was predicted, he's blundered into it. It's just crazy!"

"Solomon, there is more evidence that he's the Messiah than that he's a mutant, whether you care to admit it or not."

"Messiahs just don't pull the kind of boneheaded stunts that Jeremiah pulls," said Moore. "You've got religion on the brain, Abe."

"Have you ever considered that you might be attacking the problem ass-backwards?" suggested Bernstein.

"What are you talking about?"

"You've been hell-bent on proving that Jeremiah isn't the Messiah. You've talked with Milt Greene, you've been to the Reality Library, you've seen what Jeremiah did to Krebbs, you've matched his perform-ance against the accepted Messianic signs, and no matter how much you protest, you haven't been able to prove a damned thing. I suggest that instead of trying to prove that he isn't the Messiah, you try to prove that he is, and see what you come up with."

"I don't see the difference," said Moore.

"It's a matter of approach," explained Bernstein. "Take a cataleptic. Without a stethoscope or a fogging glass it can be pretty hard to prove that he's alive. But stick him with a pin and watch the blood flow out of the wound, and it's easy to prove that he's not dead."

"That's a pretty weak example."

"I'm not selling examples; I'm selling approaches. You have a certain amount of evidence before you, and you have been unable to prove that Jeremiah isn't the Messiah — and believe me, your experts are going to confirm everything I've told you about mutation. Therefore, why not see if trying to prove that he *is* the Messiah works a little better?"

"That's asinine," said Moore.

"Have you got anything better to do with your time?"

"Lots," said Moore. "But if it will finally shut you up about this Messiah crap, we'll give it a try."

He pressed an intercom button and told his secretary to have lunch for four sent into the office. Then he turned back to Bernstein.

"All right, Abe — what do we know about Jeremiah that leads us to think he's the Messiah?"

"His name is Immanuel, he went to Egypt as a child, and he has resurrected the dead. That's three-quarters of the signs right there."

"Some resurrection," snorted Moore. "What about his being from the Davidic line?"

"Who knows?" said Bernstein. "It's possible."

"Do you even know for a fact that David really lived?"

"There seems to be some historical evidence. But even if a man named David did not exist, that doesn't alter anything."

"Oh?" said Moore. "Why not?"

"Because we're interested in the king that the Bible refers to as David, and personally, I don't much give a damn whether his name was David or George or anything else. It's just a symbol for the man. I'll keep calling it the Davidic line because it's a handy term, but when I use it I am referring to the bloodline that traces back to the man the Bible rightly or wrongly calls David."

"Which doesn't solve anything," said Moore. "Your own rabbi said there would be four signs by which we'd recognize the Messiah. Even stretching the facts, we can only confirm three of them. And, as I recall it, he was supposed to establish a kingdom in Jerusalem. He hasn't quite gotten around to that, has he, Abe?"

"Not yet," said Bernstein.

"Then until he does, I guess the subject is closed."

"I disagree," said Moira.

"Another quarter heard from," commented Moore wryly. "Okay, let's get it all out now, and then maybe we can go back to doing something a little more practical."

"All I did," began Moira, "was follow Dr. Bernstein's advice: I asked myself if I could disprove the assumption that Jeremiah was the Messiah. To do this, I had to prove that he hadn't fulfilled what you claim are the vital prophecies. I know for a fact that the first three are true, so that left only the prophecy about the Davidic line." She paused. "Now, obviously it can't be proved either way, since no records go back more than a few hundred years — but that doesn't mean that there isn't another way to tackle the problem."

"Such as?"

"If I am assuming that Jeremiah is the Messiah, I must therefore assume that he's of the Davidic line, and then ask myself what logically follows."

"And what does?" asked Moore.

"Well, if the Messiah is from the line of David, it seems logical to assume that the line has been kept alive all this time in order to produce him. This would mean that he is the only male in the world who traces directly to David. Now, what does this imply to you?"

"That you're as crazy as Abe is," said Moore.

"No, Mr. Moore," said Moira. "It implies that if the Messiah is ever to be produced in accordance with the prophecies, Jeremiah cannot be killed. He almost died a few times of childhood diseases, but he always recovered — and your own men were also unable to destroy him."

"Then you're saying that he'll manage to keep alive until he sires a male to succeed him in the line?" asked Moore.

"No, Mr. Moore. I'm saying that Jeremiah himself is the Messiah."

" Why?"

"Because Jeremiah had a vasectomy two years ago. The line ends with him."

"By God, she's right, Solomon!" exclaimed Bernstein.

"Not so fast," said Moore. He turned back to Moira. "What if Jeremiah isn't the only direct descendant of David? What if there are fifty of them?"

"Then why couldn't you kill him?" responded Moira. "If he defies all the laws of chance and nature, there must be a reason. I've offered mine, Mr. Moore; do you have a better one?"

"Not at the moment," admitted Moore grudgingly, as a cart with four meals was wheeled into the office.

And, thirty hours later, when every biologist had confirmed what Bernstein had told him, he still didn't have a better answer.

13

Moore gradually became aware of a persistent buzzing on his nightstand. Finally he threw the covers off and groped blindly for the phone.

"Yeah?" he muttered at last.

"I'm at the office. You'd better get down here right away."

"Who is this?"

"Ben."

"What's up?"

"Moira's flown the coop."

"I'm on my way," said Moore.

It took him five minutes to get dressed. Then, accompanied by his bodyguards, he left his apartment and headed to the office, arriving just before sunrise.

Pryor was waiting for him, a note in his hand.

"From her?" asked Moore, taking the folded piece of paper.

Pryor nodded, and he opened it up and read it.

Dear Mr. Moore:
    Facts are facts. If you don't want to recognize them, that's your problem. Mine is surviving, so I'm joining the side that seems to afford me the best opportunity of so doing.

Moira Rallings

PS: If you kill him, which I personally consider impossible, you still owe me his body.

"That's what I like," said Moore dryly. "Loyalty in an employee. How long ago did you find this thing?"

"About two minutes before I called you," said Pryor. "Naomi and I are . . . ah . . . no longer roommates, and I've spent the last couple of nights here."

"I know where you've been spending them," replied Moore curtly. He tossed the note onto his desk. "We'd better move fast on this thing. I want that girl dead or alive, but mainly I want her before she can contact Jeremiah."

"*We* can't find him. What makes you think she can?"

"Things have a way of working out for that bastard," said Moore. "I think we'd better always assume the worst when dealing with him." He turned to Pryor. "Which reminds me: how's *your* loyalty holding up these days?"

"If I turn on you, it won't be to go over to Jeremiah's side," answered Pryor.

"Why not?" asked Moore curiously.

"Because if he as the Messiah, he doesn't need me. I wouldn't be doing myself any good by joining him."

"And if he's not?"

"Then sooner or later we're going to find a way to kill him."

"Reasonable," commented Moore. "The underdog will always have a bigger reward for you than the favorite."

"You think we're the underdog?" said Pryor with a disbelieving smile.

"It's sure starting to look like it," replied Moore seriously.

Nothing that transpired during the next three weeks changed that assumption. Moore increased his payroll and broadened his search, but Moira Railings was nowhere to be found. She had not used public transportation to leave the Chicago complex, but within ten days Moore was forced to conclude that she was no longer in the state of Illinois, and by the time twenty days had passed he was certain that she wasn't within five hundred miles of him.

Business was still booming, of course. The Thrill Show was doing better than anticipated, and even Dream Come True was starting to turn a profit. The city officially declared that Mr. Nightspore and Mr. Thrush had died of natural causes, and there was no coroner's inquiry into the untimely death of Willis Comstock Krebbs. Two more congressmen were in the bag, and one of Moore's royally bred three-year-olds had won a stakes race in Florida.

And yet, as the weeks turned into months, the tension among the members of Moore's hierarchy became almost unbearable. It was broken forever on the morning of June 23, 2048, when a uniformed woman, clad in maroon, entered Moore's private office.

"Yes?" said Moore, looking up from a stack of computer readouts.

"CPS, sir," she said briskly.

"Continental Parcel Service can damned well leave its goods in the outer office with one of the secretaries," said Moore, turning back to his paperwork.

"I'm sorry, sir," said the woman, "but this parcel has been shipped under the FYEO code."

"What the hell does *that* mean?" asked Moore irritably.

"For Your Eyes Only," came the reply. "I have been instructed to wait until you open it before leaving."

"All right," said Moore. "Let's have it."

The woman walked over to his desk and handed him a flat manila envelope. He opened it and withdrew a photograph of Jeremiah and Moira standing beside the wall of a nondescript brick building.

"Who gave this to you?" demanded Moore.

"My supervisor, sir."

"Where was it sent from?"

"I don't know. I can check on it and get back to you this afternoon."

"Do that," said Moore, dismissing her with a wave of his hand, and knowing full well that it wouldn't have been shipped from within a thousand miles of wherever Jeremiah and Moira were hiding.

Pryor walked into the office. "I saw CPS in here a moment ago," he said. "Anything up?"

"You might say so," replied Moore. He held up the picture for Pryor to see — and as he did so, his eyes fell on a two-word message scrawled on the back:

I know.

PART 2

14

*T*he movement began so slowly that Moore, insulated in his Chicago offices, wasn't even aware of it for a number of months — but finally the reports began to trickle in.

Jeremiah had miraculously — and with no cameras to record the feat — restored sight to a blind child in Newark.

Jeremiah had been adopted as the true Messiah by four minor Protestant sects, then by a major one.

Some two hundred American Reformed rabbis were proclaiming that Isaiah's prophecy was now being fulfilled.

Twice more Moore's men had Jeremiah seemingly at their mercy, and twice more he escaped, not unscathed but alive. If he had any headquarters, they were unknown. If his new religion had a name, it too was unknown. Indeed, his motives, his religious philosophy, his whereabouts, and his eventual goals all remained mysteries.

The press and the networks started the game of counting his followers. What was once a laughably small sect soon numbered almost a million. It was still no threat to the established order, but those in power began doing a little mathematics of their own and decided to investigate the phenomenon of Jeremiah the B.

And as the notion of a Messiah — even one it didn't believe in — began to permeate the public consciousness, dissatisfaction set in for the first time in half a century. Social mobility and innovation had remained static for decades, as apathy and boredom buried the dream of a better life and a better world more efficiently than a thousand wars had done. But now people began to understand that even if Jeremiah was a fraud, there might nonetheless be a better way; that although they didn't yet know how to manipulate the machinery of change and progress, it could indeed be manipulated.

Despite tapping this responsive chord, Jeremiah made no promises, no predictions, no prophecies. It was Moore's firm conviction that, Messiah or not, Jeremiah didn't have the brains to figure out what to do with his mass of followers, how or where to lead them.

And still the wave of belief grew. It crossed the Atlantic first, then spread through Europe and Asia and snaked its tentacles into Africa. Israel alone openly condemned him as a fraud — but Israel knew better than anyone else where his kingdom would be, if indeed he had the inclination and the power to establish it.

Soon requests began pouring in for Jeremiah to appear on television, before committees, and in private audiences with religious and political leaders. He made a few video appearances to replenish his coffers, but rejected all other public and private confrontations, stating curtly that the Messiah had no need for any such dealings.

And then, still in need of money, Jeremiah entered the only business he knew anything about: sin. With his followers nearing the three million mark, he had enough clout and enough connections to enter the pornography and prostitution business, and to make his initial purchases of some lower-echelon politicians.

Moore felt the pinch slowly at first. Pornography was down three percent, prostitution seven percent, the domestic drug traffic six percent. But within a handful of months all of his major business enterprises were down by thirty percent or more, and Dream Come True, which had been burgeoning into a healthy money-maker with offices in eleven states, was virtually bankrupt, since the populace preferred buying their dreams from a Messiah rather than an underworld kingpin.

When his gross had been cut in half, Moore tripled the reward and sent out the kill order once again — and many of the employees who would normally have been laid off because of the disastrous slump in business were kept on salary and ordered to help destroy the financial empire Jeremiah was building at Moore's expense. Moore closed his distributional outlets to Jeremiah's products — and Jeremiah established new ones. Moore had his own politicians and policemen crack down on Jeremiah's prostitution ring — and found that Jeremiah had enough politicos and cops on his own payroll to keep his girls working. Moore plugged up every narcotics route — and Jeremiah created new routes just as quickly.

Finally Moore decided that if he couldn't get at Jeremiah's businesses directly, he would do the next best thing and try to discredit him in the eyes of his millions of followers. To this end, he hired a number of research and media teams.

It wasn't difficult to make Jeremiah appear to be an uneducated, ill-mannered, and womanizing fool, for he was all of those. It wasn't even hard to dig up his financial records and show the world that he had already accumulated almost two hundred million dollars. Jeremiah not only admitted it, but stated that he planned to double that amount every six months for the next two years. His scheming, panhandling youth was made public — and far from denying it, Jeremiah took a certain measure of pride in supplying Moore's reportorial teams with some of the more salacious details they had overlooked.

But when it came to proving that Jeremiah was a fraud, the going became more difficult. He had laid his hands on a crippled girl's legs — after receiving a substantial donation from the child's grandfather — and made her walk again. In a most un-Messiahlike ploy, he had jumped, sans parachute, from a helicopter flying at a height of two thousand feet in front of a paying audience numbering in the hundreds of thousands — and though he had to be rushed to the nearest hospital with broken legs, multiple fractures of the spine, and severe internal hemorrhaging, he walked out on his own power nine days later, perfectly healthy. He visited a dying village in Baja California, and while he was there the impoverished farmers experienced rain for the first time in more than a year.

Every Sunday ministers and priests took to their pulpits to proclaim that Jesus was the only Messiah, and every Sunday there were a few less people in their congregations. A thousand authors and biographers tackled the enigma of Jeremiah, and came up with a thousand different conclusions.

Jeremiah reveled in the publicity. The only thing he wouldn't do was codify his philosophy. It was enough, he stated time and again, that he was the Messiah; all else, including his personal beliefs, faded into insignificance beside that fact.

Within another year his followers numbered more than twelve million, and his finances grew apace. Then came the revelation that Jeremiah was building a military machine, and the governments of the world, which had largely been ignoring him in the hope that he would go away, sat up and took notice. Spies of all nationalities and religious persuasions infiltrated his organization. Up to a point they were successful: he had so many men and so many weapons and such and such a military capacity. But as to why he needed an army and where he intended to deploy it, no answers were forthcoming,

Since Moore had done more research on Jeremiah than anyone else, he found himself granted amnesty for all past crimes — and, the implication went, all *future* ones as well — in exchange for his cooperation with the various agencies that had committed themselves to Jeremiah's destruction. There were a lot of them, too, since almost every religious institution found its own existence threatened by the possibility of a living, breathing Messiah.

Now, with the financial and intelligence resources of virtually the entire world at his fingertips, Moore went after Jeremiah with a vengeance. His priests and lieutenants were assassinated, his speeches and broadcasts were disrupted, much of his money was impounded — and *still* his following increased.

And then came the incident which turned the tide of events in Jeremiah's favor for the first time. It came from a totally unexpected source, but its effect was both enormous and immediate.

It was *The Gospel of Moira*, penned by Moira Rallings, and it sold forty million copies during its first two months of publication.

15

And he made a blind child see and a legless girl walk, and when the people saw him and knew him for who and what he was, then in truth did the Word spread across the bleak, unhappy land.
> — *from* The Gospel of Moira

*P*ryor's office was as cluttered as Moore's was barren. It was far larger, and every inch of wall space was covered with computer screens, punctuated only occasionally by television monitors. The office housed a large conference table, a wet bar, a pair of leather couches, and a huge mahogany desk with a leather judge's chair.

Moore entered the room, walked directly to Pryor's desk, and tossed a copy of *The Gospel of Moira* onto it.

"Well, what do you think of it?" he asked.

"She's not about to win a Nobel Prize for Literature," replied Pryor. "It's some of the worst dreck I've ever read." He opened his desk drawer and withdrew his own copy.

"It's also some of the most *dangerous* dreck you've ever read," said Moore. "Check the copyright page."

"Mine is the fifty-third printing," said Pryor without opening the book. "What's yours?"

"The fifty-seventh," replied Moore. "They must be defoliating whole forests to keep up with the demand for this thing." He sat down on one of the couches. "And in the meantime, our gross is off forty-two percent this month; and we finished the last quarter deeper in the red than ever. I think we're going to have to pull out of Kentucky and Tennessee altogether."

"I know," said Pryor grimly. "Even the legitimate enterprises are dropping through the floor."

"You wouldn't think it would be that goddamned hard to kill him," said Moore with a heavy sigh. "After all, they killed the last Messiah without any trouble."

"You know the answer to that: if they killed him, then he wasn't the Messiah." Pryor picked up the new Gospel and began thumbing through it. *"And Moira Rallings became his concubine, and thus was she blessed above all other women,"* he intoned.

"It sounds like some no-talent producer's idea of a Biblical epic," snorted Moore.

Pryor kept thumbing through the book, reading occasional snippets. *"And he went into Egypt, as the prophets foretold. . . . And he began his ministry sullied and abused, an outcast among men. . . . And in the sin-ridden city of Chicago dwelt a servant of the Devil named Moore. . . ."* Pryor looked up. "It's all here — everything but the Sermon on the Mount." He smiled. "I guess she's saving that for the sequel."

"It's not that funny, Ben. If half the people who buy this book throw it out, and half of those who keep it think it's hogwash, she'll still have gained him ten million converts in six weeks — and every last one of them is going to think Judas wasn't all that bad a guy compared to me."

"We can't keep the books out of their hands," replied Pryor. "They're not going through our agencies — and from what I've been able to find out, almost half of them are being sold by computer or through the mail."

"I know," said Moore. "Besides, with that many copies in print, I'd say it's a little late in the game to get a restraining order or an injunction to prohibit distribution. I don't see how we could make one stick, anyway." He paused for a moment, drumming his fingers on the arm of the couch. "What's the last word we have on him?"

Pryor shrugged. "As of yesterday, we have sworn statements that he's in Albuquerque, Buenos Aires, the Manhattan complex, and Iceland. Take your choice."

"Damn MacIntosh, anyway!" snapped Moore suddenly.

Xavier MacIntosh was the only agent of Moore's to successfully infiltrate Jeremiah's expanding organization and gain a position of authority. There was absolutely no question that he would have access to Jeremiah's schedule, and would probably be privy to his future plans as well. But Xavier MacIntosh had wired his resignation to Moore four days ago, explaining that he had seen the light and had elected to become one of Jeremiah's disciples.

"It's not unheard of," said Pryor. "I've been in touch with some of our new . . . ah . . . associates, and they've had pretty much the same problem. As soon as they've got a plant in a position to do then some good, he — well, he *converts.* I don't suppose there's any other term for it."

"And just how *are* our new associates doing?"

"Not very well. If Jeremiah ever commits his forces to some military objective, they may prove useful — but as things stand now, they're no better at infiltrating his organization than we are. We'd probably be better off with industrial spies and saboteurs."

"True," agreed Moore. "Except that industrial cartels don't offer amnesty; governments do. Besides, look at what's happened to our finances in the past year. No business organization is going to lock horns with Jeremiah. There may be easier ways to go broke, but there aren't any quicker ones." He paused. "Anyway, our immediate problem is that damned book Moira's written. It pinpoints me as the greatest archvillain in human history, and it's gaining Jeremiah more support than anything he himself ever did." He shrugged. "You know, it's always possible that she's right — that I am the Devil incarnate for trying to kill Jeremiah."

"I doubt it," replied Pryor seriously. "After all, lots of people have tried to kill him. The only reason you're being singled out is that you're the one who drew Moira into this thing to begin with."

"By that same token, I ought to be canonized instead of condemned," said Moore wryly. "Neither of them had any idea what he was before I got involved."

"They'd have figured it out sooner or later," said Pryor. "After all, if he really is the Messiah, it's not just because you pointed it out to him."

"I know, Ben. It's just so frustrating! Sometimes I feel like we're all walking around underwater, we react so slowly. I thought Moira would prove to be a weak spot, and she's done him more good than the rest of his group put together."

"It's just a book."

"Yeah, and Adolf Hitler was just a housepainter."

Pryor's intercom buzzed, and he pressed a button. "What is it?"

"Ben, is Solomon in there with you?" asked Bernstein's voice.

"Yes, Abe. Do you want to see him?"

"No. Just tell him to turn on a TV to Channel 9 if he wants to see an old friend."

Moore walked to a monitor and activated it.

Moira Rallings, her skin whiter than ever, sat on a love seat, a copy of her Gospel in her hand. She had added about ten pounds and displayed a hitherto unknown fondness for see-through clothing, but seemed otherwise unchanged.

She was being interviewed by Stormin' Norman Gorman (formerly Herbert Russell), a twenty-year-old entertainer who had been a pop music star during a recent revival of acid rock until continued exposure to the high decibel level had caused him to go deaf. His millions of fans wouldn't let him retire from the limelight at seventeen, so he had learned how to read lips and now hosted the nation's third-ranked syndicated noontime talk show.

". . . figures must be immensely gratifying to you," Gorman was saying.

"Oh, they are," replied Moira with more enthusiasm than Moore had ever seen her display for anything except a corpse.

"The money all goes into Jeremiah's treasury, of course. I'm just pleased and happy to know how many wonderful people have now seen the light."

"Check out that transmission and see if it's live," Moore instructed Pryor.

"And will there be a further Gospel in the years to come?" asked Gorman.

"Certainly," said Moira. "If not by me, then by someone else. Jeremiah's ministry is just beginning, Norman. He still has most of his work ahead of him."

"What, exactly, *does* lie ahead of him?" asked Gorman. "He's been very vague on that point, and I'm sure all our viewers would like to know."

"He reveals the details to no one, not even myself," replied Moira. "But it's common knowledge that he will ultimately fulfill all the Messianic prophecies."

"Does that include the establishment of a kingdom in what is now the nation of Israel?"

"It's possible."

"You're begging the question," said Gorman. "The Hebrew prophets expressly state that the Messiah must establish his kingdom in Jerusalem."

Moira smiled. "Which Hebrew prophets?"

"Isaiah, for one."

"Did he?" she said, still smiling.

"Absolutely," said Gorman. "Would you like me to quote chapter and verse?"

"Of what?" asked Moira. "Of the prophet Isaiah himself, or of the ten generations of Jews who repeated his prophecies around campfires, or of the Hebrew scholars who finally wrote it into the Torah, or the Greeks who rewrote it, or the monks of the Dark Ages and Middle Ages who rewrote it again, or of the men who rewrote it for the King James Version?"

"Then you're saying that Jerusalem is not his goal?"

"I'm not saying anything about his goals," replied Moira. "I'm sure he'll reveal them in his own good time. I'm simply saying that fulfilling a prophecy and fulfilling what people *think* is a prophecy may not be the same thing."

Pryor, who had been speaking quietly on the phone, hung up the receiver and walked over to Moore.

"Pre-recorded yesterday in Philadelphia," he said softly. "Moira showed up, spent the day doing about twenty interviews for talk shows, and vanished. Six agencies put tails on her, and she managed to lose all of them within ten minutes."

Moore nodded, never taking his eyes off the screen.

"I see that our time is almost up," said Gorman. "Have you any last words for our viewers?"

"Yes," said Moira. "I have a message from Jeremiah."

"I'm sure we'd all like to hear that."

"Solomon Moody Moore!" she intoned, staring into the camera with dark, wild eyes. "Judas! Embodiment of Satan! If you're watching or listening, I implore you: cease your persecution of the One True Messiah!" She turned toward another camera. "Members of the New Faith, believers of the New Truth: a man who would be the Christ-killer is in your midst! His name is Moore, and he would strike down the Messiah! Band together! Do not let him do this dreadful thing!"

The camera zoomed in on her until her eyes filled the screen. Moore felt they were looking straight at him.

"Repent, Judas Moore, before it is too late!"

The picture faded out, to be replaced by a commercial.

"Charming girl," said Moore, turning off the set.

"We'd better tighten the security around the building," added Pryor.

"Right. It'll give the impression that I'm still here."

"Won't you be?"

"Ben, you've been spending too much time messing around with your girlfriends," said Moore. "Don't you understand what you just heard? He's getting ready to march on Jerusalem, or at least to begin his military campaign."

"How do you come up with that?" asked Pryor, genuinely puzzled.

"Why else would Moira throw up a smokescreen like that? I bet if you get tapes from the other nineteen shows, you'll find that she gave them all the same cock-and-bull story about how the Messianic prophecies didn't necessarily refer to Jerusalem."

"I don't follow you."

"Ben, a lot of the Old and New Testaments got rewritten, and a lot of stuff was edited out for political reasons, and a lot of stuff was invented to make it seem like Jesus was the Messiah — but there is one thing you're forgetting."

"And what is that?"

"The concept itself. Abe's rabbi told me that the literal meaning of 'Messiah' is 'Anointed One,' or 'king.' By definition, a Messiah is the king of the Jews — and by definition, the king of the Jews rules from Jerusalem. If she's trying to convince anyone that it isn't true, it's because Jeremiah's getting ready to move and he wants as many people as possible looking in some other direction."

"What about the love and kisses she directed at you?" asked Pryor.

"It makes it a hell of a lot harder for me to get around," admitted Moore, "and it probably encourages a few thousand fanatics to go hunting for my scalp. We'll increase our security here for show, but I think it's time I got out of Chicago for a while."

"Where to?"

Moore shrugged. "It doesn't make much difference — but I'm going to have a little meeting with some of our associates, so fix me up something a little more luxurious than usual."

"Right," said Pryor.

"And Ben?"

"Yes?"

"Put out a contract on Moira Railings."

16

Jeremiah bellowed like a bull moose as his body jerked through the inevitable contortions of the sex act. Then, panting and sweating, he slid off the motionless figure of Moira Railings and rolled onto his back.

"Christ!" he spat. "It's getting so I have a hard time telling the difference between you and one of your goddamned corpses!"

"Learn to be a little more skillful, then," she said, pulling the covers up over her breasts.

"I'm the goddamned Messiah!" he shouted. "I'll learn what I want to learn and screw the way I want to screw!"

"Then don't complain when there's no reaction," she replied calmly.

She started to get out of bed, and he grabbed her arm, pulling her back.

"Where are you going now?" he demanded. "Off to fuck a statue?"

"One gets satisfaction where one can," she answered with no show of embarrassment.

"Which one is it tonight — the general, or the one done up like the Emperor Augustus?"

"Whichever strikes my fancy."

"That's a well-traveled fancy you've got there," he said disgustedly. "Why do you dress all those corpses up if you're just going to strip them down for action every night?"

"So as not to shock you."

"I'm pretty hard to shock," he replied with a harsh laugh. "Someday I'll tell you what I did this morning with three female members of my flock."

"Well, then," said Moira, "maybe I find them more attractive in uniform. Maybe *they* feel better about it."

"It makes small difference to the dead if they are buried in tokens of luxury," said Jeremiah in amused tones.

"Since when did you start quoting Euripides?"

"Since I read his fucking poems," he answered, reaching over to his bedtable and picking up two pills of indeterminate properties. "What the hell difference does it make to you, you damned necrophile? I read them, that's all." He put the pills into his mouth and swallowed them.

"Recently?"

"Yes, recently."

"And when did you learn what *necrophile* means?"

"Maybe I'm a little smarter than you think!" snapped Jeremiah.

"Maybe you are," she said, frowning.

"And getting smarter all the time!" he added. "Things that were incomprehensible to me a few months ago are suddenly becoming very clear."

"Like the word 'incomprehensible'?"

"What the hell are you talking about?"

"That you really *are* getting smarter every day," she replied, sitting up. "You're using words you never knew before, you're reading books you'd never heard of and wouldn't have understood, and when you take the obscenities out of your speech even your sentence construction is more complex."

"Everyone gets smarter, just like they get older," he said. "Otherwise there'd be even more stagnation than you see now. So what? Leave it to a frigid pervert to start changing the subject."

"The subject was intelligence."

He ripped the covers from her and pulled her unprotesting legs apart, "The subject is what I'm looking at, and nothing else! God and Messianic destiny are half horseshit and half hokum, cooked up for a bunch of sheep. The secret of the universe is right between your legs, and I'm getting fucking sick and tired of your clogging it up with a bunch of corpses!" He glared at her. "God! If it wasn't for that book of yours and the sequel you're writing, I'd have your ass out of here so fast you'd never know what hit you!"

She listened to him as he continued castigating her — *really* listened, for the first time in many months. She listened to the choice of words, to the concepts couched in vulgarisms, and she knew he was *changing*. It wasn't complete yet, and he wouldn't rank with Shakespeare or Einstein for a long, long time, if ever; but the signs of a growing intellect were unmistakably there.

And, being a survivor by nature, she opened her body to him when he threw himself onto her, wrapped her legs tightly around his torso, shrieked in splendidly false ecstasy, made sure she dug her fingernails into his neck and back so hard that she drew blood, performed acts that even she had never attempted before, and forced herself to beg for more when at last he lay exhausted beside her.

Long after he was asleep she rose quietly from the bed, tiptoed out of the room, and found her own special form of satisfaction. The knowledge that she was indeed on the winning side, and that that side was growing in power almost by the minute, made the experience even more exhilarating and satisfying than usual.

Jeremiah awoke the next morning to find himself in bed with the sexual tigress of his dreams. What she may have lacked in sincerity, she more than made up for in motivation and enthusiasm, as she made certain, in ways he had previously only fantasized about, that no one would soon be supplanting her at the side of the Messiah.

17

*O*fficially it was known as the North Central Caribbean Undersea

Dome, but its inhabitants called it the Jamaica Bubble.

It was a large, totally submerged structure, residing on the ocean floor some three miles southeast of Kingston and well out beyond the coral reef. The Bubble was almost a mile in diameter at its base, and the top of it came to within forty feet of the ocean's surface, where a series of elevators connected it to a floating airport.

The Bubble possessed a trio of water desalinization plants that turned out more than ten billion gallons of fresh water every twenty-four hours, barely enough to satisfy the ever-increasing needs of Mexico, the islands, and the eastern seaboard of the United States. Sharing the limited space were four compact seaweed-processing laboratories and two research institutes.

Also inside the Bubble was the New Atlantis, a luxury hotel which offered a truly impressive array of food, drink, drugs, entertainment, gambling, and sin. Solomon Moody Moore, hidden behind an impenetrable corporate veil, was its owner.

The New Atlantis was twelve stories high. On the top floor, above the bars and the nightclubs and the casinos, Moore kept a suite of rooms. Unlike the Spartan surroundings of his headquarters, these apartments were used solely for entertaining and reeked of luxury, from the spun-gold draperies and fur-covered couches to the platinum bathroom fixtures. Van Goghs and Picassos and Chagalls and Frazettas were displayed haphazardly on the walls, as were a pair of century-old original Pogo and Li'l Abner strips. In addition to the many windows that overlooked the activities of the Bubble was a huge "porthole," a circular view screen tied in to a high-resolution video camera that was perpetually trained on the sea life outside the dome.

Moore hated the place. He felt uncomfortable, as he always did when surrounded by the luxuries that blurred the dividing line between himself and the masses. He had spent most of the day sitting morosely in a whirlpool tub of Homeric proportions, got out in late afternoon for a meal of filet of sole almandine, and finally dressed himself in the style of a Tombstone gambler, complete with black sombrero and silver spurs. Then he walked into the lush parlor and waited.

Soon they began to arrive:

Caesar DeJesus, an Argentine cardinal in the Catholic Church, a surprisingly blond, fair-skinned man swathed in velvet robes; Felix Lewis, purportedly the richest investor on Wall Street and activist head of the Jewish Defense League, a small, dapper, graying man carrying his own hashish pipe; Naomi Wizner, Israel's Defense Minister, whose shaven head and slit skirt belied her fifty-six years; and Piper Black, head of the Black and Noir Conglomerate, a seven-foot-tall mulatto wrapped in gold and purple silks and wearing a jeweled turban.

Moore greeted each in turn, opened a bottle of century-old sparkling burgundy, and filled crystal glasses for everyone except himself. Then he chatted idly about sports and the weather and the wonderful results of the Bubble's technology, allowing each of them a chance to admire the artwork and the decor, and to make sure that there were no secret microphones or cameras planted about the apartment.

Finally, after some twenty minutes had passed, all four visitors were sitting comfortably in the drawing room, sipping contentedly from their glasses and staring at the viewscreen, and Moore decided that it was time to get down to business.

"I'm very glad all four of you could make it here," he announced, turning off the screen and focusing their attention upon himself. "If anyone is hungry, I can have some food sent in, and once we're through all of the attractions of the New Atlantis are at your disposal. But we've got a lot of ground to cover tonight, so if there are no objections, I think we'd better get started."

"All right, Solomon," said Black, lighting up an oversized cigar. "Just why *are* we here?"

Moore leaned forward slightly in his wingback chair. "I have reason to believe that Jeremiah is getting ready to mobilize his troops."

"What makes you think he *has* any troops?" asked Lewis.

"What makes you think he hasn't?" Moore shot back. "Look — you know the stock market; that's your field of expertise. Well, my field of expertise is Jeremiah, and I'm telling you that even if he doesn't have enough troops, he can afford to go out and buy some more." He turned to the huge mulatto. "How much are you down this year, Piper?"

"What makes you think we're down?" demanded Black.

"We're not going to get anywhere if we don't put our cards on the table," said Moore. "My own gross is off almost seven hundred million dollars in the past nine months."

"Half a billion," said Black emotionlessly.

"No one is saving any more money than they used to, so it's not unreasonable to assume that almost a billion and a quarter of our dollars, or dollars that should have been ours, have gone straight to Jeremiah this year."

"Why only Jeremiah?" asked Lewis. "Why not others as well?"

"I'm not particularly inclined to tell you all the details of my business operation, and I'm sure Mr. Black feels much the same way — but I think we can both assure you that the nature of our business is such that it doesn't encourage competitors. No one except Jeremiah could take a single dollar from us without our consent. Am I right, Piper?"

Black nodded.

"So money for mercenaries is not exactly his biggest problem," concluded Moore.

"If he's got any problems at all, I sure as hell haven't spotted them," said Black.

"That's why I've called this little meeting," said Moore. "To see if we can't create a few for him."

"You've seen him, talked to him," said Naomi Wizner. "That's more than any of us has done. What's his secret?"

"No secret at all," responded Moore. "He's got the brainpower and emotional stability of a hyperthyroid twelve-year-old. I've asked Piper to join us because his interest in Jeremiah is similar to mine: we're both getting hit in the pocketbook. But you others have been financing me and encouraging me and supporting my private little war, and the time has come to put the question to you: are you ready to come out of the closet and wage a *public* battle against Jeremiah?"

"We've been doing that!" said Lewis hotly.

"No!" replied Moore. "You've been making pious statements while my people have been in the trenches! I'm telling you that this man is going to stop being merely a religious threat and is about to become a military one. He's got more money than he needs, and he has no reason to wait. Before I commit what remains of my holdings, I want to know where you stand on this."

"He's got to be stopped," said Naomi Wizner.

"Killed," added DeJesus.

"All right, Cardinal," said Moore. "Let me put the question to you. You say he's got to be killed?"

"Absolutely."

"Isn't that just a little inconsistent with your religious principles?"

"My religious principles are the veneration and worship of the Holy Trinity," replied DeJesus. "My fealty is to the Church and the Pope."

"Even if they're wrong?" asked Moore.

"That's unthinkable!"

"Well, you'd better start thinking about it pretty seriously," said Moore. "Because every piece of evidence we have points to Jeremiah's being the Messiah."

"You could pick a better Messiah out of the phone book," interjected Black sarcastically.

"How can you claim this . . . this *animal* is the Prince of Peace?" added DeJesus.

Moore shook his head. "Will the pair of you try to get it through your heads that if he is the Messiah, then he's the Messiah of the Old Testament? He is *not* the Prince of Peace or the Son of God. He is simply the person God — or *some*one — has chosen to establish a kingdom in Jerusalem — and for what it's worth to you, once you get rid of all the rotten poetry in *The Gospel of Moira*, the facts are correct. They ought to be; she got them from me. Jeremiah *did* bring a drowning victim back to life; he *did* spend some time in Egypt; his name *is* Immanuel; and he may very well be from the Davidic line. At least, no one can prove that he isn't."

"I oppose him because I know Jesus to be the Messiah," said DeJesus. "But if in your opinion Jeremiah is the Messiah, why do *you* oppose him?"

"He's not *my* Messiah, Cardinal," said Moore. "My interest in the future of Jerusalem and the Jewish race is minimal. Besides, if he's the best that God could come up with, I don't know that I care to have anything to do with either of them."

"That's a very glib answer," said DeJesus.

"You want a better one?" asked Moore. "All right. If he's the Messiah of the Old Testament, he's just a man, nothing more. I don't give a damn what he plans to do in Jerusalem. I care about what he's doing now — and what he's doing now is trying to kill me and take over my organization. That's my motivation, plain and simple — and I'll stack its staying power up against yours anytime." He turned to Lewis. "As long as the Cardinal brought the subject up, let me ask it of you: if he's the Messiah, why shouldn't the Jewish Defense League accept him?"

"You haven't spoken to a hell of a lot of American Jews, have you?" said Lewis, taking a puff on his hashish pipe. "I don't care if he is the Messiah. He's a disruptive influence." He paused thoughtfully. "Judaism isn't so much a religion as a way of life. Our culture means more to us than the details of our religion, and this man threatens to destroy that culture. I don't care if he sets up a kingdom in Jerusalem or not; after all, there are less than five million Jews in all of Israel, and there are twelve million in the Manhattan complex alone. But if he succeeds in taking over Jerusalem, he can't help but change what being Jewish means, and we cannot allow this."

"Let me repeat this, just to make sure I've got it right," said Moore. "Neither the Jewish Defense League nor the Catholic Church — or at least those portions that are represented here tonight — will back down even if Jeremiah is what he claims to be. Is that correct?"

Lewis nodded.

"He is not," said DeJesus firmly.

"But *if* he is?" persisted Moore.

"If it seems that he is, then he is the Devil, the Prince of Liars, and we must destroy him."

Moore decided that he wasn't going to get a better answer from the Cardinal, shrugged, and turned to Naomi Wizner.

"How about you? Do you speak for your government?"

"Absolutely. For all practical purposes, if it comes to an attack on Jerusalem, I *am* the government."

"And what is Israel's feeling?"

"Israel feels like it's under attack."

"Israel always feels like it's under attack from someone," said Black with a chuckle.

"And Israel *always* defends itself!" she replied hotly. "This time is no different from all the others!"

"But it is," Moore pointed out. "If Jeremiah is the Messiah, it means Christianity has been dead wrong for two thousand years — but why won't Israeli citizens accept him with open arms? After all, you never accepted Jesus, so why shouldn't Jeremiah seem like the fulfillment of the prophecies?"

"He'll come with the sword and the fire," replied Naomi. "I'm sure God won't mind if we protect ourselves."

"That's not an adequate answer," said Moore.

"It's the best you're going to get, Mr. Moore," she said. "What do you expect my government to do — turn the country over to him on a silver platter?"

"What if he convinces your government that he's the Messiah?"

"And just how do you think he's going to do that?" she scoffed.

"By taking Jerusalem."

"Mr. Moore, do you have any idea how many times Jerusalem was conquered between the time of the prophets and the establishment of the State of Israel in 1948?"

"No."

"Well, take my word for it: it happened more often than you can imagine. We never accepted any previous conquerors as the Messiah. Why should this man be any different?"

"Because he *is* different," said Moore. "When Moira Railings writes of the some of the things he's done, she's not exaggerating. I'm not saying that he is necessarily the Messiah — but he sure as hell is different."

"You sound like you're more convinced than any of the rest of us, Solomon," said Black.

"That's irrelevant," said Moore. "Messiah or not, he's a man, and he's got to have a weakness. He's been trying to ruin me, and I'm not going down without a fight."

"Bully for you," said Lewis, clapping his hands slowly. "Now, do you have any plan in mind, or do you just like making speeches?"

"I've got a number of plans," replied Moore, turning to him. "I've come to the reluctant conclusion that whatever he is, we're not going to be able to kill him. This means that we've got to consider alternatives."

"Such as?" asked Lewis.

"Here's the simplest one," said Moore. "Let him take Jerusalem. That's all he's supposed to do, isn't it?"

"What?" cried Lewis and Naomi in unison.

"Let him have it. It's just a city. Your government can always relocate."

"It took the Jews two millennia to regain Jerusalem!" snapped Lewis. "Giving it up without a fight is out of the question!"

"Is it?" asked Moore. "He's got something like thirty million people who'll buy guns and pay their own passage over there to fight in his Holy War. Why not just turn it over to him?"

"It's unthinkable!" said Naomi. "Why not just turn Czechoslovakia over to Hitler? That's all he wants! Except that it wasn't all he wanted, and Jerusalem isn't all that Jeremiah wants. Once he's got his army, he's got to keep them fed and active. How do you think he'll do that, Mr. Moore? He'll march into Egypt and Syria and Jordan and Lebanon, and then he'll cross the Mediterranean into Europe."

"With what?" scoffed Black. "He hasn't got any planes or tanks, or even any ammunition."

"He'll get them," said Naomi. "Do you know how many churches would be happy to unload their treasuries on him in exchange for lenient treatment? How many officers would turn over military equipment to him in exchange for favored positions in his army?"

"Not that many," said Black. "He's still small potatoes."

"Is he?" she said. "This man was a penniless beggar less than three years ago. Today he's worth about four billion dollars, he's got more than thirty million followers and is picking up half a million a week, and one church out of every ten has decided he's divine. What, in your opinion, would it take to make him a *big* potato, Mr. Black?"

Black seemed about to reply, then changed his mind and kept silent.

"All right," said Moore. "Since no one wants to take the easy way out, we fight him. But you have to understand that military action is out of the question."

"Why?" demanded Naomi. "We're prepared to do battle with him down to the last man, woman, and child."

"More power to you," said Moore dryly. "But Jeremiah doesn't have a standing army yet. Where will you launch your attack? How can you cut a supply line that doesn't exist? Even if you didn't mind slaughtering civilians, you couldn't attack his home base; no one knows where it is."

"The man is right," said Black with a grin. "Until he mounts a legitimate army, there's nothing to fight."

"Right," said Moore. "So what I propose is a concerted and coordinated media attack on his credibility. We've done it in bits and pieces, but we've been working at cross-purposes. Naomi fears a military attack, the Cardinal fears that Jeremiah is the Antichrist, Piper fears a further loss of money, Mr. Lewis fears for his cultural values, Lord knows the Chinese and Indians and Africans have things to fear — but we've been speaking out as individuals, or at least as single interest groups. Jeremiah has to be discredited not just in the eyes of the Jews or the Christians or the Moslems, but everywhere at once."

"I'll commit every cent I've got," said Black. "But first there's got to be an understanding."

"What kind of understanding?" asked Lewis suspiciously.

"If we're successful, there's going to be a very healthy piece of change up for grabs," continued Black. "Don't go looking so superior, Mr. Lewis. You've still got all of your money. Do you really think I give a damn about Jews or Christians, or about who rules Jerusalem? And if Solomon cares one whit more than I do, it's because he's lost his objectivity. We're businessmen, and whether the business is sex or drugs or stopping a would-be Messiah, we expect to turn a profit."

"Are those *your* sentiments?" Lewis asked, turning to Moore.

"I have my own reasons for wanting to destroy Jeremiah," said Moore, measuring each word carefully. "He's the closest thing to a blood enemy that I've ever had, and I'm in this to the finish, with or without your help." He paused. "But, as my friend Piper has pointed out, I'm a businessman, and I certainly intend to share in the spoils if we're successful. However, I don't think we need to go into the details right now," he added. "You have my pledge that we won't take anything that anyone else wants."

He stared directly at Black, who decided to let the subject drop.

"Now," continued Moore, "if we're all in agreement, we'd better start talking about just what kind of media campaign we're going to be mounting. Cardinal, how many television stations does the Church control in South America?"

"We *own* stations, Mr. Moore," said DeJesus defensively. "We don't *control* them."

"No one's keeping notes," said Moore. "None of this will ever leave this room. In exchange for that, I feel I have the right to expect straightforward answers. Now, how many stations do you control?"

DeJesus glared at him for a long moment, then shrugged. "Between six and seven hundred," he said at last.

"And the Jewish Defense League?" asked Moore.

"Personally, I own or control five," replied Lewis. "The League doesn't control any, and that's the truth."

"Newspapers and newstapes?"

"Me, ten; the League, maybe two dozen."

"How long will it take you to raise enough money to blanket the papers and networks with a hate campaign?"

"Three months, maybe four," said Lewis promptly.

"Too long," replied Moore. "You'll have to dip into your own capital and do it in six weeks."

"Why so quickly?"

"Because if Jeremiah's getting ready to move, it's not going to take him four months to get his act together. These are religious fanatics we're talking about. If he puts out the call tomorrow, they'll start buying tickets to Jerusalem before the weekend."

"I'll see what I can do," said Lewis.

"I can't commit any funds," said Naomi Wizner. "Every penny is going to strengthen Jerusalem's defenses."

"I wasn't going to ask you for any," replied Moore. "I just wanted to make sure that you weren't planning on throwing in the towel after we've committed everything we've got. As for Mr. Black and myself, between us we control a third of the press time on the North American continent. I'm sure we can gear up to print a few billion anti-Jeremiah tracts in a matter of weeks."

"So *that's* why you pulled me in and didn't invite Quintaro!" exclaimed Black. "He's strictly drugs and whores, but I've got printing presses!"

Moore nodded. "Our contributions will be press time and distributional channels."

"Makes sense at that," agreed Black.

"You're in?" asked Moore.

Black nodded.

"Good," said Moore. "Then may I suggest that we meet here again in two weeks?"

"Fine by me," said Lewis, He stared at Moore for a moment. "Do you really think much good can come out of this meeting?"

"It's usefulness is extremely limited," replied Moore.

"Then why are we here?"

"Because I had to start somewhere," said Moore wryly. "Tomorrow I'll be meeting with a Greek Orthodox leader, the Foreign Minister of Egypt, and Henri Piscard."

"Who is this Piscard?" asked Lewis.

"Another businessman," replied Moore. "He provides pretty much the same services in France and Belgium that Mr. Black and I offer to the United States."

"And I assume you've got still more meetings lined up?"

"Six of them. I think by the time I see you again we'll have put together a pretty useful organization." He got to his feet and walked to the door. "And now, let me suggest that you partake of some of the pleasures of New Atlantis before returning home."

DeJesus, Lewis, and Naomi Wizner filed out, and Moore closed the door behind them. Then he turned to Black, who hadn't moved from where he was sitting.

"Hi, Solomon," grinned the mulatto. "We've come a long way, haven't we?"

"Hello, Piper," said Moore, sitting down and returning his smile. "Yes, we have."

"Not bad for a couple of small-time hoods."

"Speak for yourself," said Moore. "I was never small time."

Black laughed. "And here we are, fighting for Right, Justice, and the Christian Way."

"Or for Judas' seat in Hell."

"Oh, well," said Black. "I never did want to go to Heaven anyway. I *like* heat."

"I never really thought you were in much danger of freezing in the next life," said Moore.

"Which brings up an interesting point, Solomon."

"And what is that?"

"I've been an atheist all my life — but if Jeremiah is the Messiah, that sure as hell seems to imply the existence of God, doesn't it?"

"You can't have the first without the second."

"Well," said Black, "if there is a God, do you suppose He wants us messing around with His Messiah? I'm going straight to Hell anyway, and I aim to go in style, but what about *you* — you never enjoy your money anyway, so why fight God for it?"

"Don't think I haven't given it a lot of thought," Moore said slowly. "I think there's a good chance Jeremiah is the Messiah, with all that implies."

"Then why *aren't* you keeping your hands off?" asked Black. "And remember that this isn't Cardinal What's-his-name asking you."

Moore picked up an ornate platinum cigarette lighter and toyed with it.

"I could take the easy way out and say that you and I had paid our entry fees to Hell long before Jeremiah appeared on the scene," he said ironically. "But I won't. If there's a God, and Jeremiah is His handiwork, then I'm acting contrary to His wishes by trying to kill him. But, damn it, Piper — look at the other side of the coin!"

"What other side?" asked Black.

"Why now, and why Jeremiah?"

"I don't think I follow you."

"Where was God when the Jews got thrown out of Jerusalem two thousand years ago? Why did He let us blow up Hiroshima and run an Inquisition and starve eighty million African babies?"

"You expect God to take a day-to-day interest in what's going on down here?" said Black with a smile.

"If Jeremiah's the Messiah, then that's just what He's finally done!" said Moore, his rage, held so long in check, finally boiling over. "Not when we needed Him, but now! And not with a healer or a peacemaker or even a reasonably wise ruler, but with Jeremiah!"

"You know what they say: He works in mysterious ways."

"If Jeremiah is the best He could come up with, His ways are more than mysterious — they're out-and-out irresponsible!"

"Son of a bitch!" laughed Black.

"What's so funny?" demanded Moore.

"I just figured it out," said Black. "Jeremiah is just the goddamned battlefield. You've declared a Holy War on God!"

"Look around you," said Moore grimly. "There are nine billion people out there, each of them going a little crazier every day, and what does He do? He sends down a selfish, womanizing, slow-wilted moron. If He truly exists He may be *your* God, but He sure as hell isn't *mine!*"

"I didn't know you had a choice," said Black. "I mean, either He's God or He isn't. And if He is, then maybe we both ought to reconsider what we're doing and start praying to Him."

"Never!" roared Moore. "If there's a God, He gave me a brain, and then saw to it that the only way I could keep it active was to break every goddamned Commandment He created. He set up the rules for a Messiah close to three thousand years ago, and we wound up with Jeremiah. He waited two thousand years for the Jews to kick and claw their way back to Jerusalem without His help, and now He's sent Jeremiah to burn it to the ground and build a new kingdom. I'd sooner worship the Devil!"

"My, you *are* one troubled criminal mastermind, aren't you?" said Black, amused.

"Not any more," said Moore, willing his emotions back into the tortured recesses of his mind. "I know what I have to do."

"Maybe you ought to see a good shrink, Solomon," said Black, his smile gone. "Being angry is one thing, but you're *driven.*"

"Then I'm just going to have to get back in the driver's seat," replied Moore.

"God's a pretty sharp customer," said Black. "Maybe He wants you to make all this fuss about getting back in the driver's seat so Jeremiah can hang on to center stage. Maybe you're being manipulated."

"No one manipulates me," said Moore with more certainty than he felt, "Not Jeremiah, not God, not anyone." He paused. "Besides, when I'm being rational, I don't believe in any of this shit."

"Okay, but I think —"

"The subject is closed," said Moore, and now the emotionless mask was completely back in place.

Black puffed silently on his cigar for a few minutes, while Moore reactivated the viewing screen. Finally the huge mulatto stretched, placed the cigar in an ashtray, and turned to Moore.

"Ready to talk a little business, Solomon?"

"That's what you're here for."

"So how do we split it up?"

"I think we play it very, very safe," said Moore. "If we stop Jeremiah, it's going to be because we have a lot of help. I figure his weapons are up for grabs; probably Israel will wind up with them."

"And his billions of dollars?"

"We don't touch them."

"I think this artificial air has softened your brain, Solomon," said Black. "You're talking about three, maybe four billion dollars."

"Try to understand, Piper: we're being tolerated. We're a couple of pretty big operators in our own ball park, but look at who we're dealing with now — ambassadors, statesmen, cardinals, people who could land on us so heavy that we never get up again. Let them keep the money."

"Then what's in it for us?" demanded Black. "I never knew Solomon Moody Moore not to have an angle."

"There's an angle," said Moore with a smile. "Who's the biggest drug dealer in the world?"

"Piscard, or maybe me."

"The biggest pornographer?"

"You, unless Davenport in Britain has caught up."

"The biggest fence?"

"Quintaro," said Black. "What's all this getting at?"

"Nothing — except that your answers were wrong. Jeremiah is the biggest."

"I wasn't counting him," said Black. "I figure he won't be around that long and . . ." He stopped, and a huge grin spread across his face. "So we split up his sources and outlets and equipment!"

"And double whatever we were making four years ago," concluded Moore. "And we're not taking anything that could be of any possible use to any of our associates, so who's to tell us not to?"

"What about Piscard and the rest?" asked Black. "We'll have to let them in."

"We will," agreed Moore. "I get thirty-five percent, you get twenty-five, and they can fight over what's left."

"I thought we were going to be equal partners, Solomon."

"I don't take on equal partners," replied Moore, his smile vanishing. "That's my offer: take it or leave it."

"And if I leave it?"

"If you leave it, Piper, we'll just have to make do without your services as best we can — and I might add that your life expectancy will be, not to be too pessimistic about it, perhaps twenty minutes."

"What the hell," shrugged the huge mulatto. "Twenty-five's better than nothing, and that's just what I'm making with Jeremiah around — a big, fat zero."

He rose, walked over to Moore, and extended his hand. Moore took it.

"Tell me, Solomon — would you really have killed me?"

"I never joke about business or about Jeremiah," said Moore.

"I'm a pretty big guy, Solomon," said Black.

"I know," replied Moore. "That's why there are three pretty big guns trained on you right now, behind two of the paintings and that one-way mirror in the foyer."

Black threw his head back and laughed.

"Same old Solomon! You've always got every angle covered. I wouldn't want to be in Jeremiah's shoes, not with you after him!"

"He seems to be doing pretty well so far," noted Moore.

"Then he'll fall that much harder when we bring him down," said Black. "And they always fall, Solomon, no matter how big they grow. Even Messiahs."

"Let's hope you're right," said Moore. He found himself tiring of the conversation, so he walked Black to the door and gave him the number of a room that was reserved for Moore's special guests. Black grinned again and walked out into the corridor.

Moore closed the door, went into the bedroom, and began undressing, trying to decide whether to go straight to bed or stop by the whirlpool first. Then' a flashing light told him that he was wanted on the phone, and he picked up the receiver.

"Moore here."

"This is Ben. Are you sitting down?"

"What's up?"

"We've got him!" said Pryor excitedly.

"Who's got who?" asked Moore, not daring to hope.

"We've got Jeremiah! Do you want us to bring him to the Bubble?"

"No!" said Moore emphatically. "The damned plane would probably explode. Where are you calling from?"

"Cincinnati. You can figure out where."

"Hold him right where he is, and don't take your eyes off him. I'm on my way."

Moore was half dressed and halfway out the door before Pryor realized that the connection had been broken.

18

*I*n the third decade of the twentieth century, the people of Cincinnati, anticipating their city's continued rapid growth, passed a bond issue to build a subway system beneath the downtown area. Work began immediately, and continued for a few years until it became apparent that far from increasing, the population of the river city had become absolutely constant. It neither rose nor fell during the next century, and the construction of the subway was completely abandoned.

Until Moore's organization decided to open up the Cincinnati market, that is. At that time the ownership of two miles of subterranean tunnels changed hands privately, and Moore's people set up shop in the deserted and almost forgotten subway.

Moore arrived in Cincinnati two hours after receiving Pryor's call, went directly to a run-down Tudor home that was owned by a nonexistent Chicago realtor, climbed down the rickety basement stairs, opened a hidden door, and found Pryor waiting for him.

"Where is he?" demanded Moore as the two of them walked through the long, empty tunnel, their footsteps echoing off the damp stone walls.

"Relax," said Pryor. "He's sedated and under heavy guard. It'll be a while before he wakes up."

"Has anyone tried to kill him?"

"Yes."

"It didn't work, of course."

Prior shook his head. "Visconti put a gun to his temple and pulled the trigger — and the damned thing backfired and blew his hand off. I have a feeling that if we tried to electrocute hire, the whole blasted city would go dark first."

"I agree," said Moore. "How did we get our hands on him?"

"It was crazy. He called a press conference up in Dayton to push Moira's book, and we simply put the snatch on him."

"I see he hasn't gotten any brighter," remarked Moore. "But I'm surprised that he wasn't able to get away."

"That *is* the surprising part," agreed Pryor. "We got to him while he was putting on makeup in his dressing room, and he just raised his hands and surrendered. There were two other doors and a first-floor window, and based on our previous experience with him you'd have thought he would make a break for it. The bullets would collide in midair or some such thing, and he'd be on the loose again."

"It's more than surprising," said Moore thoughtfully. "It's very disturbing. He must have known that we were going to try to kill him. Maybe he doesn't die, but he sure as hell feels pain. Why put himself through it? In fact, why choose to speak in Dayton when he knows we've still got muscle in Ohio?"

"All we did was capture him," said Pryor thoughtfully. "Maybe whatever protects him is only concerned that he stays alive."

"It's a possibility," said Moore, considering the notion. "Maybe we can do anything we want to him except kill him. Lord knows he hasn't led a painless life up to now." He paused. "By the way, is Abe around? This seems like a good time to try to get some straight answers from Jeremiah."

Pryor shook his head. "He's wavering. He says he's still on our side, but just to hedge his bets he's not going to get involved with this."

"Damn it!" snapped Moore. "He's involved up to his goddamned neck! What does he think Jeremiah is going to do — absolve him?"

"He says he'll quit if you order him to work on Jeremiah."

"We'll take care of Abe later," said Moore after a moment's thought. "Right now our problem is Jeremiah. Just how tight is our security?"

"Come see for yourself," said Pryor, leading him down the corridor to a door that was guarded by a dozen armed men. The structure they entered had originally been a bomb shelter built well beneath a luxurious center-hall Colonial home which was now registered in Montoya's name, but sometime during the past century it had been transformed into a truly elaborate room. It housed an ornate Spanish four-poster bed, a number of chairs, a built-in wet bar, and a functional marble fireplace that was somehow tied in to the house's chimney. Six more armed men, including Montoya, stood within the room, while Jeremiah, naked and unconscious, lay spread-eagled on the bed, each of his limbs tied to a corner post. His right arm bore numerous puncture marks of recent vintage.

"Either you loaded him up enough to kill him," observed Moore, "or he's on the needle himself."

"Only two of those holes came from us," answered Pryor. "The rest are his own project."

"How much longer should he be out?" asked Moore.

"Maybe half an hour or so — if he's a normal human being. Otherwise, he could wake up any second."

"It's cold in here," said Moore, turning to Montoya. "Start a fire."

"But Mr. Moore," replied the security chief, "it's got to be eighty degrees."

"I don't recall asking you the temperature," said Moore. He turned to another of the men as Montoya shrugged and started passing the order for firewood. "I haven't eaten in a few hours. I'd like a sandwich."

"Any particular kind, sir?"

"Whatever's handy."

"I'll have one sent in right away, sir."

"The bread might be hard," added Moore. "I'll need a very sharp knife."

The man nodded and departed.

Moore sat silently in a corner while Montoya built a fire, and set his sandwich aside without touching it.

"Stir that up a little with the poker," he said to Montoya once the firewood was ablaze. "No, leave the poker in it. Why get ashes on the floor?"

Finally he turned back to Pryor.

"Ben, do you think there's any chance that we can kill him?"

Prior shook his head. "I don't think it can be done."

"I don't think so either," said Moore. "I don't even see much sense trying."

"Then what do you plan to do?" asked Pryor.

"Whatever I have to," said Moore grimly. "Take the men out with you."

"Leave you *alone* with him?"

"I'll be all right. And even if I'm not, the room is still secure. Then call the press and get them upstairs in the Colonial with their cameras in about three hours' time."

"But —"

"That was an order, Ben, not a request."

Pryor nodded curtly and ushered the men out, after which Moore bolted the door from the inside. He picked up a rocking chair, placed it next to the bed, sat down on it, took a bite of his sandwich, and stared thoughtfully at Jeremiah.

He hadn't changed much. There wasn't a scar on his body, except for the needle marks, and they'd doubtless vanish in a few days. As for bullet wounds, knife scars, or any of the rest, his flesh was as clean and unmarked as the day he'd been born. He had put on some weight, perhaps fifteen pounds, none of it muscle, but he still didn't appear overweight, though he was far from athletic.

Moore finished the sandwich, walked over and stoked the fire, then returned to the chair. In a few minutes Jeremiah began moaning and twitching. Finally he tried to sit up, found that he couldn't, shook his head vigorously, and focused his eyes.

"Have a nice nap?" asked Moore.

"*You!*" whispered Jeremiah.

"Who were you expecting?"

"Where am I?" demanded Jeremiah, his speech slightly slurred.

"Where nobody can find you," said Moore. "What difference does it make?"

"What are you going to do with me?"

"A much better question," said Moore. "To tell you the truth, I haven't really decided. I thought we might discuss it."

"Fuck you!" snapped Jeremiah.

Moore picked the knife up, touched the point of it to Jeremiah's foot, pressed, and cut a deep gash the length of the arch.

Jeremiah howled in pain.

"Stupid," commented Moore calmly. "Very stupid, Jeremiah. If our positions were reversed, I sure as hell wouldn't speak to *you* like that."

Jeremiah spat at Moore, who applied the knife to his other foot with similar results.

"Just like training a puppy," he said. "Repetition is the key."

Jeremiah bit his lip and glared at Moore.

"As I was saying," Moore continued, "we've got a number of things to discuss. Let me know when you're ready to start."

"All right," muttered Jeremiah.

Moore pressed the point of the knife next to one of the gashes. "I didn't hear you."

"*ALL RIGHT!*"

"Better," remarked Moore dryly. "I have to admit that you're something of a problem. I've got a feeling that nothing I do to you can kill you."

"Nothing can kill the Messiah!" Jeremiah shouted.

"You're possibly right," said Moore calmly. "However, I don't know of any reason why I shouldn't be able to keep you tied to this bed for the next twenty or thirty years. What would you say to that?"

"It'll never work!" hissed Jeremiah.

"Oh yes it will," said Moore. "I think that if we try to starve you to death it won't work; something or someone doesn't want you to die just yet. But I have a feeling that as long as your life isn't directly threatened, you're as powerless in that position as anyone else."

Jeremiah made no reply, but Moore could tell that he was considering the idea.

"And, after all," continued Moore, "why should I want to kill you? I'm considerably older than you are, I have no wife or children, and to be perfectly honest, I don't care if the whole world goes to hell in a handcart five minutes after I'm dead. Can you come up with any reason why I shouldn't follow this course of action?"

"My followers will find me," said Jeremiah. "And when they do, I won't leave enough of you to burn or bury!"

Moore pressed the knife into his foot again.

"You keep forgetting who's in control here," he said, raising his voice to be heard over Jeremiah's screams. "I find this procedure every bit as distasteful as you do, but on the other hand, you probably find it more painful. I think you'd be well advised to keep that in mind and stop making threats, or else you'd better be prepared to suffer the consequences. Look at the discomfort you're suffering, and then consider that we haven't even begun talking about alternatives yet."

"What alternatives?" grated Jeremiah.

"Oh, there are always alternatives," said Moore. "I think I can keep you here as long as I want, but I could be wrong. You think no one can hold you prisoner for arty length of time, but *you* could be wrong. It seems to me that the logical thing to do is search for some common meeting ground."

"For instance?"

"Well, for starters, you're worth a great deal of money, a lot of it mine. I'm not a greedy man; I think I'd settle for half."

"You go to hell!" snapped Jeremiah.

Moore reached out with the knife and put another gash on Jeremiah.

He waited until the young man stopped cursing, then continued speaking in a conversational tone. "This is a time for negotiation, not for threats. I'm a little rusty at this kind of thing; there's always a chance I might lose my temper and turn the world's greatest lover into a eunuch. If I were you, I'd really try to avoid making me mad." He paused. "Shall we get back to the subject at hand?"

Jeremiah glared at him and nodded.

"Very reasonable," commented Moore. "I think I should tell you, Jeremiah, that even though I'm a dedicated businessman, there are a lot of things that I care about more than money. One of them, for instance, is my life. I think that as a gesture of good faith you might pass the word to your rather fanatical disciples to take my name off their hit list. Certainly a man of your particular qualities isn't afraid to show a little Christian charity."

He placed the point of the knife just below the young man's left ear.

"I agree!" yelled Jeremiah.

"Excellent," said Moore. "Now we're making some progress." He paused. "Still, I can't help wondering just how this message will be passed to the ranks of your followers."

"I don't know what you mean."

"Well, I can't just let you walk out without it having been done," said Moore. "After all, what guarantee do I have that you'll keep your word — your honest face? Your past history of generosity to me and my organization?"

"What guarantee do you want?" rasped the young man.

"Oh, I'm sure if we put our heads together we'll think of something," said Moore pleasantly. Suddenly he snapped his fingers. "I think I've got the solution to our problem!"

"What?" asked the young man, eying him fearfully.

"Why do all these wild-eyed fools follow your orders in the first place? You're a beggar and a thief, a gambler and a dope addict, you seem intent on bedding every woman on the face of the earth, and to be perfectly candid about it, you haven't the intellectual capacity of a retarded barn swallow. So why should your word have any weight with the masses?"

"You know why!" snapped Jeremiah.

"Yes I do," admitted Moore. "They seem to think that you're the Messiah."

"I am!"

Moore jabbed him gently with the point of the knife.

"Please don't interrupt me. Now, it seems to me that if they didn't think you were the Messiah, they wouldn't be so all-fired anxious to do your bidding. Does that make sense to you, Jeremiah?"

"What are you getting at?"

"Simply this: if the people decided that you weren't the Messiah, they'd stop listening to you. They wouldn't want to kill me, they wouldn't try to drive me out of business, they might even consider throwing down their weapons and going about their normal daily business. Do you agree?"

Jeremiah glared silently at him.

"Well, at least you don't disagree. So while I appreciate the fact that you're going to sign over half your treasury to me and order your people to leave me alone, the crux of the matter still comes down to this misconception the masses have about what you are." He paused. "Now, who do you suppose can set the record straight? Certainly not me. If I tried to tell them you weren't the Messiah, they'd probably shoot me down in cold blood before I got the first sentence out. Moira? No, I have a feeling that they wouldn't believe her either." He paused again. "Who can we get to do it, Jeremiah? Who is the one person they might believe?"

"Never!" screamed Jeremiah. "I don't give a damn what you do to me! Rip my eyes out of my head, it won't make any difference!"

"Who said anything about your eyes?" asked Moore. "For one thing, you'll need them to sign half of your money over to me. For another, we wouldn't want you looking anything less than your best, since you're going to be making a television address in a couple of hours."

"That's what you think!" snarled Jeremiah.

"Wrong," said Moore, walking over to the fireplace and withdrawing the poker. "That's what I *know.*"

The hideous screams that followed continued for almost forty minutes. At last Moore, his face ashen, unlocked the door, walked out into the tunnel, and slammed it shut behind him. The security men backed away from him, and even Montoya seemed to regard him with a mixture of awe, disapproval, and terror.

"Give him about twenty minutes," he told Pryor. "Then get him dressed and carry him upstairs to the house's living room. How soon do the newsmen get here?"

"An hour or two."

Moore nodded, walked to a makeshift bathroom, and vomited. He rinsed his face off and emerged a few minutes later.

"One of you men," he said to the security team, "get a thin piece of wire about five feet long. Picture-hanging wire will do just fine. Then bring it to the living room."

Pryor came out of the room, looking sick.

"My God, Solomon — what did you do to him?" he said shakily.

"Nothing he won't recover from."

"It's awful!"

"Sometimes people have to do awful things."

"But his body — it's all . . ."

"It won't be for long," said Moore grimly. "When he gets upstairs, sit him in a stiff-backed chair so that he doesn't slump, and use the wire you'll find there to tie his legs to the chair so he can't make a run for it."

"*Run?*" repeated Pryor. "I don't even know what's keeping him alive."

"Just do it, Ben."

Pryor nodded numbly and went off to attend to Jeremiah. Moore rinsed his face again, waited a few more minutes to regain his color, then climbed up the basement stairs and walked into the living room, where Jeremiah sat motionless on a ladder back chair. The young man's face was still unmarked, and a loose robe covered all traces of his recent ordeal.

Moore walked up to Jeremiah and placed a hand under his chin. "Can you hear me?"

Jeremiah nodded.

"Good," said Moore. "Now, in a few minutes the press will be here. Do you remember what you're going to tell them?"

"Yes," whispered Jeremiah.

"Have you tried to walk?"

Jeremiah shook his head.

"Take my word for it: you can't. I'm sure the thought has also crossed your mind to say something other than what we agreed upon. Let me assure you that if you do the story will never leave this building, and what I do to you afterward will make the last couple of hours seem like a Sunday-school picnic."

Jeremiah nodded.

"Ben, have someone get him a little water to drink."

Within a few minutes the color began returning to Jeremiah's face, and ten minutes after that Moore was convinced that he was coherent enough to make the brief statement.

The press finally arrived, late as usual, and Moore waited upstairs while Pryor led them into the living room. There were two cameramen, who immediately went to work setting up their lights, and a reporter who kept dabbing powder onto his face.

"No questions tonight, please," said Pryor. "Jeremiah has a brief announcement to make."

The reporter looked disappointed, but stood back while the cameras were trained on Jeremiah. Finally one of the cameraman nodded his head.

"My name is Jeremiah the B," said the young man, "and I want the world to know that I am making this statement freely and under no coercion from any quarter." He stared directly into the nearer of the two cameras. "I am a fraud. I am not the Messiah. I was never the Messiah. I never believed I was the Messiah. I can no longer live with my conscience. I can no longer look at the worshipful faces of my followers without feeling guilt and remorse beyond measure. I apologize for what I have done. Such monies as I have accumulated will be distributed to those I have robbed and misled. Believe me, I meant no harm — but also believe me when I tell you that I am not the Messiah."

He fell silent, and pandemonium broke loose.

"My God, what a story!" exclaimed one of the cameramen.

"Who's forcing you to make this statement?" demanded the reporter.

"No one," said Jeremiah.

"Why did you come to Cincinnati to make it?" persisted the reporter. No answer.

"How are you dividing the money?"

Before Jeremiah could respond, Pryor had the security guards clear the room over the outraged protestations of the reporter, and then signaled Moore to come downstairs.

"Very good, Jeremiah," said Moore. "I'm quite proud of you."

Jeremiah, groggy from the effort of addressing the cameras, merely glared at him.

"We're going to keep you under lock and key for about a week," continued Moore. "Long enough for every television station, every radio station, and every newspaper to run that story over and over. After that you're a free man."

He walked out the front door, followed by Pryor.

"I'm going back to Chicago. Keep him on ice until the story gets out."

"And then?" asked Pryor. "Do you really intend to let him go?"

"Why not? Who believes discredited Messiahs?" Moore smiled. "Someday I'll have Abe's rabbi tell you the story of Sabbatai Levi."

"You're the boss," said Pryor, a troubled expression on his face.

"Relax, Ben," said Moore confidently. "It's all over now."

But, of course, it wasn't.

19

From WHTB (Hartford):

"So you now recant your recantation and claim that you are the Messiah? Is that correct?" The interviewer had a condescending smile on his face.

"That's correct," said Jeremiah, looking soulfully into the camera. "I was tortured into making a false denial."

"You're telling me that God allowed His Messiah to be tortured?" scoffed the interviewer.

"If you're a Christian, you believe that God allowed His Messiah to be crucified," said Jeremiah with a smile.

"But really . . ."

"What the hell do you know about Messiahs?" demanded Jeremiah impatiently. He raised his hands above his head and intoned: *"LET THERE BE RAIN!"*

And, instantly, the rain came.

Jeremiah looked wildly at the camera. "How do you like them apples, Moore?" he bellowed.

From KPTO-TV (Denver):

"This is Jeremiah the B. You know who I am and what I am. Senator Caldwall Burke would deny me. He runs for reelection the day after tomorrow. He has publicly stated that I am not the one true Messiah. Can you guess what I want you to do?"

Burke lost by half a million votes.

From BBC-3 (London):
"And you've been blind from birth?" asked Jeremiah, standing at center stage of the New Palladium.

"Yes, Lord," said the old woman.

"And you will pledge your everlasting fealty to me and turn all your worldly goods over to me for the gift of sight?"

"Yes, Lord."

He laid his hands on her eyes. "Then so be it."

He removed his hands and the woman slowly, fearfully, opened her eyes. She blinked a few times, and then a torrent of tears burst forth. "My God, I can see!"

"Take that and stick it in your ear, Moore!" shrieked Jeremiah, his face flushed with triumph.

From WQRQ-TV (New York):
"Who am I?" he cried to the wildly cheering throng of people who had gathered in Times Square.

"JEREMIAH!"

"And *what* am I?"

"THE MESSIAH!"

"The day is fast approaching when the Messiah must lay claim to his throne. Will you help me?"

The answer was so loud that it blew every circuit in WQRQ's sound system.

From WLKJ-TV (Miami):
Jeremiah looked up from the burn victim, whose skin was already starting to heal.

"Who am I, Moore?" he gloated, grinning into the camera.

From UBS Radio (Network):
"Do you hear me, Moore?" he screamed into the microphone. "Calling a sheep's tail a leg doesn't make it one, and torturing the Messiah into renouncing doesn't make him any the less a Messiah! I am the Expected One, and nothing else counts! Blow it out your ass, Moore!"

From KFD-TV (Seattle):
"I don't need your support, but I do want it! The Messiah is a law unto himself, but those who support me will be remembered and rewarded — and those who oppose me will be remembered even better! Start saying your prayers, Moore — I'll be listening!"

20

*T*ake a look," said Moore, tossing the handwritten letter onto Pryor's desk.

Dear Solomon:

I am not ungrateful for all the years I have worked for you, but it seems to me that the handwriting is on the wall. I am a Jew, and I can no longer oppose the man who seems to be the living culmination of my religious beliefs.

I have been in constant contact with Moira Rallings for the past week, and have been granted an amnesty of sorts in exchange for my pledge of allegiance to their cause. This I have freely given.

I shall divulge none of your plans to which I am privy, nor will I give them any details of your past actions in reference to Jeremiah.

I wish you well, but urge you to call off your vendetta before it is too late. I know you are a resourceful man, but face facts, Solomon — he is the Messiah!

Abraham Bernstein

"Not exactly a surprise," commented Pryor, putting the letter down.

"I suppose not," admitted Moore. "But damn it, Ben, I hate to lose another of our insiders to Jeremiah!"

"I know. How long do you think he'll keep his word about playing dumb?"

"Twenty minutes, tops," said Moore. "It doesn't matter. He can't do us any harm. Get Piper Black on the phone for me.'"

Moore returned to his office, pacing the floor restlessly until the light atop his telephone flashed.

"Hello, Piper," he said.

"Solomon."

"How are things coming along at your end?"

"You've got to be kidding, right?"

"I'm quite serious," responded Moore. "We've got a PR campaign to begin."

"Come off it, Solomon," said Black. "You had that son of a bitch in your hands and you turned him loose. Not only that, but he's saying that you tortured him until he signed over half his money to you."

"It'll never stand up in court," said Moore. "I just did it to tie up his funds while we're fighting him."

"Sure you did, Solomon," said Black. "Listen to me, you bastard! We had an agreement, and you broke it by trying to cut me out. Fight him yourself!"

"All right, Piper," said Moore. "I tried to cut you out. So what?"

"What do you mean, so what?"

"What's changed?" asked Moore. "Is your business any better? Is Jeremiah any less of a threat? We've still got to work together, unless you expect him to just up and vanish."

"Oh, we can still work together, Solomon," said Black. "But this time I make the bargain."

"Name your terms," said Moore.

"Forty for me, twenty for you, and forty for the rest of them."

"Done."

"What did you say?"

"I agree."

"Too fast, Solomon. What's the catch?"

"No catch," answered Moore. "Maybe I just want to break him more than I want to break you."

There was a long pause.

"Okay. I can accept that," said Black at last. "But you tell that little bloodsucker Pryor what we agreed to. I'll have my brother get in touch with him tomorrow and take care of the details. It's all going to be recorded and put under lock and key — and God help you if you try to pull anything fancy."

"God isn't exactly who I'm worried about," said Moore, breaking the connection.

21

Moore sat in a leather wingback chair in his apartment atop the New Atlantis. He stared at the fish in the viewscreen for a long moment, marveling at how they seemed to preen for the camera, then turned back to his associates. Naomi Wizner had been here before, but it was his first meeting with General Josef Yitzak of the Israeli Army.

"So he's definitely on the move," said Moore at last.

"There's no question about it," replied Naomi Wizner. "He's got about a quarter of a million volunteers in Egypt and Lebanon, and probably five times that many just across the Mediterranean."

"They're not very well organized," added Yitzak. He paused thoughtfully. "Of course, there is no reason for us to have supposed that they would be. Nothing we've been able to learn about Jeremiah indicates that he possesses any knowledge of the techniques of modern warfare."

"It doesn't make any difference," said Moore. "What's harder to fight, General — five trained soldiers who want to live to fight another day, or one untrained fanatic who wants to die for his cause?"

Yitzak nodded. "This has been our most serious problem — the knowledge that they're going to be vying with one another for the privilege of throwing themselves in our line of fire."

"What kind of firepower has he got?"

"Strictly conventional," replied Yitzak. "But we're not here to discuss military strategy with you. The Israeli Army is quite capable of taking care of itself."

"If the Israeli Army was capable of taking care of itself, you wouldn't be here," Moore pointed out. "Now, what can I do to help you?"

"I must know more about him," answered Yitzak, electing to ignore Moore's comment. "You know him better than anyone else who opposes him. You may have some knowledge of how his mind works that could prove useful to us. Who knows — you may even be able to suggest a weakness."

Moore laughed. "He was my prisoner six weeks ago. Does it appear to you that I've discovered any weaknesses in the man?"

"Why did you let him go?" asked Naomi.

"Why not? Since I couldn't kill him, I thought that I could at least discredit him. As it turned out," he concluded dourly, "I was mistaken."

"Then you can suggest nothing?" said Yitzak.

"Not at the moment," admitted Moore. "I keep coming back to the notion that if you can't stop him — and it looks like you can't — then you ought to concentrate on unconverting his followers."

"How do you unconvert an army of religious fanatics that is massing on your border?" asked Yitzak ironically.

Moore shrugged. "I wish I knew."

"Can you give us any other information that might help us prepare for Jeremiah's attack?" asked Naomi.

"Not a thing," said Moore. "You probably know more about the disposition of his army than he does."

"This is no time for levity," said Yitzak sternly. "I'll let you know when I'm joking," replied Moore.

"Jeremiah has no interest in learning how to deploy his forces, nor will he especially give a damn if ten million of his followers must die to get him what he wants."

"I find that difficult to believe."

"I don't doubt it," said Moore. "But if Jeremiah thought and acted like a normal man, he wouldn't be knocking at the door to your city. By the way, exactly where is he now?"

"We aren't sure," admitted Yitzak. "We know he's not in Egypt or Lebanon, but we haven't been able to pinpoint him yet."

"You probably won't, until he decides to attack," replied Moore. "He can stay hidden better than any man I've ever known."

"Then in your opinion he's just going to magically appear at the proper psychological moment to lead his troops to victory?"

Moore shook his head. "You still don't understand him. My own guess is that he won't appear until *after* Jerusalem has fallen. Why should he be a target if he doesn't have to be?"

"Your advice, then, would be to make Jerusalem all but impregnable?" persisted Yitzak.

"Eliminate the words 'all but,' and you've got it," said Moore. "Leave him an opening and he'll have his foot in the door before you can slam it shut. Look at what he's done in less than four years." He grimaced. "Give him another four and he could probably pass a constitutional amendment proclaiming his divinity."

"What will he do if we fight him to a standstill?"

"If you fight him to a standstill, he's already won," answered Moore. "How many new citizens emigrate to Israel in a year? Less than Jeremiah picks up in a day. If you fight to a draw it's all over, because he'll be back twice as strong six months later. You've got two choices: beat him decisively the first time you meet him, or sue for peace. There's no third alternative."

"And not a government in the world has offered to stand with us," said Naomi Wizner bitterly.

"We have always stood alone against our enemies," said Yitzak. "Why should this time be any different?"

"That's the wrong attitude," said Moore. "They're not giving out prizes for bravery this season. He's already got twice as many followers as you have citizens. You're going to have to get help."

"From where?" asked Yitzak with a bitter laugh.

"How the hell should I know? Arm the Catholics and the Moslems. Get ITT to finance an army. Tell the Chinese they're next on his hit list. But do *something!*"

"You're right, of course," interjected Naomi hastily. "And I won't be revealing any secrets if I tell you that we have been actively trying to rally support to our cause — thus far without noticeable success." She paused. "However, these are definitely not your problems, Mr. Moore. What we would like you to do is come to Jerusalem in an advisory capacity."

"I don't know anything about fighting a war."

"We are aware of that," said Yitzak.

"Then what do you need me for?"

"Of those people committed to the defense of Jerusalem, you are the only one who has ever met Jeremiah face to face. I realize you think you have told us everything you know about the way his mind works, but there is always a chance you have overlooked something — or, more likely still, that you will be able to improve some section of our defense based on facts and insights that we do not possess. To this end, we are prepared to offer you a temporary commission in the Israeli Army if you will come to Jerusalem and let us pick your mind as best we can."

Moore considered the offer for a moment, then turned to Yitzak. "And what if you become convinced that he's the Messiah?"

"Then I shall do his bidding," replied Yitzak promptly. He held up his hand as Moore began to speak. "But let me add that the only way he can convince me is by defeating our army in battle, at which point the entire matter becomes academic."

Moore walked over to the viewscreen and studied the fish for a few minutes. Finally he turned back to the two Israelis.

"All right," he said. "I'll go. And you can keep your commission; I'm no soldier."

"It will get you preferential treatment and quarters of your own," said Yitzak.

"I don't know any protocol," protested Moore. "And I have a feeling that I won't like saluting fellow officers."

"Israeli soldiers don't salute — they *fight,*" said Yitzak, not without a trace of pride. "From this moment on, you are Colonel Solomon Moore. You are responsible to no one but myself, and your sole duty will be to analyze Jeremiah's actions and advise me on how best to respond to them." He smiled wryly. "I cannot promise to take any of your advice, but I *do* promise to listen."

"Fair enough," said Moore.

Yitzak stood up. "How soon can you be ready to leave?"

"I've got some business affairs to put in order," replied Moore. "It'll take about a day. I don't think I'll be returning to Chicago, so I'll catch the next flight to London from Kingston, and make connections there."

"Nonsense," said Yitzak. "I'll have my own plane ready and waiting for you twenty-four hours from now. We are about to become inseparable companions."

"Whatever you say."

Moore led them to the door, then picked up the phone and began putting his affairs in order.

First he instructed his lawyers to place what remained of his personal holdings into a blind trust. While he was waiting for them to fly out to the Bubble for his signature, he called Pryor on his vidphone.

"What's up?" asked Pryor, adjusting the picture he was receiving. "The last time you bothered with video contact was the day you bought out the Portofilio Family."

"We've got a lot to talk about, Ben," said Moore. "I thought it might be more comfortable to do it this way."

"Fine by me," said Pryor, pouring himself a drink.

"I'm leaving for Jerusalem tomorrow."

"Good! Either you'll kill him, or I'll wind up in charge of things. Either way I'm happy."

"How touching," remarked Moore dryly.

"You don't really want me to lie to you, do you?" asked Pryor easily. "How long before Jeremiah attacks?"

"Soon. A week or two at most, based on what our associates have told me. However, that's neither here nor there. I called to give you some information you're going to need if I don't come back."

Pryor turned on a tape machine. "Shoot."

For the next two hours Moore listed the politicians, criminals, businessmen, newsmen, and religious leaders who were either owned outright by the organization or at least beholden to it. He spent another hour laying out the details of those enterprises that he had never committed to paper, and noted with some satisfaction that even Pryor was surprised by the extent of them. All were hurting at the moment, but few of them were so moribund that Jeremiah's demise couldn't bring them back to glowing health and solvency in a year's time.

"And Ben," he concluded, "I want you to understand that until you have proof of my death, nothing has changed."

"I'm not sure I understand."

"Don't play stupid, Ben; it's unbecoming. I want you to think very carefully before letting your reach exceed your grasp. I'm still in charge."

"Absolutely, Solomon."

"I don't expect to be gone more than a couple of weeks, a month at the most. You haven't time to consolidate power during that period, and I strongly suggest that you allow discretion to remain the better part of valor."

"If I were the type to move prematurely, I'd have grabbed for the brass ring before now," replied Pryor frankly. "Besides, the odds are that you'll be dead in two more weeks. I've waited nine years; I can wait half a month more."

Moore smiled. "That sounds more like the Ben Pryor we all know and love. And now let me give you a final order: take the hit off Jeremiah and Moira, and bring our operatives back into the business. It's strictly a military matter now, and our people are out of their depth. Let the Israeli Army handle Jeremiah from here on out; we'll concentrate on making money."

His call completed, he phoned Chicago on a private line that Pryor knew nothing about, and instructed a couple of spies to make sure that Pryor didn't try to jump the gun. This done, he lay down for what he anticipated would be his last comfortable night's sleep for quite some time, awoke nine hours later, conferred with his lawyers, concluded a couple of business arrangements that he had decided to withhold from Pryor, and had an order of eggs Benedict sent up to the room. He ate, showered, and donned the rather bedraggled uniform that Yitzak had sent up to his room at midmorning.

Then, at the appointed time, he took an elevator to the ocean's surface, took his private helicopter to Kingston's airport, and found Yitzak waiting for him. The Israeli general led him to a small plane, they walked up a mobile stairway, the door closed behind them, and a moment later they were airborne.

"Any change in the situation?" asked Moore, sitting down on a swivel chair that was bolted to the floor.

"We still don't know where Jeremiah is, if that's what you mean," replied Yitzak. "As for his army, they're practically knocking at the door. They're in Gaza, they're on the Golan Heights, they're at various positions in Sinai. And, of course, they're almost impossible to identify: no uniforms, no similarity of weapons, no common language. Someone is obviously giving them orders, telling them when and where to move, but we haven't been able to penetrate their chain of command."

"Any skirmishes yet?"

"No," answered Yitzak. "It's my own guess that Egypt and Jordan have made some accommodation with them which includes confining the battle to Israeli soil."

"Why play by their ground rules?" asked Moore.

"I don't believe I understand you."

"What's to stop you from attacking them now, before they reach Israel?"

"Because, as I mentioned, they are indistinguishable from the natives of the surrounding countries. The only way to wipe them out at this time would be to unleash our thermonuclear arsenal, and literally tens of millions of innocent people would die." He paused. "We, of all people, are just a little sensitive about committing genocide."

"Can't you move your army across the border and attack with conventional weapons?" persisted Moore.

"Genocide on *any* scale is unacceptable to us," replied Yitzak. "Our best hope is to capture or kill Jeremiah before it comes to that."

"It's going to come to that sooner or later," said Moore. "You're not going to kill him, and he's not going to chance being captured. So why not fight on Syrian or Egyptian or Jordanian soil? Slice them down quick enough and you might give the rest of his followers second thoughts."

"It is not my decision to make. The order has already been given. For the moment, there is to be no bloodbath."

"Stupid," commented Moore.

"Now that I've given you the official line," said Yitzak, suddenly looking very tired, "let me personally agree with you. While we have made no military alliances, we cannot be sure that the same is true of Jeremiah. The sooner we join this battle, the better."

They discussed the situation further as the plane raced toward Yitzak's beleaguered country. Finally, when they were through speaking, Moore dined on knishes and kreplach, washed them down with a red wine, positioned himself as comfortably as he could on his chair, and fell asleep.

He was awakened some time later when the plane started bucking like an untamed horse.

"What the hell is going on?" he demanded, sitting up abruptly.

"Ground fire," said Yitzak. "We're over Sinai." He tossed a parachute to Moore. "Here. Slip this on, just in case."

Moore watched Yitzak, copied his movements, and soon had his own parachute on.

Yitzak looked out a window. "We should be out of range in another minute or —"

There was a thunderous explosion, the plane shuddered convulsively, and Moore looked out just in time to see a wing catch fire. They went into a spinning nose dive, trailing flames and black smoke, and Yitzak helped Moore to a hatch.

"I'll go first," he announced. "When you see my parachute open, pull the rip cord on your own."

"Where is it?" asked Moore, surprised that he didn't feel more panic-stricken.

Yitzak pointed it out to him, opened the door, and jumped. Moore followed him a second later. It took him a couple of seconds to get his bearings, but finally he figured out where up and down were. Then he looked ahead and saw the flaming plane plunging toward the earth.

After a time he became aware that Yitzak had already opened his parachute, and he pulled the rip cord on his own. He thought for an instant that the sudden jerk on the harness would rip him in half, but it didn't, and suddenly the parachute blossomed like a giant flower and his rate of descent slowed somewhat, though he was still certain that he would be crushed the moment he hit the ground.

When he was about two thousand feet from the ground he looked once again for Yitzak's chute, and saw it about half a mile northeast of him. He became disoriented again, then forced himself to stare at the ground until he once again regained his bearings. A gust of wind hit him at fifty feet and carried him toward Yitzak. It stopped as quickly as it had begun, and he had to decide whether to attempt to land on his feet or hit the ground rolling. He opted for the latter, watched the sandy loam racing up to meet him, tried to remember how he had been taught to fall during his brief interest in judo, realized at the last second that he was positioning his body wrong, and lost consciousness the instant he landed.

22

Moore slowly became aware of the fact that Yitzak was trying to help him to his feet.

"Is anything broken?" asked the Israeli.

"I don't know," mumbled Moore. "How do you tell if something's broken?"

"If you can move your arms and legs, nothing's broken," replied Yitzak with a smile. "Nothing important, anyway."

Moore spit out a tooth and a mouthful of blood. "I must have landed on my face," he grunted.

"It's possible," said Yitzak. "Difficult, but possible. And of course you'll have a minor concussion. You can't be knocked unconscious without concussing. But on the whole, I'd say that you made an exemplary first jump under hazardous conditions. We lost the pilot and the crew."

Moore took a step, wobbled slightly, and had to hold on to Yitzak's shoulder to keep from falling. "I'm too old for this kind of thing," he said painfully.

"It could he worse," said Yitzak, supporting him. "At least we landed in our own territory."

"It's all desert," said Moore, trying to focus his eyes. "How can you tell the difference?"

"No one is shooting at us," replied Yitzak. "Besides, Israel is a tiny country. It's not too difficult to spot a landmark or two, such as that tel over there near that grove of trees."

"What do we do now?" asked Moore, rubbing his jaw and spitting out another tooth.

"We wait. The way that plane was blazing, I imagine everyone within fifty miles must have seen us. They'll be sending out search parties."

Moore began feeling dizzy, and decided to sit down and await his rescuers. They arrived about twenty minutes later in a pair of sixty-year-old Land Rovers. Yitzak issued a few terse commands, and one of the drivers helped Moore into a Land Rover and drove him straight to a hospital at the northern end of Jerusalem.

He was examined, medicated, and sent down the street to a dentist, who took one look at his mouth, shook his head dismally, shot Moore full of painkillers, and began repairing the damage. Moore leaned back, his mouth propped open, and spent the next twenty minutes concentrating on not falling off the chair. Finally the drugs they had given him at the hospital began to take effect, and he surveyed his surroundings.

The room itself was quite small. There were three certificates on the wall, all in Spanish, and that in turn led him to scutinize the dentist, whom he had originally taken to be a Semite but now, in light of the certificates, could just as easily be Hispanic. It was then that he saw the golden crucifix suspended from the dentist's neck.

"What the hell are you doing in an Israeli dental clinic?" he managed to mutter.

"Fixing your teeth," replied the dentist with a smile.

"But you're a Catholic!"

"And Catholics can't repair teeth?" asked the dentist.

"But why here? This is a battle zone."

"I know who you are, Mr. Moore," was the reply. "And you are no more Jewish than I am. Why are *you* here?"

"To fight Jeremiah."

"I, too. The false Messiah must be destroyed, and if by being here I can free another Israeli to do battle against him, then I am content."

"What makes you think that he's *false?*"

"He must be!"

"Don't bet every last penny you've got on it."

"But we must totally discredit him!"

"I'll settle for just stopping him," said Moore.

"That is not enough," said the dentist. "There must be no shred of doubt remaining that he is a fraud."

"What difference does it make, as long as we beat him?" asked Moore.

"I am a practicing Catholic, and yet I freely acknowledge that my Church has done many wicked things, Mr. Moore. The Papacy itself has been sold numerous times, and more than one Pope has littered Europe with his bastard children and the bodies of his enemies. We slaughtered millions of Moslems during the Crusades, tortured thousands of intellectuals during the Inquisition, crushed the skulls of Incan and Aztec babies immediately after baptizing them to make sure their souls would go directly to Heaven, and fought far too many Holy Wars. And yet it is precisely because of these evils that I will defend Jesus as the true Christ to my dying breath."

"I don't think I see the logic of that," commented Moore.

"My God, Mr. Moore!" whispered the dentist. "Think of how many millions of people have died for no reason at all if He is *not* the Christ! Jeremiah must be killed if for no other reason than that!"

"Well, it's a novel approach," remarked Moore.

Then the dentist leaned forward and began working on his mouth again, and he could make no further comment.

The repair job took about two hours, with instructions to return a week later for still more work, and when Moore finally got up to leave he found Yitzak waiting for him in the outer office.

"I understand that you have nothing more than a few bad bruises and some broken teeth," said the Israeli vigorously. "You should be feeling just fine by tomorrow morning."

Moore grunted. "We are not amused."

"I expect you'll want to see your quarters. They aren't as luxurious as the New Atlantis, but I trust you will find them sufficient."

"I'm sure I will," replied Moore. "The New Atlantis isn't exactly to my taste."

They walked to an ancient but well-kept apartment building, where

Moore followed Yitzak up two flights of stairs. The general unlocked a door and turned the key over to Moore.

"There's a staff phone beside your bed," he said. "Feel free to use it whenever you wish. Your refrigerator is well stocked, and if you wish, a roommate can be supplied."

"That won't be necessary," said Moore. "What are my duties, and who do I report to?"

"Your duties are simply to evaluate the situation, and you'll report directly to me. Any suggestions I find useful will be transmitted to Prime Minister Weitzel. You have free run of the city, and on your nightstand you'll find a pass that will get you into all but a handful of our military installations." He paused. "Try to get some rest now, and I'll be back tomorrow morning to show you around."

Moore thanked him, locked the door, and began inspecting his apartment. Except for the lack of books, it was very similar to his Chicago dwelling: small, comfortable, and unpretentious. He found the pass, pinned it to his lapel, and walked to the bathroom, where he undressed and took a long, hot shower.

When he emerged he went to the kitchen and checked out the refrigerator, and discovered that someone had gone to great lengths to learn his taste in food. He warmed up a frozen dinner of veal parmesan, but found that his mouth was too sore to chew, so he settled for drinking a quart of ice water. Then, suddenly very tired, he took a couple of pills the hospital had given him and collapsed on the bed while the medication went to work.

23

*J*eremiah suddenly sat up in bed.
"He's there!" he announced.

Moira stirred sleepily and opened one eye. "Who's where?"

"Moore!" said Jeremiah excitedly. "He's in Jerusalem!"

"What makes you think so?"

"I don't *think* so. I *know* it!"

"Big deal. You're just going to kill him anyway."

"Poor little necrophile!" said Jeremiah with an amused laugh. "You don't even begin to understand what's happening, do you? Moore is the last person in the world I want to kill just now. Our fates have become linked to one another."

"What are you talking about?" asked Moira, rubbing her eyes.

"You think you and that fucking book of yours are important?" said Jeremiah sarcastically. "Well, let me tell you: it makes no difference to me whether or not you ever sell another copy or write another word. It's all clear to me now. Moore is my most important ally, not you."

"Be sure to tell him that just before he blows your brains out," said Moira disgustedly.

"Oh, I will," chuckled Jeremiah. "I will!"

24

*M*oore awoke feeling very stiff, but in considerably less pain. He was in the process of cooking some soft-boiled eggs for himself when Yitzak arrived.

"How is our wounded warrior feeling today?" asked the Israeli.

"A little the worse for wear," replied Moore. "I'm too old to take up parachute jumping." He poured himself a cup of tea. "What's on the agenda for this morning?"

"A tour of the city. You can't spot our weak points if you haven't examined our defenses."

"You're wasting your time," said Moore. "I wouldn't begin to know what to look for. If you tell me the city's secure, I have to take your word for it. If you tell me there are weak spots, you'll have to point them out to me before I know they're there. I think it's a waste of time."

"I'm fully aware of this," said Yitzak. "But I've got a lot of time to spend. As you have doubtless guessed by now, my sole responsibility is to shepherd you around while listening to you and evaluating your observations."

"We're going about it all wrong," said Moore. "Finding weak spots isn't the way Jeremiah works. He's more likely to walk right up to fifty riflemen — and twenty of them will miss him while the other thirty rifles will explode."

"So you keep telling me," said Yitzak patiently. "Nonetheless, I would appreciate it if we could do this my way."

"You're the boss," said Moore. He finished his eggs and tea, and then accompanied Yitzak out into the street.

They climbed into a Land Rover and began driving around the city on the Jaffa and Gaza roads. Jerusalem, more than most cities, was a mixture of the old and the new, with fifty-story steel-and-glass office buildings towering over the Mandelbaum Gate, fast-food stands lining Jericho Road, and a rugby field buttressed up against the Lion's Gate. Only the Wailing Wall was not surrounded by new structures; it stood alone, untouched by any recent century, guarded by twenty crack Israeli soldiers.

"We've created a rectangle, the corners of which are the four Gates — Lion's, Jaffa, Zion, and Mandelbaum," explained Yitzak, pointing out the various fortifications to Moore as they drove by. "For all practical purposes, the city of Jerusalem is within that perimeter. Of course, this doesn't mean we will allow Jeremiah's army to march over the Israeli border without a fight, but Jerusalem is his ultimate target, so this has become our final line of defense. We don't know what part of the city he'll hit first, but this perimeter encompasses all of the Old City, including the Moslem and Christian shrines, plus the Knesset, the Prime Minister's palace, and the various other governmental buildings. If it's secure, Jerusalem's secure."

"Where do you expect the attack to originate?" asked Moore, gazing off in the distance.

"Not in the direction you're looking," replied Yitzak with a smile. "They'll most likely approach from Abu Tur to the south, Tel Arza to the north, and the Golan Heights to the northeast. You're looking almost due west, which is the one direction we're not too worried about, since we've got about half a million troops stationed there, halfway between Jerusalem and Tel Aviv."

They continued driving around the Old City, which an army of almost eight hundred thousand Israelis was poised to defend to the last man, woman, and child. There was sufficient ammunition for a four-month pitched battle, and the air force, geared for action, was ready to take off at an instant's notice. Radar and sonar blanketed the area, laser weapons were revved up for the conflict to come, and tanks guarded the perimeter at regular intervals.

"A mosquito couldn't get through all that," said Moore when they had arrived at Yitzak's headquarters, the nerve center of the communications network.

"You're quite sure?" asked Yitzak, escorting Moore into a nondescript office and offering him a beer, which he refused.

"I can't imagine any army launching a successful attack — at least, not on the ground. Just how good are your air defenses?"

"Excellent," replied Yitzak. "Furthermore, according to our information, Jeremiah hasn't got more than half a dozen planes."

"Fifth columnists?" asked Moore.

"I tend to doubt it," said Yitzak. "This is not the Messiah of Christianity we're dealing with here. Whether our people believe in him or not, we all know that he's not exactly coming as a Prince of Peace."

"*Do* they believe in him?" asked Moore.

"Who knows?" replied Yitzak with a shrug. "It makes no difference. This is the only homeland we have, and we don't plan to turn it over to him without a fight."

"As far as fighting goes, I'm no expert — but I don't think you've got much to worry about from Jeremiah's army. Jerusalem seems about as well fortified as cities get to be."

"Good. Tomorrow we'll tour it on foot, and see if you still feel that way." Yitzak paused thoughtfully. "Possibly we'll go well beyond the perimeter. You can put yourself in Jeremiah's shoes, so to speak, and try to foresee how he might lead the attack."

"I keep telling you — he won't be leading anyone into battle. It's not his style."

"If his army is expected to overrun Jerusalem without availing itself of his special talents, he's going to have to wait until it's larger and better-trained," said Yitzak. He turned to Moore. "I find it difficult to believe that having come this far, he'll be willing to wait any appreciable length of time."

"Could this be a feint?" asked Moore.

"What do you mean?"

"What's to stop him from attacking every other square foot of Israel first? All he has to do is keep clear of Jerusalem and Tel Aviv and assume you won't leave them unguarded."

Yitzak shook his head. "You still don't comprehend just how *small* Israel is. We could cross it in ninety minutes in that beat-up Land Rover we used this morning. Believe me, there is no place he can attack where we can't retaliate instantly, and without appreciably decreasing our security around Jerusalem."

"Then I'm out of ideas," said Moore. "I don't know what the hell he'll do next." He shrugged. "I guess we just sit back and wait."

"For the moment," agreed Yitzak.

And so they waited. For two weeks there was no change in the disposition of Jeremiah's forces. Yitzak and Moore toured the perimeter of the city daily, looking for weak spots, for anything that might give

Moore an idea as to when and where Jeremiah would strike.

They found nothing.

It was late on the night of his sixteenth day in Jerusalem that Moore decided to call Pryor in Chicago to see how the business was going. He quickly discovered that the phone in his room could only make contact with headquarters, so he wandered over to Yitzak's office to place the call from there. He nodded to the various members of the night staff, which consisted primarily of lower-echelon officers and orderlies, then let himself into the office and closed the door behind him.

He put through the call, was informed that Pryor was in Boston on business, and hung up. Since he didn't feel like going right back out into the oppressive heat of the Israeli night, he walked over to the refrigerator and poured himself a glass of orange juice that the general had started keeping for him. He carried it over to Yitzak's desk, sat down on a swivel chair, stretched his legs out, took a long sip from the glass, and closed his eyes.

"That drink sure looks good," said a familiar voice from behind him. "Mind if I join you?"

Moore spun his chair around and leaped to his feet.

"Hello, Solomon," said Jeremiah. "Long time no see."

25

"How did you get in here?" demanded Moore.

"Relax, Solomon," laughed Jeremiah. "You'll have a stroke. Now, how about that drink?"

As Jeremiah strolled over to the refrigerator, Moore quickly walked to the door and found that it was locked.

"There's nothing to see in the outer office anyway, except for a bunch of sleeping soldiers," said Jeremiah. He pulled out a can of beer. "Hope you don't mind," he said, popping the top open, "but I gave up fruit juice when I was four years old." He took a long swig of it, wiped his mouth on a shirtsleeve, and then finished it. "Good stuff. Mind if I have another?"

Moore sat back down at the desk and stared at him while he opened a second can.

"Thanks, Solomon. It's hot as hell out there. I'm not used to the climate anymore." He chuckled. "I'd forgotten just how uncomfortable the Middle East can be at this time of year."

"You still haven't answered my question," said Moore. "How did you get in here?"

"I just walked in."

"Don't give me that shit!" snapped Moore. "There are a million armed men and women out there!"

"Nevertheless," said Jeremiah, breaking out into a huge smile.

"I didn't hear a single shot."

"There weren't any. I walked straight from my camp to this office. Nobody saw me, nobody heard me, nobody tried to stop me. It was really amazing, Solomon — I simply walked right by them and they acted like I wasn't there. Then, when I got here, I just told everyone in the outer office to go to sleep, and they did." He grinned again. "I *like* being the Messiah!"

Moore slid a desk drawer out, found a letter opener, and withdrew it.

"Then I guess I'll have to kill you myself," he said ominously.

"No you won't, Solomon," replied Jeremiah, making no move to defend himself. "But *your* job is done. I can finally kill *you* — and if you annoy me, I will."

"What are you talking about?"

"Up until this moment, you've been as impossible to kill as I have, Solomon," said Jeremiah, pulling up a chair and facing him. "But you've been so concerned about killing me that you never realized it." He paused, obviously enjoying himself enormously. "Remember that day in Chicago when the plane crashed into the hangar? I got away, but you survived too. Lisa Walpole couldn't kill you, either. And while you've been trying to kill me for four years, I've had a hit out on you, too. Even shooting down your plane didn't do the trick."

"What are you driving at?" asked Moore, laying down the letter opener and staring at him.

"I thought you were supposed to be the one with all the brains," said Jeremiah. "And yet you still don't see it, do you?"

"Keep talking."

"Take a look at the record, Solomon. You've spent the past four years alerting millions of people to my presence; indeed, you've been the best advance man anyone could want. And now you've even helped to make Jerusalem totally impregnable. You did your job well, Solomon."

"*My* job?"

"Yes, Solomon," said Jeremiah. "You see, you're the Forerunner. You are Elijah, come to pave the way for the Messiah."

"You're crazy!" snapped Moore.

"No, Solomon. I'm right, and I can tell from the expression on your face that you're beginning to realize it." He paused. "How was Elijah to come to Jerusalem?"

"You tell me."

"He was to streak across the skies in a flaming chariot," replied Jeremiah. "We don't have chariots anymore, but I'd say that you chose the closest thing. *'Behold, I will send you Elijah the prophet before the coming of the great and dreadful day of the Lord!'* That's Malachi 4:5, Solomon."

"Bullshit!"

"I got a million of 'em," grinned Jeremiah. "Do you want me to start quoting them?"

Moore shook his head, lost in thought.

"I would have attacked much sooner," Jeremiah continued, "but when I figured it all out, I thought I'd wait and see just how much of the way you would prepare for me. I'm glad I did, too. I knew you'd make me a household name, but I never dreamed that you'd also present me with an impregnable Jerusalem. As I said, Forerunner, you did your job well — but your job is over now. You live or die at my whim. You're simply not needed any longer."

Moore remained silent for a few minutes while Jeremiah opened a third can of beer. Finally he looked up, a rueful smile on his face.

"In other words, if I had just ignored you . . ."

"You couldn't have, Solomon. The Messiah must have his Forerunner. It was written in the Book of Fate eons ago that you and I should play out these roles at this time and place."

"Such eloquence," said Moore sardonically.

"Oh, I know I was a pretty dumb little bastard when all this started," admitted Jeremiah. "But the Messiah must rule with the wisdom of David and Solomon. I see things more clearly these days."

"So what's next?" said Moore. "Do you establish a poverty-free utopian state?"

"Oh, no, Forerunner," said Jeremiah with a nasty smile. "First I raze civilization to the ground. I burn out the evil and put mine enemies to the sword — figuratively, of course. After all, I've got an army to do that kind of stuff for me. Then and only then do I set about rebuilding the world the way I want it."

"And what kind of a world will it be?" asked Moore.

"I really don't know," answered Jeremiah. "But I'm sure it will come to me in time. Most things do, you know."

Moore nodded. "I know." He paused. "Will your army march into Jerusalem the same way you did?"

"I haven't the slightest idea," said Jeremiah. "But I rather suspect that

I won't need them any longer. After all, you've presented me with a ready-made army."

"And what makes you think they'll accept orders from you?"

"Historic inevitability. If they don't take orders from me, then I can't establish my kingdom, can I? Unless we're to have a military bloodbath, that is — and I don't think God would want that. When all is said and done, I'm the Messiah of the *Old* Testament, and the Israeli Army represents a healthy chunk of God's chosen people."

"The wholesale slaughter of His chosen people never seemed to deter Him in the past," noted Moore dryly. "Forty days and forty nights of flooding wasn't exactly the act of a compassionate deity."

"True," responded Jeremiah. He shrugged. "Well, whatever I have to do, I'm sure the solution will dawn on me when the time is right. But right now I'm afraid I have a more immediate problem, Solomon."

"Oh?"

"What am I to do with a Forerunner who has outlived his usefulness?"

"What did you have in mind?" asked Moore warily.

"I'm not sure," admitted Jeremiah. "On the one hand, I'm certainly grateful that you accomplished your purpose so effectively. But on the other hand, you *have* been trying to kill me for four years. I realize that this was predestined, and that of course I can't be killed — but you did cause me an enormous amount of pain, Solomon. I certainly have to take that into consideration." He paused. "Have *you* any suggestions?"

"You're holding all the cards."

"True," agreed Jeremiah. "Well, I'll figure it out eventually. In the meantime, I suppose I'll let you hang around for a while. After all, you *are* my Forerunner. I owe you something for that, even if it's just another few days of existence. Just see to it that you don't leave the city."

"Thanks," said Moore ironically. "Well, who do you kill first? What city goes up in flames tomorrow — Jerusalem, or something inhabited by the infidels?"

"I think I'll play it by ear, Solomon. But this much I know: the ground will turn red with blood before I'm done. So it is written; so it must be." He finished his beer. "Now why don't you show me how the communications system works?"

He unlocked the door, and the two of them walked into the main office, where almost two dozen soldiers lay in a trancelike sleep.

"Ah!" said Jeremiah, his face lighting up with interest as he walked over to a bank of radios. "Look at all this lovely machinery. I've never understood computers and electrical systems, Solomon, but they have always impressed the hell out of me."

"What do you intend to do?" asked Moore.

"Address my people."

"They're forty miles away."

"You still don't understand," said Jeremiah. "*All* people are my people." He looked around the room. "Is there some public address system here?"

"Who do you want to reach?"

"The whole city."

"I suppose you'd have to rig the air-raid sirens to a microphone."

"And where is the control panel for the sirens?"

Moore pointed it out.

Jeremiah found the massive line that powered the sirens, ripped it out of the panel, and wrapped the exposed ends around a portable microphone that he appropriated from one of the radios.

"You'll electrocute yourself," said Moore.

Jeremiah merely laughed.

"At any rate, you'll never be able to turn *that* into a PA system."

"The Lord works in mysterious ways," said Jeremiah. "Turn the power on."

Moore flipped the appropriate switch.

"*MY PEOPLE!*" said Jeremiah, and Moore felt the building vibrate as the earsplitting sound permeated the still night air of the city. "*I AM JEREMIAH, COME TO LAY CLAIM TO THAT WHICH IS MINE. PREPARE YOURSELVES! THE EARTH WILL CATCH FIRE, AND THE RIVERS WILL FLOW RED, AND NOT A BLADE OF GRASS WILL REMAIN STANDING! THE DAY OF THE LORD IS AT HAND!*"

26

*T*he next morning — October 4, 2051 — Jeremiah set up temporary headquarters in the penthouse of a luxury hotel on the outskirts of the Old City. He ordered a general amnesty for all Israeli citizens and soldiers who had opposed him.

Moore, who had spent the remainder of the night trying to assimilate what he had learned, made a pair of long-distance calls to Rabbi Milton Greene, bought a copy of the Talmud, and vanished from sight.

On October 5, Jeremiah issued orders that Moore was to be shot if he attempted to leave the city.

Moore remained in hiding.

On October 6, Jeremiah paid a visit to Prime Minister Weitzel and accompanied him to a closed cabinet meeting and an emergency session of the Knesset.

Moore remained in hiding, and waited.

On October 7, Jeremiah called a press conference and announced that he was abolishing the Knesset.

Moore remained in hiding, and waited.

On October 8, Jeremiah summoned two hundred of his own officers from the plains and hills beyond the city and put them in charge of the Israeli Army. The remainder of his followers were instructed to return to their homelands and await the further biddings of their Messiah.

Moore remained in hiding, and waited.

On October 9, Moira Railings showed up. Ashen as ever, she remained at Jeremiah's side as he went about the business of consolidating the various branches of the government, making them more immediately responsive to his needs.

Moore remained in hiding, and waited.

On October 10, Jeremiah held another press conference and announced that he intended to make Moira his Queen. She looked as surprised as the reporters, but offered no objection.

Moore remained in hiding, and waited.

On October 11, Jeremiah executed some seven thousand Israeli men and women who still opposed him and offered an ultimatum to Syria, Jordan, Lebanon, and Egypt: accept his divinity and his authority, or suffer the consequences.

Moore remained in hiding, and waited.

On October 12, Jeremiah offered the same ultimatum to all other Middle East nations, and suggested that dissenters would do well to read the prophets of the Old Testament.

Moore remained in hiding, and waited.

On October 13 (which shunned historical tidiness by falling on a Wednesday rather than a Friday), Jeremiah presided at his own coronation in the ceremony that gave official sanction to the already acknowledged fact that Israel had crossed over the line from democracy to monarchy.

And Moore was all through waiting.

27

*J*eremiah's penthouse, situated at the eastern edge of the Old City, overlooked the broad expanse of Dayan Boulevard. Moore took a cab to the front door of the building, walked across the tiled lobby, and was approaching an elevator when two soldiers barred his way.

"What's your business here?" demanded one of them.

"I'm here to see Jeremiah."

"I'm sorry, sir," said the soldier, "but Jeremiah is not seeing visitors."

"He'll see *me*," said Moore.

"No one is allowed upstairs without a priority pass."

"Why not phone him and tell him that Solomon Moody Moore is in the lobby?"

"Moore," repeated the soldier, frowning. "I know that name. There was some order concerning you."

"The phone?" repeated Moore.

The soldier stared at him for a moment, ordered his companion to keep an eye on him, and walked to a house phone. He returned less than a minute later.

"I'm sorry for the inconvenience, Mr. Moore. He'll see you immediately. Take the last elevator on the left; it goes directly to the penthouse."

Moore thanked him, entered the elevator, and emerged a few seconds later on the top floor of the building, at the edge of a large, luxurious sitting room. Jeremiah was nowhere to be seen, but Moira Railings was seated on a plush velvet sofa, reading a magazine.

"Hello, Moira," said Moore. "It's been a long time."

"Hello, Mr. Moore," she replied. "Have you read my book yet?"

"Hasn't everyone?" he responded with a smile.

"I want to apologize for some of the less flattering references to you," she said. "I had no idea who and what you were when I was writing it. Everything will be corrected in the revised edition."

"Your apology is accepted," said Moore, as Jeremiah, wearing a white silk robe, entered the room.

"Have a seat, Solomon," he said pleasantly. "I've been wondering what happened to you." He opened a bottle of wine and filled three glasses. "Care for a drink?"

Moore shook his head. "Why in the world would I want to drink with you?"

"To help me celebrate," answered Jeremiah. "After all, I couldn't have done it without you and my oversexed little Boswell here."

"And now that you've done it, have you decided what you're going to do with *me?*" asked Moore.

"I've been giving the matter considerable thought, Solomon," replied Jeremiah. "You seem to be a little different from the rest of the sheep. They all love me these days, but I get the distinct impression that you still nurture hostile feelings."

"Maybe they don't know how many people you intend to kill," said Moore.

"It's got to be done, Solomon," said Jeremiah easily. "Millions upon millions must die. But that's beside the point, said point being what I intend to do with you. I must confess that you are turning into an embarrassment to me. I mean, after all these years of futility, you still harbor thoughts of killing me. Don't bother to deny it; the bulge under your coat is unmistakable."

"You mean this?" asked Moore, withdrawing a wicked-looking revolver.

"What good would it do, Solomon?" laughed Jeremiah. "I can't be killed. Hell, I don't even have my soldiers inspect visitors for concealed weapons."

"I know. I made sure of that before I came."

"If you shoot me," continued Jeremiah, totally ignoring the revolver, "I'll lie near death for a day or two, and by the end of the week I'll be as good as new. And my retribution will be considerably harsher than what you did to me back in Cincinnati."

Moore shook his head and sighed. "When Moira writes of your last days on Earth, she's going to point out the basic tragedy of your nature: that your intelligence, despite its admittedly rapid gains, never quite caught up with the rest of you." He pulled a silencer out of his pocket and screwed it onto the muzzle of the gun.

"You're crazy!" snapped Jeremiah. "Nothing can kill me! You know that!"

"I've spent a lot of time thinking about that," said Moore. "That's why I've been avoiding you until today — because I didn't want you to force me to act before I was ready."

"What the hell are you talking about?" demanded Jeremiah.

"*Why* can't you be killed?" asked Moore, cocking the hammer.

"Because *nothing* — not you, not anyone, not anything — can stop me from establishing my kingdom in Jerusalem!"

"Very good, Jeremiah," said Moore, pointing the pistol at him. "And what particular event took place today?"

Jeremiah merely stared at him, wild-eyed, for a long moment. Then a look of dawning comprehension and terror slowly spread across his face.

"That's right, Jeremiah," said Moore softly. "And that's why I didn't want to see you before now. But as of this afternoon you are the King of Jerusalem, indeed of all Israel. You've done what you were destined to do, you've served your purpose and fulfilled the prophecies — and now you're fair game."

"No!" screamed Jeremiah. "It can't end like this! First the sword, then the fire, then —"

"An interesting theory," said Moore. "Let's put it to the test."

He fired the pistol.

Jeremiah staggered backward into a wall, clutched at the rapidly spreading red stain on his chest, and collapsed to the floor. He moaned twice, convulsed, and then lay still.

Moore walked over to him, picked up his hand, and felt for a pulse. There wasn't any. He put four more bullets into Jeremiah's temple, then turned to Moira.

"I made you a promise a long time ago," he said quietly. "Do you remember?"

Moira nodded, her eyes aglow with excitement.

"I'm keeping it now," said Moore. "He's all yours."

Moira scurried across the room, no trace of sorrow or remorse on her face, and knelt down beside Jeremiah's body. She lifted his bloody head to her lap and began stroking it passionately, murmuring words that Moore couldn't quite make out. He watched her for a moment, grimaced, and then looked around for a telephone. He found one, and placed a call to Chicago.

"Pryor here," said a familiar voice a few minutes later.

"Hello, Ben."

"Solomon!" exclaimed Pryor. "How are things out there?"

"Everything's under control. I killed Jeremiah not five minutes ago."

"How?"

"I'll tell you all about it when I get home."

"Uh . . . Solomon?"

"Yes?"

"Maybe you'd better tell me about it on the phone."

"Trouble?"

"Not exactly . . . not for me. But I've waited a long time to sit in this chair, and I don't think I want to give it up."

"I see," said Moore softly.

"You always encouraged ambition, Solomon."

"I know I did, Ben."

"It's nothing personal," continued Pryor. "But as soon as I hang up the phone, I'm putting out a hit on you. It's *business,* Solomon."

"No hard feelings, Ben," replied Moore. "But you've just signed your own death warrant."

"We'll see, Solomon," said Pryor. "But for your own good, stay away. I've uncovered your spies and taken care of them, and I just entered into a partnership with Piper Black. He'll be putting out a hit, too."

"Fair enough, Ben," said Moore. "But you've got something that's mine, and I'm going to get it back."

"You're welcome to try."

"No quarter asked or given?"

"None," agreed Pryor, sounding just a little less sure of himself.

"I'll be seeing you soon, Ben," promised Moore.

He hung up the phone and walked to a window. Hundreds of soldiers and civilians were scurrying about their business, completely unaware of what had happened three hundred feet above their heads.

"Moira?"

"Yes, Mr. Moore," she said, wiping some of Jeremiah's blood from her face.

"I kept my promise to you. Now I want you to do me a favor."

"What favor, Mr. Moore?"

"Give me a six-hour head start before you tell anyone what happened in here. Will you do that?"

She looked down at Jeremiah's body for a moment, then met Moore's eyes.

"Six hours," she said, nodding her head.

He took one last look at them, the corpse-lover and the corpse, and then, tucking the pistol into the back of his belt, he entered the elevator.

28

*H*e stole a Land Rover that was parked near the building and drove to the southwest, passing into Egypt and continuing on for another four hours before he ran out of gas. Then he got out, pushed the vehicle into a small gorge, and started walking.

By midday the heat had become oppressive, and, slightly dehydrated, he climbed into the foothills of a nearby mountain, seeking out the slowly shifting shade. When darkness fell he decided to spend the night there rather than chance meeting his pursuers on foot in the desert. The temperature fell sharply, and he gathered some shrubbery and built a small fire, huddling over it to keep warm.

Finally he lay down, pillowing his head on his right arm, and went to sleep.

Sometime later he awoke with a start. The moon was directly overhead, the stars shone down brightly, and there was no trace of wind. Yet *something* had awakened him, and he got to his feet, prepared to search for intruders.

Then he noticed that one of the bushes he had set fire to some hours earlier was still burning, and he walked over to it. It shimmered with a cold glow and seemed to pulsate with energy.

And suddenly, within his head, he heard a voice speak out in stentorian tones.

"Why hast thou killed My Messiah?"

"Who are you?" demanded Moore.

"I am that I am."

"I must be dreaming," he muttered to himself, looking into the shadows beyond the fire for a sign of life.

"Solomon Moore, why hast thou spilled the blood of him that I sent?"

The bush became brighter with each word.

"Where are you?"

"I am here, where I have always been, for before this was Mount Sinai it was Mount Horeb, and it was here that I spake to Mosheh."

"Then why didn't you send someone like Moses?" said Moore bitterly. "Why a bloodthirsty fool like Jeremiah?"

"I owe you no explanation. It was enough that he was the one, and you slew him."

"And I'd do it again!" snapped Moore. "Where were you when we needed you? Why didn't you send a little help during the Inquisition, or save your chosen people from the Nazis? What kept you?"

"Thou hast killed him."

The unspoken words grew louder, and the light of the fire became so bright that Moore couldn't look at it.

"Yes, I killed him!" yelled Moore in an cold fury. "But *you* chose him. Which of us is guiltier?"

"I hereby annul my covenant with man! Never again shall I concern myself with your affairs."

"We'll get by!" Moore shouted at the skies. "We got along just fine when you were too busy to bother with us, and we'll get along now!"

There was no answer, and, unable to sleep, he wandered through the foothills for the remainder of the night. Then, as the sun began rising, he stepped out into the desert.

The coming days and months and years weren't going to be easy ones. Pryor controlled what was left of his organization, and probably had fifty hired killers out after him already. Black would have fifty more. Behind him an entire nation would be mobilizing its army for the sole purpose of finding and executing him. Thirty million people across the face of the planet would be screaming for his blood.

But, regardless of their numbers, they were just people, and he had made his fortune by his ability to manipulate them. He thought of the events of the past two days, of what he had done and what company he had kept, then raised his eyes and sought out the horizon.

Somewhere out there, beyond the vast expanse of desert, was the Gulf of Aqaba. Beyond that was the Red Sea, and the Suez Canal, and a way home. Along the way he would have to evade tens of thousands of enemies and reclaim a financial empire. But at least he wouldn't die of boredom — and in this day and age, on this world that he had inadvertently helped to shape, that was sufficient.

He took a deep breath, released it slowly, and began walking.

He looked forward to the challenge.

Afterword

About a week after I agreed to let Wildside Press reprint this book, I received the following e-mail from Josep Guirao:

Hi, Mike,
   Just wanted to let you know that the movie was shown yesterday at the festival . . . people loved it!!!

"The festival" was the South Beach Film Festival in Miami. The film was *No Pronunciaras el Nomere de Dios en Vano*, which translates as "Do Not Pronounce the Name of the Lord in Vain." More to the point, it was Josep's film version of *The Branch*.

I first heard from Josep a few years back. He put through a transcontinental phone call to explain that he was an independent producer in Andorra (yes, I had to look for it in my Atlas), and that he had fallen in love with *The Branch*, and desperately wanted to make the movie.

I'd never dealt with a foreign filmmaker before, but *The Branch* had been in print for more than a decade, and while I'd had a couple of nibbles from Hollywood, the fact of the matter was that no one was breaking down my door to produce it, so we negotiated a two-year option.

And I didn't hear from Josep for two years. Then he called back to tell me he simply hadn't been able to raise the money for a full-length feature film, but he had an idea: would I have any problem extending the option another year and allowing him to make a half-hour condensation of the story that he could then show to backers and hopefully raise the funds for a two-hour feature? By now I had sold a bunch of other things to Hollywood, but they were still leery of *The Branch* and Josep clearly loved it, so I agreed.

Another year passed, and then I started getting the strangest e-mails. He was in Madrid with a copy of the film. The Andorran church had condemned him, and the government had told him that his reward for

making such a blashphemous movie was that he would not be allowed
to work in the country of his birth for the next fifteen years.

A couple of months passed, and I heard from him again. He was in
South America, still with the film clutched tightly in his hands.

Then, just about the time I was wondering if this was all a gigantic
hoax perpetrated by some friend with a strange sense of humor, I heard
from him again. He was in Miami, and he was sending me two copies
of the subtitled videotape — and sure enough, they arrived a few days
later.

And the next time I heard from him, it was the message that started
off this Afterword.

So who is Josep Guirao and what is this all about? He's graciously
allowed me to quote (and edit just a bit) from his web page.

> *About the script: It is adapted from the novel* The Branch *by Mike
> Resnick, regarding the arrival of a new Messiah in the 21st Century. A
> fictional thriller, full of real information and historical references.*
>
> *I was advised by the Ministry of Culture of Andorra not to touch the
> topic of religion in any script. I therefore decided to write a script in which
> religion was the main topic. The presentation of the film was unofficially
> prohibited; no commercial movie house offered to exhibit it, and they also
> refused to rent out their facilities. So we had to debut it in an almost
> clandestine fashion in a theater, with a portable projector and screen. (I
> myself and the leading male actor put up the posters the night before on
> the streets of Andorra.) I got some interview spots on the radio and
> television a few hours before the debut, and a half hour after we opened
> the doors, so many people had arrived that we had to turn them away.*
>
> *When the movie was over, the three hundred people that were there stood
> and applauded for several minutes. It had been a success. The next day,
> the press was censored and there was no mention of the event, as if nothing
> had happened. (The only write-up was in a politically conservative news-
> paper that devoted a half a page to mentioning the failure of the picture
> and my lack of professionalism.) Several journalists apologized to me for
> not having been able to publish anything, as the orders had come from
> above.*
>
> *I wrote this script respecting not only the source material but the opinion
> of each religion. I held several meetings with theologians and representatives
> of the Catholic and Jewish religion, and the only thing I did was
> summarize briefly in 34 minutes their opinions on a topic they have
> disagreed upon for centuries, the Messiah. Once this, which was to be the
> first part of the film, had been filmed, I imagined, based on a solid historical
> and sociological foundation, how the world would react to the arrival of
> a Messiah in the year 2046. Therefore, all the data presented in the dialogue
> between Armstrong and Emmanuel, in what would be the second part of*

the picture, is very thoroughly researched. Everything, from the different quotes concerning the world's population to who and what the process of recognizing this Messiah would be like, has been calculated beforehand.

I think it is also important to know that the character of Armstrong (Solomon Moody Moore in the novel) borders on paranoia, and that he is, at least for himself, the only god who exists. If he calls a meeting, after capturing the alleged Messiah, it is rather to determine what repercussions killing the Messiah would have on his business.

Neither is it strange that Armstrong's economic power should have gone so far as to buy certain representatives of the Vatican or some rabbi.

The alleged Messiah, Emmanuel, is a Messiah who comes from the street, from poverty, and who has become completely involved in the business of the gangster Armstrong. He has been doing so for some years, and now he is beginning to do the gangster serious harm. The reason he has become involved in such shady dealings – whether it forms part of his mission as a Messiah or if it is just due to his personal ambition – is not known. The audience should form its own conclusions, as with other questions, such as whether he was really the Messiah or not, or whose position was more logical, that of the theologian rabbi or the Vatican representative.

Evidently, in accordance with the culture or the religion of each spectator, he will be more or less in agreement with such different characters. However, these characters leave a series of questions and contradictions between "the history of humankind" and "religion," which will not leave anyone indifferent.

Of course, the excessive amount of information in the movie and the tension created on purpose evidently require a very attentive and predisposed audience.

Director's notes: 34 minutes (35mm). A personal challenge in directing actors, filmed in five days (12 hours a day). Actors taken to the limits of their abilities, with continuous dialogue, live sound, negative and limited number of takes. Two of the main characters are played by the same actor. The rest of the actors were not available every day, so that many times scenes with dialogue were filmed with only one of the actors appearing on screen, with the director providing answers off-screen. In this movie, I also play the part of the character Krack. The ending of the movie was filmed first, to make sure that it could have some interesting camera movement at the conclusion that would give it some rhythm, since otherwise I risked having to have to rush to the ending and go to a fixed camera. The budget was US$ 4,000. Everyone worked for free and the negative left over from the previous film, Confidencias, *was used. The movie was filmed without the permission of the government, so we had to film on private property – in this case, a garage. The problem is that the garage was so small, that we had to come up with all sorts of different ways to represent three different locations, and move everything from the set at every change of scene, so* *that it wasn't apparent that it was always the same place. I also chose a very zenithal type of lighting, and a very charged atmosphere. Because authorization from the government was not obtained, and fearing that they would put a stop to the shooting, I moved up the filming date, and it was shot without previous planning.*

After reading the web page, I wrote to Josep to ask if he himself was still in serious trouble in Andorra. Here's the operative part of his reply:

Andorra is now a democracy, and it is in the interest of all Andorrans that we be perceived as such abroad – especially if it continues to be a state in which, of 60,000 inhabitants, only about 25,000 are Andorrans, and the economic and political power of the country is divided among four or five leading families. (They form part of the banking monopoly, the government, and the judiciary.

The government, for its part, also controls the media (radio, television and Internet "domains.ad").

Thus situations are created in which, although it is not evident at first glance, a large network of influence brokers continues to control the system.

It is evident that my point of view differs very greatly from that of the government, as well, of course, as from that of the newspapers belonging to certain politicians or their children.

My current situation is that I have no legal problem residing in Andorra. I never have, because I am Andorran – but in reality living there is impossible because of the following:

I cannot have a business in my name, nor a bank account, credit card or property. Thus, I cannot rent a place to live or contract for telephone service, electrical service, etc., either . . . I cannot legally practice any professional activity and, it is well understood, especially not my activity as a movie director.

A few months ago I informed the Andorran Ministry of Tourism as well as the Ministry of Culture, through the Director of Tourism, Sergi Nadal, that I needed a copy of the documentaries that I made about Andorra (17) for my personal files, in VHS. This was categorically denied, with allegations that I would never have access to this material which was now their property.

And that's Josep Guirao's story up to this point. As far as I'm concerned, any guy who is, for all practical purposes, kicked out of his country and denied the ability to earn a living there, simply for making a movie out of a Resnick novel, is aces in my book. Talk about devotion above and beyond the call of duty!

Josep: If you're reading this, I want you to know that you've got a free option on *The Branch* for as long as you want it. Now go out and win some festivals and get that full-length movie made.

Postscript: As we were literally going to press, I got one more e-mail from Josep. It said, and I quote, "We won the Audience Award for Best Movie!"

— Mike Resnick